"Here we are. The guy in the blue coat is Milner, Lieutenant."

Neuman knew which one was Milner. Being so cold, having been shot at, not having eaten . . . none of that mattered as much as having to work with Milner. Thanks to a computer.

"Not a computer, Jake," Chief Inspector Lou Klinger had said. "A computer *program*. We know you and Milner have this thing, Jake."

"It's not a thing," Neuman said. "It's a deep-seated animosity, underlain by profound mutual disrespect and contempt for each other's morals and methods and reinforced by occasional but highly fraught confrontations over a considerable period of time. Those aren't my words. They're Bernstein's, more or less. *Doc*tor Bernstein?"

"The department shrink, yes, we know, Jake."

"I don't call him a shrink," Neuman said. "I call him a psychologist, which is what he is, on the theory—Bernstein's theory, but I go along with it—that if I call him a shrink I'm not taking him as seriously as I should, I'm putting him in the same category as chow or booze or butts or doing the same thing an addict does when he calls marijuana boom-boom or crack jumbo or heroin scag or cocaine soda: kidding himself that he's not killing himself."

Bantam Crime Line Books offers the finest in classic and modern American mysteries.
Ask your bookseller for the books you have missed.

Rex Stout

The Black Mountain
Broken Vase
Death of a Dude
Death Times Three
Fer-de-Lance
The Final Deduction
Gambit
Plot It Yourself
The Rubber Band
Some Buried Caesar
Three for the Chair
Too Many Cooks

Max Allan Collins

The Dark City
Bullet Proof

A. E. Maxwell

Just Another Day in Paradise
Gatsby's Vineyard
The Frog and the Scorpion
Just Enough Light to Kill

Loren Estleman

Peeper

Dick Lupoff

The Comic Book Killer

Randy Russell

Hot Wire

V.S. Anderson

Blood Lies

William Murray

When the Fat Man Sings
The King of the Nightcap

Eugene Izzi

King of the Hustlers
coming soon: The Prime Roll

Gloria Dank

Friends Till the End
coming soon: Going Out in Style

Jeffery Deaver

Manhattan Is My Beat

Jerry Oster

Club Dead
coming soon: Internal Affairs

Robert Goldsborough

Murder in E Minor
Death on Deadline
The Bloodied Ivy
The Last Coincidence

Sue Grafton

"A" Is for Alibi
"B" Is for Burglar
"C" Is for Corpse
"D" Is for Deadbeat
"E" Is for Evidence

Richard Hilary

Snake in the Grasses
Pieces of Cream
Pillow of the Community
Behind the Fact

Carolyn G. Hart

Design for Murder
Death on Demand
Something Wicked
Honeymoon With Murder
A Little Class on Murder

Annette Meyers

The Big Killing

Rob Kantner

Dirty Work
The Back-Door Man
Hell's Only Half Full

Robert Crais

The Monkey's Raincoat
Stalking the Angel

Keith Peterson

The Trapdoor
There Fell a Shadow
The Rain
Rough Justice

David Handler

The Man Who Died Laughing
The Man Who Lived by Night

M.K. Lorens

Sweet Narcissus
The Ropedancer's Fall

CLUB DEAD

A NOVEL BY

JERRY OSTER

BANTAM BOOKS
NEW YORK · TORONTO · LONDON · SYDNEY · AUCKLAND

*Thanks, again, to everyone at the Writers Room
—especially Leslie Gourse, for the jazz tips.*

*This edition contains the complete text
of the original hardcover edition.*
NOT ONE WORD HAS BEEN OMITTED.

CLUB DEAD

*A Bantam Book / published by arrangement with
Harper & Row, Publishers, Inc.*

PRINTING HISTORY

*Harper & Row edition published September 1988
Bantam edition / January 1990*

*Bantam Books are published by Bantam Books, a division of Bantam Doubleday Dell
Publishing Group, Inc. Its trademark, consisting of the words "Bantam Books" and
the portrayal of a rooster, is Registered in U.S. Patent and Trademark Office and in
other countries. Marca Registrada. Bantam Books, 666 Fifth Avenue, New York,
New York 10103.*

For Ted and Mildred Oster

CLUB DEAD

1

In sports, the Knicks, Nets, Rangers, Islanders and Devils all were winners last night. The National Weather Service forecast: Snow beginning around midday, with accumulations of eight to twelve inches before it starts to taper off about nine o'clock tonight. Strong, gusty winds will produce considerable drifting. The high today in the low to mid teens, low tonight zero to five below in the city, ten to fifteen below in the outlying suburbs. The temperature right now is a balmy seven degrees, but the wind makes it feel like . . . Iqaluit, Northwest Territories.

Twenty-seven stories is a long way down. There's nothing to do but think:

Think that maybe the snow on the sidewalk will break your fall.

Think what a stupid thing to think.

Think that there must be someone who would pay a lot of money for your testimony—or how about a book, a miniseries?—that it isn't your whole life that's passing in front of your eyes as you drop down, down, down, down, down—just the last six months, beginning on an acrid summer Monday morning back before the ice age set in, back before there was a foot of snow on the ground and another in the forecast, back before a sled and a team of huskies would be useful—the Monday morning when you got your orders to do a number on Frances McAlistair.

Frances McAlistair off whose penthouse terrace you just did a swan dive.

Think that it's almost Valentine's Day, and you never got around to getting her a card.

1

2

Air Sax played an Illinois Jacquet riff. "So what're you doing, Ed? I mean, tonight."

Dead Eddie Milano put a hand in his pocket and juggled his balls. "What I'm doing is soon's you get outta here, some trim's coming over."

"You're yanking my chain," Air Sax said.

"Am I?"

"Who? Who's the trim?"

"Two sets a twins."

"You're yanking my chain."

"Am I?"

"*Two* sets?"

"Raven and Misty and Kristen and Inge. Raven and Misty're nineteen and Kristen and Inge're twenty-six."

"Coming over how? I mean, there's snow all over the floor. 'S why I *can't* get outta here. The time I get outta here, get home, it'll be time to turn around, come back. Coming over how?"

"In a snowmobile stretch limo."

"You're yanking my chain."

"Am I?"

Air Sax played some Paquito D'Rivera. Then he said, "Are they coming over at, you know, the same time, the trim?"

"You mean, are Raven and Misty *and* Kristen and Inge coming over at the same time?" Dead Eddie said.

"Yeah."

"No."

"They're not?"

"I just said, no, Sax."

"So which two're coming over, you know, first?"

"What's it to you, Sax?"

"I just wanna know, that's all."

"And I just wanna know what it's to you,"

Air Sax played some Jimmy Heath. "Eddie?"

"Yeah?"

"When you're, you know, doing it wit Raven, is Misty in the rack witch you, I mean, watching? And is Inge in the rack witch you when you're doing it wit Crystal?"

"Kristen."

"Is she? Are they?"

"Be hard for 'em not to be," Dead Eddie said.

"Hard for 'em not to be 'cause otherwise you can't, you know, get, uh, turned on?"

"The fuck d'you think I am, Sax, some kinda faggot?"

"Hey. Who? Me? No. I mean, I just wanna know why you said it'd be hard, that's all."

"'Cause Inge and Kristen're attached to each other, just like Raven and Misty're attached to each other, that's why."

Air Sax said, "Attached?"

"Attached."

"Attached like, you know, Siamese twins?"

"Not *like* Siamese twins. *Siamese* twins."

"You're yanking my chain, Eddie."

"I am?"

"I mean, aren't you?"

Dead Eddie got up and put on his camel overcoat. There *wasn't* snow all over the floor, they *had* snowmobile stretch limos, he *had* two sets of twins coming over, he had *one* piece of trim coming over and she was a fucking dog, Rosalie, shoulda been a professional wrestler, would find out about it, would fucking *smell* it, would get over here *yester*day, grab ahold of his ears, pull his head outta his shoulders, serve it on a platter to their fucking kid, who's gonna grow up to be a pansy faggot hairdresser.

"You got problems at home, Ed?" Air Sax said. "Is that what you're saying?"

"You don't mind my changing the subject back to business instead of this bullshit," Dead Eddie said, "the Valentine's thing set up, or what?"

"No, it's not set up," Air Sax said. "We still got some

work to do—not a lot but a little. Account a there's snow all over the floor and they're saying there's gonna be more snow, we got a rethink how we're gonna get the shooters away from the scene. Cars, vans, taxis, the usual, ain't gonna work; we're gonna have guides, like, for the shooters."

"Guides."

"Guides, like, yeah. To get them to subways and bars where we got back rooms and stuff. It'll be set up at the end a the week, which is what we figured."

"I guess I'll go home then, I can get a cab, you being on top a things and all. I'll prob'ly have to walk, get frostbite, freeze to death. You gonna sleep here tonight, or what?"

"Nah, I'll prob'ly go home too, I can get a cab. I'll prob'ly get frostbite, freeze to death too."

"I'll see you in the funeral home then, I guess, Sax."

"Night, Eddie."

"Yeah."

"Hey, Eddie, you know what I'd pay a lotta scratch to see?"

"The snatch and the boobs a a couple a sets a twins?"

Air Sax laughed. "The face a Artie Roth this Valentine's thing goes down."

"Yeah," Dead Eddie said. "Yeah, on top a the scratch I already paid on account a every time I turn around Artie Roth's breathing down my fucking neck, I'd pay some more scratch to see his face this thing goes down."

"You know what else, Eddie?"

"What, Sax?"

"This thing goes down, I'd pay to see the face a Frances McAlistair too."

"Yeah," Dead Eddie said. "Yeah, I'd pay to see her face too." And come to think of it, Frances McAlistair being a prime piece of trim, especially for a fed, *her* snatch and *her* boobs.

"Night, Eddie."

"Yeah."

Air Sax played some Hamiett Bluiett and thought what a dumb fuck Dead Eddie was, he could say what he wanted he *had* problems at home, which was why he was always making up stories about trim he was gonna have and yanking Air Sax's chain, 'cause he thought Air Sax was a dumb fuck who never got any trim. He wondered what Dead Eddie would think if he knew Air Sax had been hired by a piece of trim to berk a guy for fun and profit.

Not *just* for fun and profit. For the experience. To put on his résumé. 'Cause, face it, he wasn't getting any younger and he sure the fuck wasn't getting any richer working for Dead Eddie, the cheap son-of-a-bitch, eight yards a week he paid Sax for what other guys his age, his experience, his particular skills, like, were getting eleven, twelve, fif*teen* yards a week.

Not that the trim paid him all that much to berk this guy. The trim knew he was new at this kind of thing, which was why she called him up. She called him up and said, *Donald Dubro, please*, and he almost said, *The fuck's Donald Dubro? No Donald Dubro here, babe*, 'cause nobody called him Donald Dubro anymore, sometimes he forgot that was his name, Donald Dubro.

Donald, I understand you're looking to make a career move. I have a job that needs doing that could go a long way toward establishing you in some exciting new areas. We should talk. Don't ask me a lot of pointless questions, Donald, about how I heard about you and who am I and all the rest. Just tell me, yes or no, if you're interested in killing someone for a fee of five hundred dollars; if yes, then we can get down to the details.

What was he gonna say, no? No. Five yards wasn't really what he was thinking about when he thought about a career of berking people, he was thinking *twenty*-five yards, but five yards *was* five yards, the *twenty*-five yards would come when he had a rep, which he was going to have for sure 'cause of what he thought of while he was sitting in the fifth row of the Eighty-sixth Street Sixplex, playing a little Bennie Cotter, waiting for the lights to go out so he could berk Michael Corry, whoever he was, sitting two rows in front of him, eating one of them big buckets of popcorn, big enough to put over your head, which was what Air Sax thought he'd do with it after he berked the guy, because if he was gonna make a career out of berking people, it'd make a good, you know, trademark, like.

Hey, he wasn't saying he'd *al*ways put popcorn boxes on the heads of the guys he berked, 'cause he wasn't planning on making a career outta berking guys in movie theaters, guys who ate popcorn, *buck*ets of popcorn; but he could put *some*thing on the guys' heads, something different every time but that every time people saw it they'd, you know, know right away he was the one that berked the guy.

That wasn't even the best part. The best part, the part that would be the knockout part of the book they'd write about him and the movie they'd make outta the book, was when he waited till the lights went out, then slipped up into the next row and along it until he was right behind Michael Corry, and when the thing came on the screen that said *Welcome to the 86th Street Sixplex* he waited for the part that said *Talking during the movie is fucking inconsiderate, so don't the fuck do it*, and then in real big letters said SHHHH!, then he put the silencer of his Walther P38 9mm West German police pistol, two yards used at a place in Bayonne, up under Michael Corry's ear, not quite touching him, and said, "Hey, Mike," and Mike said, "Yes?" and "Who're you?" and "I'm sorry, I think you must be mistaken," and Sax said, "Shhhh! No talking," and berked him.

And then he dumped the rest of Michael Corry's popcorn outta the bucket and put it on Michael Corry's head and walked outta the movie, like the Sly Stallone flick that came on wasn't the flick he paid to see, he paid to see the Care Bears or something, these fucking sixplexes, you was always walking into the wrong movie.

Looking for things to do to put off going home to Rosalie and the kid, Dead Eddie went back in his office to see that the safe was locked and saw on the switchboard that Mary Elizabeth Indelicato was on call with a client. He sat down to listen to it.

Mary Elizabeth heard the telltale click. Knowing that she knew calls could be transferred from the office to the girls' homes, did Dead Eddie really believe it didn't occur to the girls that he could listen in? She thought about breaking the mood for a moment and telling Eddie to get the fuck off. "I'm so wet, Earl," Mary Elizabeth said. "Do you want me to get undressed now?"

"Wait," Earl said. "Sit up in the window. Sit sideways, with your back against the frame and your feet up on the sill."

On her stomach on the bed in sweat pants and a faded work shirt, her hair damp from a shower and up in a towel, Mary Elizabeth finished with the business section of the *Times* and reached for the science section. "Like this?"

"Pull your skirt up over your thighs."

"Like this?"

"Pull down your panties."

"I'm not wearing panties, Earl. You told me to never wear panties."

"Spread your legs a little. So someone looking up at the window can see you're not wearing them."

"Like this?"

"Is there someone down there looking up at you?"

"I think there is, Earl. Yes, yes, there is. Who is that, Earl?"

"A friend of mine."

"Ooh, I like that. You sent him over to see me?"

"Just to look. Not to touch."

"You're the only one who'll ever touch me, Earl."

"Do you mean that?"

"Of course I mean it."

"Touch yourself," Earl said. "Pull down a strap of your camisole and touch your breast. You're wearing the black camisole, aren't you?"

Mary Elizabeth turned to the 47th Street Photo computer ads. "Just like you told me to, Earl. Oh, Earl, that feels so good."

"Pull on the nipple—stretch it."

If the price of the XT with a 20-meg hard drive came down any farther she couldn't afford not to get one. "Oh, Earl." Unless she went for the Toshiba; she liked its size.

"Now the other breast. Do them both at once, one in each hand. Stretch them hard."

"He's watching me, Earl."

"Yes."

"He's very good-looking."

"Yes."

What had Dolan said about the Maxum? That it was the best of the clones, or the worst? "But not as good-looking as you, Earl. Maybe someday . . ."

"What?"

"The three of us could . . ."

"Could what?"

"I could take you in my mouth, Earl, while he was in me from behind." A *tergo*, as Freud said. Her officemate, Susan Sullivan, had come back from lunch the other day with her finger marking a place in a book of Freud's case studies that she read from time to time to take her mind off the law and to keep her own neuroses in perspective, and said, "Mary Liz, you studied Latin, right? What's a *tergo*?" "It's been a hundred years," Mary Elizabeth said. "What's the context?" "A boy saw his parents fucking—'engaged in intercourse *a tergo*.'" "From behind," Mary Elizabeth said. Susan said, "Ah."

Earl said, "Gloria."

"Yes, Earl?"

"Gloria."

"Yes."

"Gloria."

"Yes, Earl, yes."

"Gloria, Gloria, Gloria, Gloria, Gloria. Glor. I. Aaaaaaaaa."

"Yes, Earl, yes."

". . . Thank you, Gloria."

"You're welcome, Earl. Thank you."

"Was it . . . was it good for you?"

"It's always good, Earl."

"I'll be calling you soon."

"I can't wait."

"Goodbye, Gloria. Is that really your name—Gloria?"

"Goodbye, Earl."

"Is it?"

"Earl, you know the rules. Do I ask you if your name's really Earl?"

"It is. It is Earl."

"Then goodbye. Earl."

"Are you really a redhead?"

"Didn't you ask for a redhead, the first time?"

"Yes. A redhead with a perm."

"And that's just what you got—a redhead with a perm. Now goodbye, Earl. Time's up."

"Goodbye, Gloria. I'll be calling you."

"I'll be waiting."

"Goodbye."

"Goodbye."

After Earl hung up, Mary Elizabeth listened to Dead Eddie's breathing for a while, trying to hear if he'd come too, then to his trying to put the receiver down soundlessly. She remembered that she hadn't proofread the copy for the new *Voice* ad.

She got off the bed and unwrapped the towel from her waist-length black hair and draped it over a chair and went into the kitchen and got the ad copy out of her briefcase:

4-BIDDEN FONE FANTA-CEES

X-plore Your Wildest Erotic Depths
X-Pose Your Undermost Sensorial Secrets
Rap With Our Rapturous Telefantasy Experts
Gorgeous Girls of Scandinavian, European
and Asian Extraction
As Well As All-American Beauties

***

TRY OUR FEBRUARY SPECIAL
ARE GIRLS ARE HOT WHEN THE WEATHER IS NOT

***

Ask about our special services
* Two-fers *
* domination, light and heavy *
* TVs, Pre- and Post- Ops *
All major credit cards excepted

*Ex*cepted. God. *Are* girls. Dead Eddie wrote the copy and every month asked her to proofread it, on the assumption, Mary Elizabeth assumed, that she'd be impressed, that she'd fall in love with his prose, if that's what it was, and with him, never believing—as he apparently didn't believe she knew he eavesdropped—that his prose, if that's what it was, made her want to strangle him. Maybe she could get him indicted for his diction.

Mary Elizabeth smiled. Maybe at the morning brainstorming she'd suggest that the way to nail Dead Eddie Milano wasn't to go after him for pornography or prostitution or loan sharking or extortion or usury or tax evasion or selling long-distance phone codes or—Dead Eddie's latest creation—wholesaling guaranteed drug- and AIDS-free urine and blood; the way to nail him was to indict him for his diction. Even Frances McAlistair, straight arrow Frances McAlistair, the WASP's WASP, would think that was funny.

Wouldn't she? Or would the professional in her swat aside the joke and say, *Why, Mary Liz. What's a nice girl like you, a staff lawyer in the office of the U.S. Attorney for the Southern District of New York, doing hanging out with scum like Dead Eddie Milano?*

3

Nothing to do but think.

Think that on that acrid summer Monday before the ice age set in, Quinlan didn't *tell* you to do a number on Frances McAlistair, not in so many words.

Taking that morning's paper off a pile on his desk and holding it up like a newsboy, he said:

"Convictions against seven Mafia capos, two congressmen, one state senator, one borough president, one deputy mayor, twelve arbitragers and thirty-five highway superintendents. That's just this year. Pretty soon, if you *haven't* been indicted by her, people're going to think you're not all that important. Which is no excuse for a piece like this, that her press agent would've toned down. That's why I asked you up here. Chuck. I want an in-depth profile, and I don't want Metro to do it. Karen Auburn's a good reporter, but you live in the forest, you get too tight with the trees."

You took a paper off the pile and looked at the cut that went with the story. "Attractive."

"You must be getting old, Chuck. For a federal prosecutor, she's a piece of ass."

"It's what we always call her, it's her epithet: 'Frances McAlistair, the attractive U.S. attorney.' Attractive's too formal, though; but if beauty's truth, she's not beautiful, either. She has poker player's eyes."

The intercom buzzed and Quinlan, fearful of allusions and metaphors, grabbed for the receiver. "Yeah? . . . Put her on." He swiveled around to face the window. "Hi. . . . Me too. . . . I'd like that."

You didn't come up this high that often, and you took the opportunity to get the lay of the land. The title on the door said *Executive Editor*, and while the decor didn't

11

contradict that, it betrayed an uncertainty (shared by the entire staff, in fact) as to just what an executive editor did. There was a view, but of Roosevelt Island and light-industrial Queens beyond; the imposing desk, the big leather swivel chair, the two oak-and-leather visitors' chairs, the sofa and coffee table, had all been chosen according to a purchasing department budget, not a decorator's taste—and certainly not an occupant's.

The desktop was a working stiff's, littered with newspapers, magazines and the knickknacks of authority: Quinlan's old White House press pass preserved in plastic; a gold-plated pica rule; a digital clock that regurgitated hundredths of seconds; a plaque that said *El Jefé*, a photograph of Quinlan with an arm around Sigourney Weaver, who had been the subject of a cover story in the Sunday magazine. But there was no typewriter or computer console, and the only pen was part of an expensive desk set—a gift from a mother-in-law or similar species: nothing got written on this desk; nothing got edited.

Into the phone, Quinlan said, "I will. . . . So do I. . . . Bye." He swiveled back and hung up. "So how *are* you, Chuck? Christ, it's been a long time."

"I'm fine. How's Audrey?"

Quinlan flinched. "Why?"

"It's been a long time."

"Still live in the Village?"

"A prisoner of rent control."

"That's funny."

"People don't laugh anymore. They just say, 'That's funny.'"

Quinlan grabbed for his newspaper and read from it disdainfully. "'For all the talk of a female Rudy Giuliani or Mario Cuomo or Pat Moynihan or Al D'Amato, the most frequent and perhaps inevitable comparison is with John F. Kennedy. Many a Washington socialite has been heard to wonder lately whether a President McAlistair might not someday reign over another Camelot on the Potomac.'" He lowered the paper. "Bullshit."

"And anyway, she'd have no consort." A blank look from Quinlan, so you added, "She's single."

Quinlan tossed the paper aside. "How about you? You still single, Chuck?"

"More than ever."

"You mean AIDS, don't you? I wouldn't want to be a young guy today, just starting to, you know, branch out. Still. Marriage, kids—they've hurt my career."

"You're a heartbeat from the top, Phil. You report to Fields, who reports to his conscience. Irregularly."

"That's funny," Quinlan said.

"What's funny?" Roy Fields said.

Quinlan's tailored suit, his custom-made shirt, Italianate shoes, refulgent watch, had impressed you, in this year's version of your same old poplin summer suit, with the extent to which your respective paths had diverged since you'd been musketeers of a sort. But if Quinlan was well-dressed, Fields was splendid, reeking of affluence and influence.

Quinlan was like a puppy getting up to greet him. "Roy, you know Chuck Ives."

Fields held his hand out like at least an archbishop. "I know of him, of course, but I don't believe I've had the pleasure." Having had it, Fields retrieved his hand and turned his back on you. "I just dropped in to say that I was surprised at first when Phil proposed that you write our profile on Frances McAlistair." He pronounced the name as if it tasted faintly off. "You did an outstanding job for us in Vietnam, of course, and although that war is ancient history, our reader surveys show that your column is one of our most popular features. You haven't covered much politics, but I don't want this to be a political piece. Yes, it's inspired by the speculation that Frances McAlistair might be presidential timber, but I don't want to know where she stands on what issues, what her chances are in this part of the country or that. I want a piece about *her*, about the kind of woman who has the . . ." In the caesura, you heard *balls*. ". . . the courage to take on the kinds of people she has—from the gnomes of Wall Street to the kings of Queens to the princes of Bath Beach."

Fields paused so you and Quinlan could appreciate his prose as much as he did. "I also want a piece about the *wom*an, the woman behind the public exterior. Phil says you're the man for the job."

You opened your mouth—to say what, you didn't know.

"Good," Fields said, and headed for the door. "I'll leave the details to you. I like my chief and his braves to map their own strategies."

You waited for things to settle down from the backwash. "Does that mean we're on the warpath . . . Chief?"

Quinlan picked up the newspaper and scanned the profile. "Brearley, Radcliffe, Harvard Law. Phi Bete, magna cum, law review. Then the humble bit: Peace Corps *and* VISTA. Union organizing, Legal Aid, public defender, blah blah blah. Facts, but no juice. You read *Playboy*, right?"

"You mean because I'm more single than ever?"

"There was a piece this month on the drug business in Colombia. A billion dollars a year. That you knew. A lot of Americans're getting rich down there, some of them former Peace Corpsmen. That maybe you didn't know. She was in the Peace Corps in Colombia. Does she know any of them?"

"So we *are* on the warpath."

"Take as long as it takes." Quinlan gave the back of his hand to the piece in the paper. "Everybody'll have crap like this in the next six months. I want something that'll answer all the questions. . . . Like why isn't she married?"

"Aha."

"She's forty-six years old."

"So am I."

"Run for President, people'll start asking why you're not married."

"She has lots of boyfriends, according to Karen Auburn."

"*Escorts*. She calls them *escorts*."

"Is there something you're not telling me, Phil?"

Quinlan spread his arms like a man who never didn't tell everything. "I just want a story."

"No. There's something you're not telling me. Customarily around here—or since the circulation dropped, anyway—"

"It's back up, Chuck."

"—stories're written as quickly as possible and chased

only as far as necessary. Unless they have recipes in them."
You pulled a section from the paper and held it out. "This
is one of the longest stories in today's paper; it's three times
as long as the story on McAlistair's latest indictments or the
one on the mayor's changing his mind—again—on the
Times Square redevelopment thing. It's about endive. Or is
it ahn-deeve? All these words, and it doesn't even say."

"What's your point, Chuck?"

You turned a page. "Here's a piece I missed. On
repairing plaster ceiling rosettes."

"They break."

"I wouldn't know. Since the circulation dropped, cross-
ing a river has been like going overseas. I went to Princeton
last month and put in for a car and tolls and lunch and got
the third degree from Stasio about why didn't I get the story
on the phone. He seemed to understand, when I explained
it to him slowly, that the governor's wife's thoroughbred
horse wouldn't *come* to the phone."

Quinlan laughed. "That was a funny piece. . . . You
rented a car to go down there?"

"But now you're telling me to take as long as I want and
to go to Colombia if I have to."

Quinlan held up a frugal hand. "Well, Colombia . . ."

"No one's going to tell me on the phone, Phil, if
Frances McAlistair was a narcotics kingpin."

"I'm not saying she was in*vol*ved in it, for Christ's sake.
I just want to know what she thinks about some of her
ex-fellow idealists making a bundle off it."

"What I infer, Phil, is that the people upstairs—I
forgot; I *am* upstairs—is that the people up here don't want
Frances McAlistair to go any further than she's already gone
and maybe don't want her to count on staying where she is
for very long."

Didactically, Quinlan said, "It's customary for a newspaper to have an editorial point of view as well as objective
news columns. You're right—they don't like her. They've
never liked her. But that has nothing to do with what you
write."

You got up and went to the wall on which were hung
blown-up photographs of some vivid moments from recent
history—macheted Latin Americans, emaciated Africans,

hopeful astronauts alongside the extravagant puff of smoke
that testified to the vanity of their hope, a disputed infant,
a triumphant athlete, a giant panda. You studied a photograph of a woman wailing over the bodies of four children,
but you couldn't tell what had killed them. You turned to
Quinlan. "Phil, you know me. I eat lunch at my desk. Once
a month, maybe, I go to Eddie's for stuffed cabbage, but I
take a book or a magazine, I don't stand at the bar. I swim
at the Y after work. I go home and read or watch a movie on
TV or go to one in the neighborhood. I don't read *People*
magazine—not even at the barbershop. By the time I'd
heard about Vanna White, she was ancient history—just
like Vietnam. My friends're settled types who mostly talk
about endive and just how *much* quality time they should
spend with their kids. I don't hear a lot of gossip. If there's
gossip about Frances McAlistair, I want to know what it is."

Quinlan shrugged, like *Okay, I didn't want to say this,
but you made me*. "Fields thinks she's gay."

You laughed.

"He *met* her. At some dinner. Look, Chuck. Find me
a decent-looking man or woman who isn't married and
doesn't date and who people don't sometimes wonder if
they're, you know, gay."

"Me."

Pointedly, Quinlan said, "You do live in the *Vi*llage,
Chuck."

"Am I supposed to've been deaf and blind to the phone
call you got a little while ago from a woman not your wife?"

Quinlan flushed. "Don't jump to conclusions, Chuck."

"Good. You're con*cerned* about people jumping to
conclusions. If I find out that McAlistair's clean, that she's
qualified, that she's what she seems to be—dedicated,
hardworking, humane and humanistic, single because she
feels a marriage couldn't stand up under the strains of a
career like hers—"

"It's not for you to decide if she's qualified, Chuck.
That's for the pols and the voters to decide."

"—if I find out all that, are *they* going to fiddle with the
story, add some *juice*, or take some out, to make an editorial
point?"

Quinlan waved a hand. "Just get me a story, Chuck."

You started for the door. "I'll send you a postcard from Colombia."

"Chuck?"

"Don't worry. If I go to Colombia, I'll take a bus."

"If McAlistair's not"—Quinlan waggled his hand—"you know, I don't want you getting mixed up with her. Not like the last time."

"Last is superlative, Phil. There wasn't any last time, only the one time."

"So you know what I'm talking about then."

Think that you might not be in this fix if you hadn't involved DeBree.

DeBree—just DeBree; sometimes spelled (by him as well as by his detractors) Debris—was the paper's gossip columnist, an improbably fat man (woman, said some of those detractors—and some of his fans—and, sometimes, he himself—or, in that case, she herself) with a tiny, beautiful, entirely bald head. He wore a beaten gold hoop in his left ear, Savile Row double-breasted gray suits all year round, Jesus sandals or Timberland boots, depending on the weather. The former were on his feet when he appeared at the door of your cubicle that acrid summer evening, fanning himself with a piece of folded copy paper. "Got your love letter, Chas. Gauche of you to send it by copyperson. You might've dropped it by in the flesh—or phoned."

"Your line's been busy all day. I stopped by once, but you were on the phone then too—wearing your sleep mask."

"Fluorescent lights, Chas. They're sapping what eyesight I have left—them and the damned computer consoles." DeBree pointed at your typewriter, an ancient, well-cared-for Underwood. "Where did you get *that*?"

"In the storeroom."

"*Store*room?"

"It's where they put the typewriters when they automated the newsroom."

"I *know* they automated the newsroom. That's my point. Where's your goddamn computer?"

"I can't work on one. I like to rip a copy book out and

ball it up when things aren't going well, and I like the way
a stack of books looks when they are. I give one of the news
clerks a few bucks to put my final drafts into the computer.'

"Luddite." DeBree held up his right hand. "See this
finger—the one that looks like a sausage? I smashed it
horribly the other day imploring my computer to cough up
some copy it had swallowed prematurely. It refused, and a
bit of misinformation perpetrated by my legman, the
incompetent, wound up in the paper. He assured me that
Joan Collins was having lunch with Donald Trump at La
Côte Basque. Well, yes, she was, but she was merely *a* Joan
Collins, from the Landmarks Preservation Commission or
some such. I had to run a correction, my third this month.'

"I always enjoy your corrections. You apologize the
way the rest of us admonish."

DeBree sniffed. "Famous people—and aspirants to
fame—must understand that they have a responsibility to a
gossip columnist, a responsibility to be where I said they
were, and with whom." He flapped your note again. "But
what's the meaning of this? Have you decided that it's time
we became lovers? Do you just *have* to know the truth
about my gender?"

"I'd like to take you to lunch someday soon."

DeBree rolled his eyes. "Lunch can mean only one
thing; You want information. *I* crave rapture induced by
your tender ministrations, and *you* want information. I'll
tell you this much and save you the cost of a Big Mac:
Frances McAlistair's no dyke."

You laughed. "Word's out."

"Oh, yes."

"I got the assignment this morning."

"It's nearly dark outside, Chas."

You pointed to the morgue envelopes on your desk.
"I've read most of the background. I'd like to know what's
between the lines."

DeBree sat on a filing cabinet and crossed his legs like
a starlet on a steamer trunk in a cheesecake photo from a
time gone by. "Every now and then someone comes along
who has nothing to hide and therefore nothing to be found
out. God knows it doesn't happen often, or I'd be schlep-
ping shopping bags around the Port Authority, and when it

does, most of the time it's because the guy's a bore . . . or the gal, though more often it's a guy, because, I've always felt, guys're transparent—present company excepted, of course—they don't have much in the way of an inner life. They know lots of facts and the names of things; they can go into hardware stores and say they want a . . . I don't know, Chas. You're a guy—what's something you'd know the name of if you went into a hardware store?"

"A cleat."

"There. You see? A cleat. What the *hell* is a cleat?"

You made a figure-eight motion in the air. "A thing you do this with—with a cord from a window shade, for example."

"I'll be damned. I've got one. In the bedroom. I hope it breaks, so I can get a new one. 'I'd like a cleat, please, and be quick about it. Don't stare at me like that, you swine. You think just because I'm a pederast I don't know what a *cleat* is?' I can't wait to see their faces."

"But Frances McAlistair, speaking of faces, is no bore, is she, Chas? She's interesting, very interesting, but I've never heard anyone say anything about her that I tripped over myself to determine the truth of because it would look good way up high in a column and give me an excuse to run a picture of that face—such a pretty face. I don't think I've ever had an item on her that wasn't just chitchat, not gossip at all, just, you know, that she was one of a hundred at this party, one of a dozen at that dinner, and not too many of those. She's a workaholic—God, I hate that word—and as I said, Chas, if she's gay you couldn't prove it by me, although if I were, as some would have it, a woman, I wouldn't kick her out of bed any more than I would if I were a man—if you follow. I give you my blessing, Chas, should you fall in love with Frances McAlistair.

"It *has* happened, Chas. You *have* been smitten by women you've written about. Okay, so it happened only once, but it was so dra*mat*ic. Don't get me wrong, Chas, love's a wonderful thing, and far better to love the people we write about than to hold them in contempt, which is what Roy Fields would have us do.

"Roy dropped in to visit just the other day; it was only the third or fourth time I've seen him on this floor; I

thought at first that he was an insurance salesman or
something. Aluminum siding. It seems someone had had
the dubious taste to invite him to a dinner party; among the
guests, it seems, was Frances McAlistair; he wanted to
know if she was"—DeBree waggled his hand—"'you know.'
He didn't have the balls to say it, of course. He just
said"—another waggle—"'you know.'"

"Quinlan mentioned the party," you said.

"May they both die slow, painful deaths in some stalled
commuter train . . . or better yet, suffer simultaneous
coronaries while committing sodomy—Fields, I think,
would be on the receiving end—in the executive wash-
room. It's people like them—*men* like them—who give my
métier a bad name. Good, clean gossip never hurt anyone;
but slander, the kind of unsubstantiated and unsubstanti-
atable hogwash they're always rooting in the garbage
for—Christ. Is that your assignment, Chas, to find the
smoking gun, the panting nymph? Not your usual beat.
How come Karen Auburn didn't get tapped?"

"Meaning?"

"Meaning why else is she sleeping with Quinlan if not
for the plum assignments."

"I try not to know about things like that."

"You probably don't believe me," DeBree said, "but so
do I. There are those of us, though, for better or for worse,
to whom 'things like that' adhere as do old newspapers to
the shins of certain pedestrians on blustery days."

"What can you tell me about her escorts?"

"You make it sound like a dirty word, Chas. There *are*
women—upstanding, reputable, decent, moral women—
who *need* escorts. It's *treyf* to show up at too many dinners
alone when you've been asked to bring a guest. There
might be thirteen at table—or a hundred and thirteen—and
such a woman can't bring a lady friend, old pal or heart-
throb, because *men* like Fields and Quinlan will always
assume she's the latter, and jerk off into their napkins at the
thought of what they're going to do when they get back to
the old boudoir; so such a woman gets an escort, unless she
wants to sit home alone watching *The Golden Girls*. Escort
doesn't mean gigolo, Chas; it means someone who talks
good and doesn't eat with his fingers. It helps if he's

attractive, but it's not a *sine qua non*, and he should know how to tie a bow tie, because those ready-made jobs with the little clasps in the back, well, they're for waiters and trombonists."

"The names I've come across—"

"Tom McNally, magazine magnate, Himalayan climber, nature photographer; Joe Briles, importer of God knows what, but people must be buying it, because you can't live in Hohokus, Dering Harbor, Palm Beach and Juan-les-Pins on promises; Eric Freedman, realist painter of nudes, they look like goddamn photographs, but none of Frances—not that he displays in public, at any rate; Paul North, Grand Prix racing driver, onetime movie actor, savior of whales, eagles, seals, and goddamn stray dogs, for all I know—those're the front four, Chas. And to your next question, has there ever been talk of her marrying any or all of them, the answer is no, she's a professional, for Christ's sake, she doesn't have time for marriage or a family. It's only men who think you can run a business—or a country—and also run a household, and that's because they don't have to run it—the household. . . . You're not writing any of this down."

You picked up some notes you'd made. "There's a chunk of time that's not accounted for in the clips. A year, more or less, in the early seventies."

"She was having a sex-change operation, Chas. Or on the road with Ozzy Osbourne. Or murdering little boys and cutting their things off. You'll find a necklace made of them in the back of her dresser drawer."

"Between the time she left California—she was a public defender in Oakland—and came to New York, to the D.A.'s office. Any idea what she was doing?"

"Ask her," DeBree said, then put out a hand. "I'm sorry, Chas, I don't mean to be snotty. Of course you'll ask her, and I know how it is—sometimes you like to know what the answer's going to be before you ask the question, but I've had it up to here with the likes of Fields and Quinlan and their assumption that any woman who wants to tread where only men have gone before can't possibly be qualified, and even if she were, she's still going to *menstru-*

ate every month—even dykes *men*struate—so who does she think she is, behaving as if she has *balls*?"

DeBree hopped off the cabinet and went out the door, calling back over his shoulder: "I'll have a look at my files, Chas, but don't hold your breath. As I said, Frances McAlistair's a mensch, or I'm a Samoan. Don't call me, Chas, I'll call you. Or drop by, darling, I'm not going to bite you. What a vision of loveliness you'll be. Ta, love. See you around the quad."

Think that—

4

Knicks over Seattle, Nets over Houston, Rangers over Montreal; Devils and Islanders both losers. The forecast from the National Weather Service: Snow, beginning as flurries sometime this morning, increasing this afternoon, with accumulations of three to five inches. High today around twenty, low tonight zero to five above in the city, five to ten below in the 'burbs. Right now it's four degrees, and with wind from the west at twenty-two miles an hour, it feels like . . . Big Eddy, Manitoba.

"You guys hear the one about the three junkies?" James Jones put his arm on the top of the front seat and turned all the way around to look at Jake Neuman, sitting on his ragg-wool-mittened hands, his ragg-wool scarf up around his nose, his ragg-wool watch cap pulled down over his ears, the hood of his down parka up and the drawstring drawn as tight as it would go.

"Watch the road, Jonesy," Neuman said, even' though there was no road to watch, only a white hole in the white world.

Jones faced front. "Two of the junkies're shooting horse behind. Third junkie comes by—"

"Behind what?" Matt McGovern said.

"Behind means they're sharing works," Steve Federici said. "Right, Jonesy? When bloods talk about smoking behind, drinking behind, they mean sharing a butt, a J, a bottle, right?"

Jones nodded. "Third junkie comes by, says, 'Don't you muh'fuhs be shooting behind. Ain't you muh'fuhs heard a AIDS?' First junkie says, 'Chill out, bro. It's solid. We can't get AIDS. We's wearing condoms.'"

Federici and McGovern laughed and Jones turned all
the way around again to look at Neuman. "Come on,
Lieutenant. Chill out."

Neuman *was* chilled out. Frozen solid. Colder than
he'd ever been in his life. He was that cold all the time, day
and night, indoors and out. Some people seemed to be
adjusting to the cold and the snow: his wife, Maria, born
and raised in Puerto Rico, was one of them; Jones, born and
raised in Durham, North Carolina, was another; Federici
and McGovern, born and raised in Bay Ridge, Brooklyn,
and Richmond Hill, Queens, respectively, were two more,
which meant that where you were born and raised probably
had nothing to do with it. Neuman, born in Park Slope,
Brooklyn, and raised in Sunset Park, Brooklyn, was not one
of them. But then he'd been shot at recently, which set him
apart from Maria and Jones and Federici and McGovern
and most of the rest of the human race regardless of where
they were born.

"You guys hear about the woman who put her husband
in a wood chipper?" McGovern said.

Federici, sitting next to Neuman, leaned his forearms
on top of the front seat. "Let's hear it."

"It's not a joke. This guy in Canada or something was
missing for two years, it turned out his old lady put him in
a wood chipper."

"Moose Paw, Canada," Jones said. "I read it too. In the
Star."

"Moose *Jaw,*" McGovern said. "It was in the *Post* too,
and the *Post* said Moose *Jaw.*"

"I don't care if it was Moose Twat," Neuman said. "I
don't want to hear about it." Didn't want to hear about
people who put other people into machinery, then pretended that they'd disappeared. It was too much like
someone who strangled his wife, then raped her (putting on
a condom—or maybe he'd already been wearing it—so
there'd be no semen), then pretended he'd come home
from a business day trip and found her dead and violated in
the kitchen, the back door lock broken and a bunch of stuff
stolen; then when a cop who'd bought his story along with
everybody else came around one day months later to tell
him a would-be rapist had gotten nailed with his dick out

and they'd found a lot of hot merchandise in his apartment and could he please take a look at it and see if any of it was his, because if it was, it could mean it was the scumbag who nailed his wife; but for some reason he thought the jig was up, and before the cop could say why he was there he reached under this ratty old gray sweater he was wearing and whipped out a Star 30PK 9mm fifteen-shot lightweight and pointed it at the cop—Neuman—and pulled the trigger and missed the cop—Neuman—by about this much.

And didn't want to hear about Canada, either. There was some jerk on the radio who was always saying it was so cold it *feels like* someplace in Canada, someplace Neuman had never heard of but that sounds colder than hell. If Neuman ever ran into the jerk, he was going to cuff him and take him to the nearest butcher and make him sit in the freezer closet for about a week.

Federici was staring at him. "Jesus, Loo. I've never heard you talk like that. You're really ticked off about this Milner thing, aren't you?"

Neuman looked out the window at the whiteness. "Are we there yet?"

"We're still in the park," Jones said. "Couple of minutes."

Central Park? It didn't look like Central Park. It looked like the North Pole. Or maybe the South. Whichever one was colder.

"I saw a headline in the *Star*," Jones said. "I didn't read it, I just saw the headline. It said, 'Donor Wants Kidney Back.'"

Federici laughed. "Jen saw one that said, 'Infant Born Pregnant.' It freaked her out. What do you guys think of Vanna?"

"I'm sick of Vanna," McGovern said.

"I mean for my kid's name," Federici said.

"Vanna Federici," McGovern said. "Sounds funny."

"'Specially if it's a boy," Jones said.

"I told you a hundred times, Jonesy," Federici said, "it's going to be a girl. Jen had amniocentesis."

"You'd never know it," Jones said. "She looks healthy as a mule."

McGovern hit Jones's arm backhanded. "Jonesy, I ever

tell you what we used to call Steve back before he got married, started getting a gut? He was so fucking skinny we used to call him the Italian Scallion."

"What d'you mean, 'we,' you fat Irish fuck?" Federici said.

"Jennifer's Jewish, right? So what does she cook for dinner that's giving you that gut—matzo balls and stuff?"

"What're you running for, Matty—bigot of the year?"

"What did I say? I said 'Jewish.' To you that makes me a bigot? You just called me a fat Irish fuck."

"And you just called me an Italian Scallion."

"Enough," Neuman said.

"You guys hear about the DOA with the bucket of popcorn on his head?" Jones said. "McIver and Bloomfield pulled it. Guy in a sixplex movie theater on East Eight-six got whacked with a silenced nine-millimeter. Right behind the ear. A pro job, a mob-type hit, except the DOA's clean, he's nobody, he's just a guy. But his wallet was still in his coat, a fair amount of cash in it, his watch was still on his arm.

"Thing of it is, the dude that whacked him, after he whacked him he put one of those big buckets of popcorn on the DOA's head, left him sitting there propped up like that. Two shows he sat like that, nobody said anything, nobody called the manager, nothing. It was a Stallone flick, zillions of people. One of the ushers scoped the guy out, said he'd seen a lot worse, people fucking, even, shooting up, he didn't think it was any of his business if a guy wanted to sit there with a popcorn box on his head. Finally, some kids started razzing the guy, throwing stuff at him, paper and stuff. One of them threw a wadded-up cup, it knocked the box off the guy's head, they saw the blood, the bullet hole, they called the manager. Two shows. Four fucking hours."

"Maybe the guy was eating his popcorn too loud," Federici said.

"A Stallone movie," McGovern said. "It figures. Fucking Italians."

"Don't start," Neuman said.

"We're here," Jones said. "Fifth Avenue."

Neuman pulled his left hand out from under himself and rubbed at the side window; he erased the frost from the inside of the window but could do nothing about the ice crystals on the outside. Personally, it was the other way around: He could melt the frost on the outside from time to time, could walk around like a normal human being, conduct normal conversations, tell a joke or react to one; but he could do nothing about the ice crystals on the inside, the ones that had formed almost audibly as the bullet passed his left ear, making a noise of its own—a low, slightly annoyed moan. The second bullet, the one the man who'd strangled his wife, then murdered her, then pretended someone else had, the one he fired into his own mouth after the first bullet missed, Neuman hadn't even heard; he'd only seen the contents of the man's head sprayed on the wall of the foyer of the man's semiattached house in Douglaston.

Jones had to roll his window down to see—or make a stab at seeing—if there was any traffic headed south on Fifth: Santa and his reindeer, maybe, out for a post-Christmas training run. Born somewhere north of Moose Jaw and going full stride by now, the wind salted snow all over the inside of the car.

"Shut the window and go for it, Jonesy," Federici said. "If anybody hits us we'll just end up in a nice soft snowdrift."

"Tell it to this guy Ives," McGovern said as Jones shut the window and went for it. "This newspaper guy. One of the uniforms in the situation whitetop said he landed in a snowdrift, he looked like Chinese takeout, they scraped up as much of him as they could, but we should watch where we walk, there's still pieces of brain lo mein sticking out of the snow."

"Nice, Matty," Federici said. "We didn't eat yet."

"So don't eat. Fuck do I care?"

"I got to eat regular. I'm pregnant too, is what Jen's doctor says."

"Cop Born Pregnant," McGovern said.

"Here we are," Jones said. "The guy in the blue coat is Milner, Lieutenant."

Neuman knew which one was Milner. Being so cold, having been shot at, not—now that Federici mentioned

it—having eaten . . . none of that mattered as much as
having to work with Milner. Thanks to a computer.

"Not a computer, Jake," Chief Inspector Lou Klinger
had said. "A computer *pro*gram."

Deputy Chief Inspector Miles Easterly had said, "Soft-
ware," but not with conviction that that was the right term.
He added, "We know you and Milner have this thing,
Jake."

"It's not a thing," Neuman said. "It's a deep-seated
animosity, underlain by profound mutual disrespect and
contempt for each other's morals and methods and reinforced by occasional but highly fraught confrontations over
a considerable period of time."

Easterly looked at Klinger, who looked out his window
at where the Tombs had been the last time he'd been able
to see more than a few feet, before it started snowing all the
time.

"Those aren't my words," Neuman said. "They're
Bernstein's, more or less. *Doc*tor Bernstein?"

"The department shrink, yes, we know, Jake," Easterly said.

"I don't call him a shrink," Neuman said. "I call him a
psychologist, which is what he is, on the theory—Bernstein's theory, but I go along with it—that if I call him a
shrink I'm not taking him as seriously as I should, I'm
putting him in the same category as chow or booze or butts
or doing the same thing an addict does when he calls
marijuana boom-boom or crack jumbo or heroin scag or
cocaine soda: kidding himself that he's not killing himself."

"Okay, Jake," Klinger said. "I get your point. *Our*
point—"

"Let me finish, Lou. Sir. Please."

Klinger sighed and shrugged and spread his hands
more helplessly than invitingly.

"I don't want to put Bernstein in the same category as
those things because I don't want to not take him seriously
because I figure if the department's going to have a
psychologist I should take him seriously—as seriously as
I take the M.D. and the phys ed instructor and the

substance-abuse counselor and the chaplain and the other specialists."

"Since when do you go to the chaplain, Jake?" Easterly said, and laughed. "*Or* the phys ed instructor?" He laughed harder, and his eyes implored the others to laugh too, to get this thing back on the joking level that he (who had called a shrink a shrink) was most comfortable with.

"Jake." Klinger got up and came around to sit on the front of his desk. "Jake, think about this: If you're taking these specialists so seriously—Bernstein, Capiello, the rest—you ought to take Podell seriously too."

"Podell's the computer guy, Jake," Easterly said.

"Jake knows who he is, Miles," Klinger said.

Easterly began to sweat.

"You see what I'm saying, Jake? Podell's come up with a program that matches detectives according to their skills, their backgrounds, their personalities, their off-duty interests. Okay, Jake, you're making faces, but it might surprise you to learn that you and Milner have quite a few of the same off-duty interests."

"I doubt that," Neuman said. "I doubt that because I don't spend my time off in men's stores, electronics stores, sporting goods stores, auto supply stores, every other kind of store, flashing my badge, putting my hand out, taking free suits, free golf clubs, TVs, tires, mufflers, salamis, free everything you can think of, and calling it community relations. Just for starters."

Softly, Klinger said, "Jake, if you have evidence that Lieutenant Milner's on the take, on the pad, shaking down merchants, whatever, it's your duty as both a private citizen and a public servant to make your allegations to Inspectional Services."

"Milner's a creep and a bum and a lousy cop," Neuman said. "I'll tell that to anybody who'll listen."

Klinger swung around to get a file off his blotter. He swung back and opened it and paged through it. "Did you know you and Milner're both taking art history courses?"

"*Dave* Milner? Slick Dave Milner?"

Klinger smiled. "He said, '*Jake* Neuman?' You both put in for transfers to Art Theft and both cited by way of credentials art history courses—yours at the Metropolitan

Museum, his at Brooklyn College. How is that course, Jake? Gladys was thinking about taking it."

"I don't know. I couldn't go to the first class 'cause I pulled a job, and I couldn't go to the second, third and fourth 'cause of the weather. The fifth is tomorrow, and it's supposed to snow again, right, and it looks like I'm pulling another job, right? *Dave* Milner put in for a transfer to *Art Theft?*"

"For the same reason you did, I suspect: There's not a lot of flying lead in Art Theft. You both had recent looks down the wrong end of perps' weapons. Every time a cop gets thrown down on—or often, anyway—they start liking the thought of the absence of flying lead in Art Theft, we start getting applications for transfers."

Neuman looked doubtful. "I didn't hear anything about Milner getting thrown down on."

"A junkie snitch," Klinger said. "He thought Milner laid some Peruvian rock on him, he threw down on him. His piece jammed. It's not really a hell of a lot different from what happened to you."

Before Neuman could demur that it was a *whole* hell of a lot different: that a junkie snitch was someone you were kid-glove careful around; that he'd been thrown down on by a man who'd convinced a team of detectives, a team of prosecutors, a grand jury and every police reporter in town that he'd been on the Southern State Parkway on his way to sell ornamental ironwork to a contractor in Valley Stream while his wife was being choked and violated in the kitchen of the semiattached house in Douglaston, a man he'd called on in the spirit of compassionate commiseration and in the hope that by maybe ID'ing a stolen microwave or something he would get some small measure of revenge, a man whose piece didn't jam, didn't jam *twice*—before he could say that, Klinger said, "Did you know you and Milner both have Hispanic wives—both named Maria?"

Neuman blinked. "Milner's wife is Sonya or something, and her brother's a rabbi."

"She died, Jake. About six years ago. He's been married for four years to a Venezuelan woman—also widowed. Has an eleven-year-old daughter by his wife's first marriage."

"The Slick Dave Milner who used to chase sixteen-year-old parochial-school girls? His wife better lock the kid up."

Klinger smiled. "People change, Jake. I remember a time when you'd've walked a beat in Far Rock before you'd go to a, uh, psychologist. Milner sees Bernstein too."

"*Dave* Milner?"

"Every week, in fact. You go only twice a month." Klinger tossed the file behind him and picked up the flimsy of an unusual. He spoke quickly, while Neuman was still back on his heels. "Charles Ives, a reporter for the *Herald*, died last night in a fall from the roof or a high floor of an apartment building at Seventy-fourth and Park—"

"A fall or did he jump or was he pushed?" Easterly said. "And was the high floor any high floor or was it the penthouse of Frances McAlistair, the world-famous federal prosecutor?"

"I heard it on the radio," Neuman said.

"Yes," Klinger said. "Well. Notwithstanding that Miles has already formulated an opinion, we'd like to conduct an investigation. The roof door's jammed shut by snow, so it's really just for form's sake that we're saying roof; McAlistair's apartment has a terrace on the south side, the Seventy-fourth Street side, and there were some indications that somebody went over the ledge, but nothing conclusive, nothing anything like evidence. The wind sweeps that part of the terrace pretty clean most of the time. Plus Crime Scene said the uniforms from the situations cars and the precinct squad both were a little slow on the uptake, McAlistair being who she is and all.

"The M.E. put the time of death at midnight, give or take an hour. McAlistair got home about ten-thirty and was asleep by eleven-thirty. She says Ives wasn't in her apartment. He'd been up there before, though—professionally and as a guest; he did a piece on her for his paper a couple of months back and did a bunch of interviews. He'd also been back more recently; one of the doormen told the precinct squad Ives was one of several guys McAlistair would have over for dinner. Not all at once; one at a time. McAlistair says the last time she had Ives over was about a week before, for cocktails with a bunch of other people.

"We want to take this away from the precinct squad, Jake. It's too hot. The computer program indicates you and Milner might be ideally suited for the job. We're not turning control of personnel deployment over to some machine, Jake; you needn't worry about that. And it isn't what some smartasses're calling the dating game. We're not looking for personal compatibility here; we're just trying to get the best matchups for certain cases—especially ones where there's going to be a lot of media attention.

"Dave knew Ives. I don't know all the details, but a few years ago—seven or eight—Ives covered a murder Dave'd pulled. Ives got involved with the victim's widow and got in the way of Dave's investigation."

It was Dave now, just like that. Dave and Jake. Old friends. Like that song Maria liked—*his* Maria: Willie Nelson and Roger Miller and somebody else. Playing croquet and pitching horseshoes and sitting on park benches, telling lies about old girlfriends. He and Milner could tell lies about mobsters and mass murderers and other lowlifes they'd nailed.

"Ives was a loner," Klinger said. "Single, parents dead, no siblings, no close friends, not even at work. At the time Dave knew him, he had a girlfriend Dave remembers as being smart, hip, knew her way around. He thinks if he can find her, maybe she knows what Ives was up to lately. Dave can tell you more about it. . . . You've handled some politically sensitive cases, Jake, is the reason why the program flagged you, Podell tells me. You see, you *can* ask a human being to evaluate what the program's done. It's not a case of the blind following after the inanimate."

Nicely said. Who had said it to him? Neuman wondered, for it wasn't the way Klinger usually talked. It was the way Bernstein talked, and the way Neuman talked when he talked about what he'd talked about *with* Bernstein, and the way the couple of other cops he knew who admitted to going to Bernstein talked when *they* talked about what they'd talked about with Bernstein. Maybe *Klinger* was going to Bernstein; maybe more cops than he realized were going to Bernstein; maybe every cop in the department was going to Bernstein, in which case he wouldn't be the only one to say what he was about to say—something Bernstein had taught him it was not only all right but vitally important to say when the occasion demanded. "No."

Klinger cocked his head. "No, what, Jake?"

"No, I'm not going to partner with Milner."

"We're not talking about a permanent matchup, Jake. We're doing this on a case-by-case basis. That's the point."

"No."

Easterly said, "Jake."

"You say the blind shouldn't follow the inanimate; I say the sighted shouldn't follow the assholes."

"Jake." Easterly again, almost out of hope.

Klinger got off his desk and went back around it to his chair. He sat. "That's an order, Lieutenant Neuman. You follow it, or you go out in the fucking snow and find yourself another line of work. Instead of studying art history, maybe you could start stealing paintings; I hear there's money in it. Miles, on your way out, ask Christine to come in here."

Milner said, "Well, well." He looked as though he'd been called away from a table at Joe & Rose or The Post House—a table full of swells and high rollers and big spenders, guys who called Sinatra Frank; he was bareheaded and shod in expensive-looking black tasseled loafers, and somehow neither his hair—his expensive-looking razor-cut hair—nor his feet were wet; he had the collar of his expensive-looking navy overcoat turned up and wore an expensive-looking gray cashmere scarf around his neck. He smiled at Neuman's parka and watch cap and L. L. Bean boots. "You look like Nanook of the fucking north, Neuman."

"Step over here for a sec, will you, Milner?" Neuman led Milner to the doorway of a doctor's office at one side of the front door. He turned his back to the wind so that Milner would have to face it, and when he ducked his shoulder into it, Neuman said into his ear, "One provocation, just one, and you'll get a bullet in the kneecap."

Milner laughed, opening his mouth to the snow and inhaling it like some fantasy monster. "I read that piece in the *News* about the guy throwing down on you, Neuman. You've got to be very careful when you talk to the media, because they've got it in for everybody, and they can make you smell like shit. Whoever wrote that piece—it wasn't a regular police-beat guy; you shouldn't talk to guys who aren't regular police-beat guys—whoever wrote it, he had it in for you, he made you sound like you were inarticulate, almost. It makes it hard for everybody, Neuman, because it makes it look like we're all a bunch of dumb fucks—you know what I'm saying?"

"Just one," Neuman said. "We won't count this one, so starting now. Just one."

Milner took his left hand out of his pocket—he wasn't wearing gloves—and looked at his watch, his expensive-looking gold watch. He looked at his expensive-looking diamond pinkie ring, too, and twisted it slightly back into plumb. "I hope you've got something halfway decent-looking under that stupid fucking coat. We've got a date with the sexy fed in about two minutes. You want to look around, or will you take my word for it that nothing happened down here except this is where he landed?"

In the best of weather, on one of those rare spring days when the city looks like an arboretum and all the women on the street look as though they have long legs and are hurrying to cocktails with Robert Redford, Neuman would have taken the word of just about any cop he could think of that there was nothing to be seen at the bottom of a building from which someone had jumped or fallen or was pushed. In the prevailing weather, with his toes so cold he wasn't sure he still had toes, he would have taken the word of some cops he wouldn't trust to give him the right time that there was nothing to be seen at the bottom of a building from which someone had jumped or fallen or was pushed. In the prevailing weather, with Slick Dave Milner giving his word that there was nothing to be seen, he said, "You go inside. I'll have a look around."

5

"Two, uh, homicide cops're on their way up," Bill Dolan said. "We've got about five minutes."

Frances McAlistair nearly rebuked him for the particle but let it pass. "To get our story straight?"

Dolan folded his hands like a priest, which automatically put a brogue on his Brooklynese. "Frances, you have nothing to worry about."

She quoted him back at himself. "'Anyone who has to be told he has nothing to worry about has a shitload to worry about.' Or she."

Dolan got a file out of his briefcase—something to take her mind off the shitload she indeed had to worry about. That reporters and photographers and television crews weren't scaling the building to get a look at the setup was due only to the weather; that they were imprisoned in their dreary offices, where the tasteless jokes of their colleagues and the paranoia of their bosses goaded them to speculate wildly, was even more worrying.

Dolan had a fractional preference, among the news accounts he was aware of to date, for those that tried to make something of the three years Charles Ives had spent as a correspondent in Vietnam; he had even made some calls to reporters, reminding them that Ives had written a roman à clef that contained this illuminating passage:

> Severn worked in Saigon for three years, came home for what he had intended to be a vacation and found that he was a casualty. O'Neill escorted him to a private office, sat in its chair as if to demonstrate that it swiveled and said that the readers weren't interested in places halfway around the world, that they were

*interested in the city and its people. When Severn said
that the war was coming to an end, O'Neill said,
"Exactly." When the end came and Severn asked to go
back to cover the aftermath, O'Neill said, "It's over."*

*Severn worked in his private office for a year,
writing about the city and its people and growing dull.
In Saigon, half a day ahead of New York, he had felt as
if he were riding the world's prow and was the first to
sense changes in its speed and bearing; back in New
York, he felt as if he'd missed everything by the time he
got up.*

Vietnam: what a handy scapegoat. *Look, fellows,
you're asking me to speculate here and I don't care to. But
I will say this: Ives was in Nam voluntarily for a lot longer
than most guys were ordered to be. He clearly liked it, and
he just as clearly developed a view of himself as, well, as a
kind of cowboy journalist—an older, more mature Sean
Flynn, if any of you are old enough to know who he was.
Sneaking in buildings, climbing around balconies—those
might've been things he learned over there. I don't know
why he did them, or what he was after; I'm just saying that
he had a romanticized view of the job. And he probably felt
the same sense of dissatisfaction and betrayal that a lot of
combat vets feel. We've been hearing about post-traumatic
stress disorder among nurses, entertainers, rear-echelon
support personnel of all kinds; it shouldn't surprise any of
you to hear about it among correspondents.*

Bullshit, sure, but the-best-defense-is-a-good-offense
bullshit. Anything that headed off speculation about romance, sex, sin and so forth. Send them back into Ives's
past was Dolan's strategy, so that they wouldn't look too
closely at his and Frances McAlistair's present.

"Everything's in place for the Valentine's sting," Dolan
said. "There've been thirty-nine RSVPs—including several
of our most desirable targets. Artie Roth tumbled like there
was no tomorrow. There's absolutely no indication of
leakage. The bogus travel agency is in operation and has
handled not only numerous inquiries from targets but also
several from innocent civilians. The latter have been
referred to the legitimate agency that's been advising us.

The armory has been secured; the staff has been vetted to ensure against connections with the targets. Additionally vetted were . . ."

And on and on. But Frances McAlistair was no longer listening, was no longer in the study of her penthouse apartment at Seventy-fourth and Park, a blindfold of snow wrapped round the windows; she was in her office downtown last summer (The Last Summer, some pessimists were starting to call it), meeting, for the first time, Charles Ives.

Dolan, brisk, efficient, windswept even indoors, was there too: making the introductions; removing from the tape deck the cassette Frances McAlistair had been listening to (the Police, *Synchronicity:* did Ives notice: did he see irony there? would his readers?) and putting in a blank; rigging a microphone on a stand on the desk; explaining that while they were agreeable to Ives's request that no aides be present, they wanted to make a recording of the interview for their records; promising that he'd return in forty-five minutes to turn the cassette over; leaving.

Then an awkward moment, like that that stupefies a couple on their first date. She was thinking that he was unexpectedly handsome in his tan summer suit and blue shirt and yellow paisley tie; and more than that, interesting, especially with his battered leather briefcase, which looked as though it had been to hell and back. And she knew now, now in the dead of winter, that he was thinking, as he would one day write of her: *Frances McAlistair shakes a visitor's hand a little longer than necessary, a manifestation—literally—of her welcome. Her hand is big, her fingers long and spare, her grip expert. That is the right word, for the visitor's hand in hers is like a tool in a craftsman's. She is, after all, a public figure, and the visitor, a reporter, is useful.*

"The couch isn't as comfortable as it looks. Please sit in the chair." She sat on the couch. "I was a fan—if that's not too trivial a word—of your reporting from Vietnam. And then you took a leave of absence for a while, didn't you?"

Ives sat in the wing chair and put a cassette in his portable tape recorder. "I quit. I got tired of writing about what other people do." He set the recorder on the table. "I haven't used this in a while, and I'm not sure if the mike's working right. If you could please say something." He pressed the record button. "And thank you for saying you've read my work."

"You're welcome." She fidgeted and flicked a hand and shrugged and flicked the hand again and finally laughed. "I never know what to say."

Ives smiled. "Just say, Testing, one, two, three, four."

She got her composure back and said instead, "You wrote a novel about Vietnam. I read it too. I liked it."

"Thank you," Ives said, and stopped the tape and rewound it and played it back.

"*And thank you for saying you've read my work.*"

"*You're welcome. . . . I never know what to say.*"

"*Just say, Testing, one, two, three, four.*"

"*. . . You wrote a novel about Vietnam. I read it too. I liked it.*"

"*Thank you.*"

Ives stopped the tape and rewound it again and started to say something, and there was a knock on the door and Dolan put his head in. "I'm sorry, but I need a moment of your time. The Hale Mohalu matter."

France McAlistair stood and apologized to Ives and said it *would* just be a moment. She waved at the bookcases. "Feel free to browse. I've had some of those books since I was a girl. The map on the wall there was a present on my twelfth birthday."

And she went out and while she was out—she knew now, now in the dead of winter—Ives did browse. (*Snoop*, she'd almost said playfully, and *snoop* was the word he would one day use when he told her that's what he'd done.) She knew it because Ives had told her, but even if he hadn't told her she would have found out, because she'd played the tape back, just this morning, she and Dolan, and she had heard Ives saying, to his tape recorder but also to theirs:

"*Lots of books about women. Some of them young-adult biographies. Helen Keller, Anne 'Frank, Florence Nightingale, Eleanor Roosevelt, Joan of Arc, Sacagawea, Queen Victoria, Queen Elizabeth—the First, Amelia Ear-*

hart, Victoria Woodhull, Isadora Duncan, Zelda Fitzger-
ald, Golda Meir, Marian Anderson, Princess Grace, Billie
Jean King, Catherine the Great—thank God she has some
prurience—Loretta Lynn, Dolley Madison.

"And by women: *Jane Austen, the Brontës, Emily*
Dickinson. Friedan, Greer, Brownmiller, Rich, Sontag,
Steinem. Beatrix Potter, E. Nesbit, Isak Dinesen, Made-
leine L'Engle, Annie Dillard, Kathleen Raine, Margaret
Atwood, Beryl Markham, Anaïs Nin, Simone de Beauvoir,
Colette, Françoise Sagan, Lady Murasaki, Edith Wharton,
Francine du Plessix Gray, Agatha Christie, P. D. James,
Alice Munro, Phyllis Rose, Lillian Hellman, Marianne
Moore, Janet Malcolm, Shana Alexander—on Patricia
Hearst but not, that I can see, on Jean Harris—Diana
Trilling on Jean Harris . . .

"By men, I see only . . . *Kleist.* Kleist? *Mailer, on*
Marilyn Monroe. Bret Easton Ellis—good God. Styron,
Sophie's Choice. *And me.*"

Then there was nothing on the tape for a while. Just
the sound of pages turning—him looking at her copy of his
book, probably; feeling a little proud, perhaps, to be on her
shelf, to be in the company of (even) Kleist, Bret Easton
Ellis, Mailer and Styron; looking to see if she'd marked any
passages, perhaps, or left any interesting scrapes of paper
between the pages. Then a silence that she knew now (now
in the dead of winter) meant he was looking at the map, the
map she practically invited him to study, to snoop at; noting
the pinholes in the corners, testimony to how long it had
been part of her baggage, to how many walls and bulletin
boards it had been affixed; noting the single, solitary
pinhole *in* the map, a dot on the second *i* in *Louisiana.*

Then on the tape there was the sound of the door and
of her coming back in with a tray of coffee things, of Ives
making room on the coffee table and her setting the tray
down.

"That was more than a moment," she said. "I'm sorry.
An old friend in Hawaii asking for some professional advice.
We've been trying to connect for days. The six-hour, I think
it is, time difference. Are you going to write about my taste
in books?"

"If you don't mind. Your library's very different from mine. I have several copies of my book."

She smiled and he did too, and she asked him to please sign his book, and he did and handed it back to her. "I felt on seeing it the way I do whenever I come across it in a store—usually on a remainder table: that it's a forgery. I don't remember writing it. That's a new copy; you must've gotten it from my publisher."

She flushed. "If you mean did I just read it, yes. I thought I ought to know a little about you. Bill phoned your publisher."

"I'm glad they still have copies. They carefully guarded the fact of its publication."

Frances McAlistair put the book back on the shelf and sat back down. "Cream or sugar?"

"Nothing. That is, no coffee. Thanks."

She poured herself a cup, black. "I thought all newspapermen drank coffee. Black coffee."

"They do."

She heard the implication that he was not *all* newspapermen. "Well. Where would you like to start?"

"At the beginning."

She smiled, but her voice got cool. "Bill said you were writing a long piece. Your newspaper isn't exactly a supporter of mine, Mr. Ives. Short shrift is what I get in the news pages, and cavil from your editorial writers."

"It's not my newspaper," Ives said. He leaned over and depressed the pause button. "I'm not quibbling. A newspaper's editorial page—any paper's—no more speaks for its staff than do its movie reviews. And if you haven't gotten as much coverage as you'd like—"

"*And* I haven't liked the coverage I've gotten."

He sidestepped: "A newspaper's put out by people. Their foibles, their taste, their preferences, determine what the paper looks like every day more than any Citizen Kane-like statement of principles. I've written stories that were as fair as I could make them, and as thorough, and they were simply too long. Some of them got spiked by news editors, who believe that if you can't tell it short you shouldn't tell it at all; some got compressed by copy editors, who regard all reporters as enemies of style and sense, anyway; some got amputated in the composing room by makeup editors, who don't care what a story says or where it ends as long as it fits.

"Most editors are men, and many of them—especially the women—are misogynists, and in your case it's likely that along with the stories that got spiked and the stories that got trimmed there were stories that got thrown in the garbage out of a conviction that a woman who wants her name in the paper ought to act like a lady—or act not at all like one."

Frances McAlistair didn't let on that she was both enlightened and entertained by his explanation. "How is it a woman wasn't assigned to do this story? Karen Auburn's beat includes my office."

"Which makes her part of the same establishment you're part of. The piece she wrote speculating about your political aspirations was boosterish. And why not? Why should she rain on her own parade? I'm an outsider; I have a different perspective from Karen Auburn's. Not better, just different. As to why a woman *other* than Karen Auburn wasn't assigned, I can't say. I didn't ask. It didn't occur to me to ask."

"You thought you were the man for the job."

"The person."

"The person."

Silence. She played with her glasses, about which, she knew now, now in the dead of winter, he would one day write: *The visitor had once interviewed a Nobel laureate whose thick rectangular glasses seemed to help him see not only better but more. Frances McAlistair's glasses make her seem to be seeing. She wears them like safety goggles, as proof against entreaties. When she's at ease, they are parked up in her hair, or dangle by an earpiece from her pursed lips, or are discarded altogether on her desk. But confronted by a stranger, a petition, a tough question, and on they go; she seats them carefully with her fingertips against the temples, like a racer adjusting a crash helmet.*

She motioned at his tape recorder. "Do you want to turn that back on?"

He did, and Frances McAlistair said: "To begin at the beginning, my first memory is of being licked in the face by a large black dog. I was three, and playing on the lawn of my parents' summer home in Southampton. It was at the end of a road called Wyandanch—pronounced Wyan*dance* by natives, and named after a chief of the Montauk Indians. The dog must've been a neighbor's, because we had cats—three Abyssinians—and a Shetland pony. . . ."

6

The present intruded, in the form of Dolan, trailed by an investment banker and a Baxter Street bail bondsman.

The banker—his clothes looked edible, his jewelry on fire—took a step forward and bowed almost formally. "Lieutenant David Milner." He made a gold ballpoint pen materialize from an inside pocket, a leather-covered notebook from another, and—not like a banker now; like a maître d', if that's the word and of course it's not, at a funeral parlor—put a hand under her elbow to guide her toward a tea table and two Windsor chairs in a bay of the study.

"Uh, Milner?" the bondsman said. He looked as though he had been dressed by his mother—with care and love and at some expense—but could no more keep the flaps of his suit coat pockets untucked or the aprons of his necktie the proper length than he could hold his stomach in or train his cowlick. He had on his feet a pair of serious foul-weather boots.

Milner stopped and rolled his eyes, smiling at Frances McAlistair as he did, as if to say there was nothing to do but humor someone with such boots.

The bondsman motioned at the couch and the pair of armchairs around the coffee table. "Let's sit over here so there'll be room for all of us."

Milner sighed but turned back, putting a hand on Frances McAlistair's arm again.

She got free and stood her ground. "Whoa, now. First of all, who're *you?*"

The bondsman shuffled his boots. "Uh, Neuman, ma'am. Lieutenant too."

Milner snorted. "That's lieutenant *also*, Counselor."

43

"I think she got it," Neuman said.

"You do, hunh?" Milner said.

Frances McAlistair said, "Do you two know each other?"

For an answer, they sat in the armchairs at opposite ends of the coffee table. She sat between them on the couch, putting on her glasses (*wears them like safety goggles . . . seats them carefully . . . like . . . a crash helmet*). Dolan got one of the Windsor chairs and sat behind the couch at her left shoulder, the better to counsel the counselor.

Milner crossed his legs and checked the crease in his pants. "You're going to think you already answered the questions we're going to ask you, Miss McAlistair. And you have, some of them, and there's not much we can do about that. As you're well aware, one investigator's line of questioning isn't always another's: You start out being questioned by the uniforms from the situation whitetop, who've got an unusual to fill out and don't always ask about more than's on it; then you're questioned by the detectives from the precinct squad, who don't use forms so much, but there're progress reports and updates and like that; and then, in this case, anyway, you're questioned by Homicide, who don't use forms, either, but do do progress reports and updates too, but who don't always do things the way the precinct squad does them because Homicide's borough-wide and sometimes city-wide, in certain cases, as you of course know, and the precinct's the precinct, meaning a tight little island, with priorities and personalities and a precinct way of doing things, and the squad keeps that foremost in their minds at all times. Things're looser with Homicide, in a manner of speaking."

"I understand, Lieutenant," Frances McAlistair said.

Neuman understood too, and was interested, fascinated, bowled over, was having his socks knocked off. What had Milner, Dave Milner, Slick Dave Milner, *David* Milner yet, said to him about looking bad in the papers by sounding inarticulate, almost? *It makes it hard for everybody, Neuman, because it makes it look like we're all a bunch of dumb fucks—you know what I'm saying?* Looking bad in front of a witness who was maybe a suspect by sounding inarticulate, almost, wasn't such a good idea, either, but what Neuman understood was that Milner, Dave Milner, Slick Dave Milner, *David* Milner yet, was scared.

Not that Neuman wasn't scared too; he'd interrogated some heavy people in his day—a borough president, a city councilwoman, a couple of commissioners, some rogue cops, a criminal-court judge, a lot of movers and shakers, a lot of people who were famous in their circles (which were rarely the circles of the other famous-in-*their*-circles people, so fame, like everything else, was relative), nuns, priests, ministers, rabbis, gurus; and he shouldn't forget the one who had impressed an awful lot of people, including his wife, Maria, the most: a TV game show host—but never a prosecutor and never a fed. He, who usually talked too much, didn't feel like saying anything; Milner, who was usually pretty tight with the words, had a case of motor-mouth.

"I was at my office last night until seven-thirty," Frances McAlistair said. "A government driver took me to Mazza's, on Kenmare Street, where I had dinner. I was there until about nine-thirty—"

"Dinner with?" Milner said.

"A friend."

Milner uncrossed his leg and crossed the other. "I didn't imagine you having dinner with an enemy, Counselor. Oh, I suppose you might if it was business, but you'd probably do business at lunch, and you probably wouldn't do it in a place like Mazza's, where there're just as many bad guys eating lunch as there are good guys."

Dolan: "If there's a direction to this line of inquiry, Lieutenant, it might be helpful if you'd state it."

He can't help it, Neuman thought. You're lucky what he's saying looks anything like a line at all, you're lucky it doesn't look like a pretzel, like a bad dream.

Frances McAlistair put a hand up to check Dolan. "My friend's name is Tom McNally, Lieutenant. But you know that: it's on the unusual. And it's not relevant. You want to know times here, Lieutenant, and you don't need Mr. McNally to verify them. There are waiters, cashiers, drivers, doormen."

Milner made squiggles in his notebook. "He's a publisher, McNally, right? I seem to remember reading something about how he's a publisher."

"Yes, he's a publisher."

"A sports magazine or something? It's a sports magazine he publishes, isn't it?"

"A mountaineering magazine."

"Mountaineering. Right. Mountaineering. I've never done any mountaineering. Golf's my game."

Golf and graft, Neuman thought. Golf and graft and, now, gab.

"Not very good weather for golf," Frances McAlistair said, and Neuman wondered what was behind her saying it: Was she trying to elevate the conversation, or was she slumming?

Milner made a gesture that she would understand, she who lived on Park Avenue and went out with publishers of mountaineering magazines but also made life miserable for dons and shysters and other assorted maggots, a gesture like what could you do: if you could you'd be down in Augusta, out in Palm Springs, at Pebble; but there was work to be done and you were the only one who could be counted on to do it.

"Not very good weather for eating out, either, is it, Miss McAlistair?" Neuman said.

They all stared at him. He would've too if he could have, if there'd been a mirror handy.

"Meaning what, Lieutenant?" Dolan said, but Frances McAlistair put a hand up again. "I get it, Lieutenant Neuman. Mr. McNally and I had been seeing each other for about six months. It was time, from my point of view, to break things off. No, it was no night to be out late in a restaurant, but it had to be done, and it's the kind of thing that's best done when it has to be done *and* in a public place."

"And?" Neuman said.

Frances McAlistair tucked her chin defensively. "I'm afraid I don't understand."

"It had to be done: Did you do it? *Was* it best that you did it in a public place? Did McNally get the message? Did he take a walk? None of that's any of my business, probably. But what *is* is, did you go home alone?"

She came out of her huddle. "As it says on the unusual, yes."

Milner flapped the cover of his notebook, but Neuman kept right on. "You said you were at Mazza's till around nine-thirty. Kind of weather it is and all, it must've taken you a good hour to get home from Little Italy."

"Forty-five minutes," Frances McAlistair said. "I got here about ten-fifteen. The government driver brought me; his name is Glatter, Lester Glatter; Detective Luizzi of the precinct squad has his address and phone number. Felix, the night doorman, was on. I got my mail and spent a minute or two, or maybe five, going through it at a table in the lobby, so that I could winnow out the junk and throw it away before I went upstairs. I *went* upstairs, got my boots off and my coats and sweaters—you know how it is these days—checked my phone messages, made some tea. It was the first chance I'd had to look at a newspaper, so I skimmed through one while I was standing there in the kitchen waiting for the water to boil."

"Which brings us to what?" Neuman said. "Ten-thirty, or quarter to eleven?"

"I was planning to watch the late news," Frances McAlistair said, "and was aware that it was something shy of eleven, but not how much."

"Go ahead."

"I got a phone call from Tom."

"McNally?"

Dolan: "Really, Lieutenant."

"Saying?"

"Saying I hadn't given him an opportunity to tell his side of it, that—"

" 'It'?"

Dolan: "Jesus."

"It's all right, Bill," Frances McAlistair said. "Our re*lation*ship, Lieutenant."

"Your romance?"

"I wouldn't call it that."

"I noticed you didn't. But was it? Was it a, uh, you know, an affair?"

"You mean, did we have intercourse?"

"Yeah."

"No."

"No?"

Dolan, sternly, emphatically: "Lieu*ten*ant."

"So you hadn't given him a chance; did he want the chance then?" Neuman said.

"He said he wanted to come over, yes."

"And?"

"And I told him no. It was late. It was far. He lives on Sutton Place."

"But he doesn't just *pub*lish the magazine, he *climbs* mountains, right? Mountains with snow on them a lot of the time, probably."

"Yes. So?"

Neuman shook his head. "Go on."

"I went to bed."

"You had a cup of tea, then you went to bed? I have a cup of tea, I'm up half the night. I have a *sip* of tea . . ."

"It was herbal tea, Lieutenant. Emperor's Choice."

"Emperor's Choice? I'll have to try some of that. So you didn't watch the news?"

"The phone call upset me. I didn't need another dose of calamity."

Neuman nodded. He liked that; that was what life was, wasn't it? Certain lives, anyway: his, hers, *David* Milner's. A couple of vitamin C's, some calcium and a dose of calamity. "Go on."

"I was awakened at one o'clock. Policemen knocking on my door. A man had jumped or fallen to his death; the doorman believed the victim to be an acquaintance of mine; did I know anything about it?"

Milner leaned forward. "Were there any phone messages?"

Frances McAlistair stared at him. It was the question of someone who'd fallen way behind; what had happened to the banker, to the mortuary maître d'?

"You checked your phone messages. Were there any?"

Neuman thought Milner's a good question, the question of someone who'd taken a step back to look for chinks and rough edges and loose ends; and he thought the time as good as any to ask it. It was a question he hadn't thought to ask and might not have, not today; maybe on another go-round he'd have thought to ask it. But not today, and today was the day the questions mattered most, not the order you asked them in. And the answers, not the order you got *them* in. Mattered most because the daily dose of calamity was still fresh in the mind of the answerer.

"There're *always* messages," Frances McAlistair said.

"Any from, uh, Charles Ives?" Milner said.

"No."

"Do you have the tape?" Milner said.

She flicked a hand. "It's in the machine. It's been recorded over."

"Because you went out this morning?"

"No. I stayed in. But I had the machine on at times, so I could get some work done."

"But only at times, so there's a chance some of yesterday's messages might *not*'ve been recorded over. You wouldn't have gotten as many calls in a morning, is what I'm saying, as you did all day and into the night yesterday."

Dolan: "There've been a lot of calls, Lieutenant, from concerned friends, colleagues—even a few concerned rivals. The White House chief of staff called, on behalf of the President."

Milner looked at Neuman, who met his look and saw in it that Milner wasn't going to go any farther with this, that Neuman should pick up the ball again.

This was a little weird: He and *David* Milner didn't work half bad together. Beginner's luck, probably. "The doorman you mentioned, Miss McAlistair, who you said believed the, uh, victim was an acquaintance of yours—is that the Felix you mentioned before who was on when you got home?"

"No. Felix goes off at midnight. The regular overnight doorman is Juan, but Juan's on vacation and his relief man's name I don't know."

"Menendez," Dolan said. "Roberto Menendez. He's a regular relief man at a bunch of buildings in the neighborhood. He's clean."

Neuman said, "Clean, sure, but smart we don't know,

right? Like maybe he doesn't know all the tenants for sure by sight, he maybe lets people in he shouldn't."

"I wouldn't know, Lieutenant."

"So after you woke up, what did you do, Miss McAlistair? Did you go downstairs and ID the body?"

"Yes."

"And?"

"And it was Charles Ives."

"What I mean, I guess," Neuman said, "is how did you feel about it?"

Dolan stood. "I think we're going to wrap this up for now, gentlemen."

"Sit down, Mr. Dolan," Neuman said. "Please."

Dolan sat.

Neuman got his notebook out and searched three pockets for a pen before finding one. He opened the notebook, took the top off the pen and scribbled on the pad to get the pen going. It took a while and he almost thought he was going to have to ask *David* Milner if he had a pen he could borrow. "You left Mazza's around nine-thirty, Miss McAlistair, you got here around ten-fifteen, you got a phone call a little before eleven; how long was that call?"

"Ten or fifteen minutes," Frances McAlistair said. "I was another ten or fifteen getting ready for bed. I was probably in bed by eleven-thirty."

"Go to sleep right away?"

"Pretty quickly, yes."

Neuman looked at Milner and Milner at Neuman, trying to work out without saying it out loud which of them should say: *You expect us to believe it was pretty quickly even though you just told your boyfriend of six months— okay, so you weren't sleeping with him; something was going on—to take a hike and he didn't like the sound of that, he wanted to come over here in the middle of a fucking blizzard, maybe was on his way over even though you told him not to . . . that is what you told him, isn't it, Counselor?* Without saying it out loud, they decided neither of them should say it.

Instead Neuman said, "And at one A.M. some cops knocked on your door?"

"Yes."

"And according to the unusual, they'd been called about twelve-thirty by the overnight doorman, Menendez. He went out to shovel the sidewalk as far as the corner and found Ives's body."

Dolan: "Lieutenant, so much of this is—"

"Nobody saw Ives go in the building: not Menendez, not Felix—whose last name, according to the unusual, is Marcial—not any of the tenants . . . or not any who've come forward to assist in our investigation, at any rate, although we've got men going through the building right now, however, asking people if they saw anything.

"Okay, so maybe Ives went past one of the doormen when his back was turned. Okay, so there're a couple of service entrances, and with delivery guys coming out, it would've been easy enough for Ives to slip in without being seen, and maybe that's what happened. Of course, for that to happen it would've probably had to happen way back in the afternoon sometime, when the stores were open, unless they were liquor store deliveries, Chinese food. Or maybe what happened is that he was already in the building, for a long time maybe, like maybe so long no one remembers his coming in because he'd already been in so long no one remembered."

"Meaning you think he had been a guest of mine, Lieutenant?" Frances McAlistair said.

There was a rule wanting formulation—a would-be Neuman's Law—that when someone asked a question like that, starting by saying *meaning* and their voice going up and up and up the scale, and ending by saying *Lieutenant*, or whatever your rank was, in a certain kind of way that was almost like saying *Sonny* or *Buster* or *Mac* or *Buddy* or *Pal*, they were guilty. Period. Well, not guilty guilty but . . . faulty, flawed, imperfect, defective. And sometimes they were proud of it, almost, or arrogant, or determined at any rate not to do anything to change, but other times (and he thought this was one of them) they were asking you to help them repair the fault, the flaw, the imperfection, the defect—or at least not to come down on them too hard while they did the patching up themselves. "Was he?" Neuman said.

"No," Frances McAlistair said.

"But he had been," Milner said.

Him again. Frances McAlistair turned toward him. "He had been in my apartment, yes."

"I know," Milner said.

Frances McAlistair opened her mouth, but nothing came out.

Milner grinned. "I know because I know the guy."

Dolan: "Lieutenant—"

Frances McAlistair cut Dolan off. "Then presumably you know that he was in my apartment because he did a number of interviews for a profile he wrote for his newspaper."

Milner shook his head. "I didn't know that, no. I just know the guy. And when were the interviews?"

Then there was this Neuman's Law: Grill somebody long enough—even a prosecutor, even a fed—and a case of motor-mouth would run its course and the questions you asked would be good, hard questions.

"The interviews were last summer," Frances McAlistair said. "The profile was in the early fall. Wasn't it, Bill?"

"November," Dolan said.

"So when the doorman said he thought Ives was an acquaintance of yours, he was talking about an acquaintance from last summer?"

"I don't know what the doorman thought," Frances McAlistair said.

"I know what *I* think he thought," Milner said. "I think he thought Ives was an acquaintance of yours from right now."

"What makes you think that, Lieutenant?" Frances McAlistair said.

"I told you, I know the guy. Not the doorman—Ives."

Dolan: "Would you like to put your innuendo in the form of a question, Lieutenant Milner?"

Milner said, "Sure. The question is did you tell McNally to get lost because you were making time with Ives?"

Frances McAlistair smiled. "No, Lieutenant Milner, I was not making time with Charles Ives. Nor with anyone else. I stopped seeing Tom McNally because he wanted to get married."

"And you don't?"

"No."

"Not to him, anyway?"

"Not ever."

"Ever. Hmm."

Neuman took a turn. "You ever give Ives a key to your apartment, Miss McAlistair? Yes, Dolan, I know there's no evidence Ives was *in* the apartment. Did you ever give him a key, Miss McAlistair?"

"No. And no, I never gave him a key temporarily, from which he might've made a copy."

"Yeah, well. That was my next question."

"And if he somehow smuggled a key out—*stole* a key, whatever—I know nothing about it."

"Yeah, well. I was going to ask that too."

"The last time I saw Charles Ives was at a cocktail party I gave here last Wednesday. There were eight other guests; I can give you their names if you like. The first guest arrived at six-thirty; they were all gone by nine."

Neuman nodded. "That was my *next* question." And this Neuman's Law: Somebody grilled long enough—especially a prosecutor, especially a fed—would eventually start anticipating your questions and by answering them before you asked them turn the grilling to his advantage. Or hers.

Milner stood. "I think that'll be all for now, Counselor. Thanks for your time. We can see ourselves out, Dolan. We'll be in touch. Let's vamoose, Noomz."

Noomz? It *was* just beginner's luck; this was no time to leave, it was time to circle around, home in, hit her with this little inconsistency, then that one, all that.

In the hall by the elevator, Neuman said, "What the fuck, Milner?"

"That's what I was going to ask you."

"Meaning what?"

"You mean you don't have anything?"

"Have anything? I've been on the case half a day. *You* knew the guy."

Milner put on his overcoat and turned the collar up, checking the effect in a floor-to-ceiling mirror. "You know what they're doing right now? They're making sure there're no messages on that tape from yesterday, because she knows one of those messages—I don't know if Dolan knows it; I can't figure yet what Dolan knows—she knows one of the messages was from Charles Ives, saying he had something to tell her, he was coming over, it didn't matter if she was out, he'd wait till she got back, the doormen knew him, he probably had a key. Ives had a ring of keys: Eight'll get you five one of them's hers."

"*You* knew the guy," Neuman said.

"That's right," Milner said.

Neuman laughed.

"Fuck's so funny?"

"You sure were fucking scared in there."

"Meaning the fuck what?"

"Watch my lips, *Milns*. You sure were fucking scared in there."

"You're a fucking asshole, Neuman."

"Kiss my ass."

"Scared? Shit. You see her face? *There's* someone who's scared. This thing'll be wrapped up in a couple of days. A couple of days, she'll cave."

"'Cause you're on the case? Shit, she's up there laughing right now."

"Don't push it, Noomz."

"Don't call me Noomz."

"Asshole."

"Motherfucker."

Milner tapped at the call button with a fist, like a fighter at a speed bag. "Where's the fucking elevator?"

"I'm going to walk," Neuman said. "Maybe I'll run into my guys, see what they came up with."

"Your guys couldn't come up with a snowflake." Milner laughed.

"Jesus, Milns, you're a piece of work."

"You would know, Noomz. You would know."

"Scumbag."

"Motherfucker."

"Down, gentlemen?"

7

Rangers over the Devils, Islanders downed the Bruins, Knicks beat the Nets. National Weather Service forecast: Cloudy and cold, high fifteen to twenty. Tonight, snow, accumulations of two to three inches, with temperatures in the low to mid teens. Right now it's twelve degrees and partly cloudy; with the wind from the northwest at twelve miles an hour, it feels like . . . Rimouski, Quebec.

"So they're gonna what?" Dead Eddie Milano said. "Indict her, Frances McAlistair?"

"She hasn't done anything, Eddie," Mary Elizabeth Indelicato said. "Along with a presumption of innocence, the American people are granted freedom from indictment when they haven't done anything."

"Yeah, well, she was home when he took his tumble, the reporter."

"Quite possibly, Eddie, you've never been in an apartment like hers. It has more than just a lot of rooms; it has . . . dimension."

"Dimension? Oh, hey, sorry. I didn't realize it had dimension. I thought we were talking about, you know, a regular apartment what regular people live in, not a apartment wit dimension. How could I of been so fucking stupid? Dimension."

"Keep your voice down, Eddie. Val's on a call. A man who's been her customer for *seven* years."

For seven months Dead Eddie had been horny for Mary Elizabeth Indelicato; how the hell could a guy be horny for a piece of trim for seven *years?* If that's what he was, horny, the guy on the phone with Val. Dead Eddie didn't know what the guys who called his girls were when it came to, you know, being horny. He didn't know if they got off the way they got off because they couldn't get off any other way or if they got off the way they got off because that was the way they liked getting off, thanks, and not only that they liked it more than a little bit, they liked it a lot.

Shit. Dead Eddie didn't like the sound of that. He usually managed to convince himself that the guys who called his girls got off the way they got off because they couldn't get off any other way and therefore didn't feel very good or very good about themselves—and especially didn't feel very good about the girls who helped them get off. If that was the way they *liked* getting off, thanks, and not only that they liked it more than a little bit, they liked it a lot, it probably meant they not only felt good *and* good about themselves, they also felt good—*very* good—about the girls who helped them get off.

Which meant that the guy on the phone with Val, the guy who'd been calling her for seven years, didn't feel sorry for himself, or frustrated. He felt great, on top of the world. *And* meant that the guys who called Mary Liz, some of who'd maybe been calling her ever since she started working there (he oughta check the logbook, the credit card receipts), might not feel sorry for themselves, either, or frustrated, they might feel great, on top of the world, because for all intensive purposes they were getting *laid*, which was more than *he* could say, even if he *was* Dead Eddie Milano.

Dead Eddie Milano, the baddest motherfucker. The meanest dude. The woist of the hombres. Long before he was Dead Eddie, when he was Edward to his mother and to the nuns at Our Lady of Pompeii and Ed or Eddie or snotnose to his brothers and sister and friends and no-good punk to his father, he went to the Loew's Sheridan (gone for years now; who even remembered that it had been there?), not too far from where his family lived on Sullivan Street, and saw *Shane*. And whereas every other kid Edward or Ed or Eddie knew came out of *Shane* wanting to be Alan Ladd or the kid, Brandon de whatsis, Eddie wanted to be Jack Palance. Jack Palance dressed all in black, with a black glove on his shooting hand to keep it warm and limber in case he had to berk one of the sodbusters; Jack Palance,

who looked so mean riding into town for the first time on a
horse as mean as he was that the old fart sitting in front of
Eddie (sitting a seat away from his old fart wife because
that's the kind of old fart couple they were), turned to his
wife and said of Jack Palance:

He's the woist hombre.

And Eddie knew then and there that if it took him the
rest of his life, he was going to do things that would make
people—not old farts; people who knew stuff—say that
about him.

At first, what they said about him was, *That stupid
fuck Eddie Milano slept on a fire escape last night on
account a it's so hot, he fell off, didn't even get hurt—'cause
he landed on his fucking head, prob'bly.*

Or: *We're playing punchball on Spring Street, right,
Eddie Milano's playing outfield, Ant'ny Piscatelli punches
one all a way to Thompson, Milano goes back under it, this
taxi turns the corner, he smacks right the fuck in a it, goes
over the hood, doesn't even get hurt—'cause he landed on
his fucking head, prob'bly.*

Or: *We wave the piece under the clerk's schnoz, he
hands over everything in the till, we head for the door,
everything's golden, 'cept Eddie Milano, instead a going out
the fucking door the way we come in, he goes through the
fucking plate-glass window, it breaks all over the fucking
place, everybody hears it, turns around, I'm standing there
in the middle a A'lantic Avenue wit a fucking piece in one
hand, a fucking paper bag full a money in the other. We ran
like hell, I'll tell you, and you know what? Fucking Eddie
doesn't even get hurt—not one fucking cut; says he was a
little sore the next day, that's all.*

And finally: *Fucking spook says, "Beat outta my way,
muh'-fuh," Eddie says, "Kiss my ass, you jive shvoog,"
spook says, "Say what?" Eddie says, "You heard me, you
lowlife scumbag slime-bucket nigger pansy," spook pulls a
fucking three-fifty-seven magnum outta his pants, points it
at Eddie, pulls the trigger, thing sounds like a fucking
cannon, man, I think it's the fucking end a the fucking
world, man, thing of it is, it misses him, or maybe it goes
right through him, I don't know, one or the other, all I
know is fucking Eddie doesn't have a fucking mark on him,*

he reaches out, takes the three-fifty-seven outta the spook's hand, throws it on a floor, he hits the fucking spook in the fucking nose wit the heel of his hand, fucking breaks it, the spook's nose, walks away. Fucking son-a-a-bitch, man, I thought he bought it, Eddie.

You know what else I think, man? I think the reason Eddie never gets hurt or nothing—remember the time he fell off a a fire escape, the time he got hit by a taxi, the time he walked right through the fucking plate-glass window, remember all a them times?—I think the reason Eddie never gets hurt or nothing, killed or nothing, 'is the son-a-a-bitch is already dead. *You dig where I'm coming from, man? I'm saying the reason Eddie Milano never gets hurt or nothing or killed or nothing is he's already dead. Like, you know, in a horror flick or something—he's going a, you know, live forever or something on account a he's already dead.*

"I ax you something, Mary Liz?" Dead Eddie said.

Mary Elizabeth was looking through *American Lawyer*. "Because it's there."

"Fuck does that mean—''cause it's there'? Oh, I get it. You think I want a ax you how come you work here, you having a law degree and all, having a nice pad, nice clothes, coming from a good family, a good neighborhood, not like Val and them, Val and them're fucking lowlifes from fucking Queens, Staten Island, fucking Norma's from fucking Valley Stream, man, you can't get lower than that. Well, I don't want a ax you that, I know why you work here. You told me a hundred times. You work here 'cause you, you know"— how it hurt to say it!—"like it. I wanna ax you what you know about this guy, Ives."

"Just what I read in his obit. And his columns."

"Yeah, well, I read his obit, it didn't tell me nothing a*bout* him, it just told me, you know, when he was born and stuff. Wisconsin. The fuck gets born in Wisconsin? And I never read his columns, I don't read the *Herald*, I read the *News*, the *Racing Form*, so clue me in, will you—what did he write in his columns, Ives?"

"He wrote about being forty and single and living in New York."

"People read shit like that?"

"He was a reporter in Vietnam in the sixties. He wrote quite often about those days—about things he wasn't able to write about when he was there, things he didn't think at the time were news, things that were news but that've stayed vivid for other reasons."

"Oh, yeah, *viv*id? So did him and McAlistair have a *viv*id thing going, Ives?"

"Frances doesn't have *things* with men. She has men around her because she's beautiful—beautiful, wearable men. And I suppose I can see her, if she weren't a public figure, having a strictly sexual, fuck-your-brains-out-once-a-week affair with a hunk, a bodybuilder, a biker. But somebody like Charles Ives, I think, is somebody you'd have a relationship with, and relationships aren't possible for Frances. They take time, and quite simply, she doesn't have time."

"Yeah, well, what I'm axing really is how does this thing impact on the Valentine's Day thing?"

Mary Elizabeth slowly lowered the newspaper. "'Impact'?"

"Yeah. You know."

Mary Elizabeth laughed.

"What?"

She shook her head.

"*What*?"

"I explained to you, Eddie, that McAlistair hasn't been arrested or charged or indicted. As far as I know, there's no suspicion that she committed any crime. So there's no change in the situation. None. She was at her desk this afternoon; the vacation giveaway is proceeding as planned." She raised the newspaper again. "What about your end?"

Dead Eddie made the little move with his head that Danny De Vito always made in movies when he wanted to buy a little time. Danny De Vito was Dead Eddie's favorite actor; he thought Bobby De Niro should have the lead in *The Dead Eddie Milano Story*—the slim, trim *Deer Hunter* Bobby De Niro, not the fat slob *Raging Bull* or *Untouchables* Bobby De Niro—but for plain old laughs and also a couple of tears, give him Danny De Vito. Maybe Danny De Vito could play Air Sax, except that would truly be a fucking waste of talent, except maybe *The Dead Eddie Milano Story* would stretch the truth a little—a lot—and give its Dead Eddie a sideman worthy of the woist hombre, not to mention a piece of trim—two or three pieces of trim— worthy of the woist hombre too, not some fucking hairback shoulda been a professional wrestler.

Dead Eddie took a step toward where she sat on the office couch, her legs tucked up under her, her hair spilling over her shoulders, over the back of the couch. "Whattaya mean, what about my end?"

"What about *your* end?"

He took his .38 Smith out of his shoulder holster and pleated the top of the newspaper. "Whattaya mean, Mary Liz?"

"Put that away, you dumb wop."

"You axing on account a you want to tip Frances McAlistair off to what's going down, maybe?"

Mary Elizabeth put the newspaper down and pressed the tips of her middle fingers against her eyes.

Dead Eddie put the gun barrel between her hands and separated them.

"Don't do that, you dumb wop. Guns go off."

"You axing on account a you want to tip Frances McAlistair off to what's going down?"

"I heard you, Eddie."

"You heard me, how 'bout answering me?"

"It wasn't a question, Eddie, it was irrational ranting. Tip McAlistair off to what—that to keep myself in cocaine, compact disks and chocolate-chip cookies I've sold out to the mob?"

Dead Eddie wished she could see that if she let herself she could see it differently—that she'd done it for love. "You're not tipping Frances McAlistair off to what's going down, maybe you're tipping Artie Roth."

Mary Elizabeth looked right at him as she took the barrel in her left hand and put it in her mouth.

"Hey, Mary Liz."

She made a ring of her right thumb and forefinger and slipped it slowly up and down the barrel.

"Mary Liz."

She slipped it faster and faster.

"Lizzie."

She took her left hand off the barrel and lifted her dress up over her thighs and grasped her panties and pulled them tight against her crotch.

"Hey, babe. I mean, you know, pieces go off."

She put a finger inside her.

"I'm leaving, Mary Liz. I mean, if you want the piece, I'm leaving it witch you, but I'm not gonna stand here holding on a it while you're, you know, beating off."

She took the barrel out of her mouth and her finger from inside her and adjusted her panties and pulled her dress down and picked up *American Lawyer.*

Dead Eddie put the .38 back in his shoulder holster and went to the window. Snow. Snow on the ground, snow in the air, snow in his heart.

After a while, Dead Eddie said, "Slow night."

"It's early yet."

"You want something to eat? Chinese or something?"

"Aren't you going home for dinner?"

"Don't remind me, all right?"

"No, thanks. I'll have something later."

"No Chinese?"

"No, thanks."

"Pizza? How 'bout a pizza?"

"No, thanks."

"A hero? We could get a hero from the corner. A little salami, a little prosciutto, a little provolone, some nice tomatoes, a little oil and vinegar. They make a good hero, for Koreans. It's nuts, ain't it—every time you turn around, a place used to be Italian's all of a sudden Korean. How 'bout it?"

"No, thanks, Ed."

"You mad at me?"

"No."

"You're mad at me."

"I'm not, Ed."

"You're mad at me on account a you thought I was going a ax you again why you work here. I've axed you before, you always say, 'Cause it's there,' I should know by now that's the answer."

"I'm not mad, Eddie."

"You're mad 'cause I said you was gonna tip Frances McAlistair, Artie Roth, to the Valentine's thing. The fuck would you do that, like you said? I mean, you know. I just said it, I don't know why."

"I'm not mad."

"Then go to bed wit me, will you, for the love of God."

Mary Elizabeth laughed.

"Oh. Now you're laughing. Now it's funny or something."

"I'm sorry, Eddie. I'm not making fun of you. It's just that the way you said it, it startled me, it was a nervous laugh."

"Yeah."

"I'm sorry."

"Yeah."

"You want some Chinese?"

"Nah. I gotta go home."

"Some wonton. Some ribs."

"Nah."

"Some mooshu pork."

"I don't know."

"It's my treat."

Dead Eddie did a Danny De Vito. "Well, all right."

The phone rang.

"Shit," Dead Eddie said. "*Now* they call."

"Call the restaurant, Eddie. By the time they get here, I'll be done."

"You gonna go in the other room?"

"Of course."

"You could stay in here."

"Eddie, really."

"Shit."

"Call the restaurant. I'll have some wonton and a spring roll. Or no—maybe I'll have ribs."

Dead Eddie put his hand over his genitals. "You want some meat? Have a bite a this."

"Don't be vulgar, Eddie," Mary Elizabeth said, and went into the next room and answered the phone and got the caller's American Express number. She put him on hold, got a silver Tiffany's snuffbox and a silver spoon out of her bag and did two toots of cocaine. She got back on the phone and told the client how she would trim her middle fingernail to a point so that she could put her finger all the way up his asshole while she licked his balls and while he was masturbated by another woman he said should be black and for whom Mary Elizabeth made up the name Indigo.

8

"Mr. McNally?" Milner said.

Tom McNally laughed, which they figured meant he wouldn't try to kill them with his bare hands, which was good, because he could have, he was that big and that strong—big enough to dismantle mountains if he wanted to, if he didn't feel like climbing them. All over the wood-paneled walls of his office were photographs of McNally on tops of mountains that he'd climbed and axes and coils of rope he'd climbed them with and in not one of the photographs did McNally look the least bit happy or triumphant—or even tired or strung out or lucky; in most of them he looked annoyed, as if it had just occurred to him that he hadn't had to climb the son-of-a-bitch, that he could simply have used the axes and ropes to dismantle it.

He was big enough and strong enough as well, Neuman and Milner said to each other with a look, to slog or mush or maybe even ski or snowshoe uptown in the middle of a blizzard (there were snowshoes on McNally's wall too, and photographs of him wearing skis and a variation on his dismantle-the-son-of-a-bitch look, a look that said, *As long as we're this high up, let's see how fast we can get down*) and throw someone off a penthouse terrace if he wanted to, if he didn't feel like having that someone going out with the woman he'd been going out with until she told him it had gone on long enough, or whatever it was Frances McAlistair had said.

"Cops, right?" McNally said.

"Un hunh. Yes. That's right," Neuman said.

"It's all right, Missy," McNally said to his secretary, who had stayed in the doorway behind them. She went back to her desk, shutting the door behind her, which was

64

fine with them because she didn't look like a Missy, she looked like she'd dismantled a few mountains in her time, and would again, and wouldn't mind practicing on a couple of guys trying to see her boss without an appointment, forget about their being cops.

"So you're just here to ask me a few questions, is that it?" McNally said.

"Uh, yes," Neuman said.

"So? Ask."

Milner stepped around to the side of McNally's desk. "We'll ask, but first why don't you ask us to have a seat, offer us a cup of coffee, pre*tend*, anyway, that you're, you know, a little bit nervous about having us up here, prying into your private life, your business life, asking questions, nosing around. 'Cause you've got something to hide. Pad on Sutton Place, office at Five-seven and Park, of course you've got something to hide, it goes with the territory."

McNally looked at Neuman. "He's the bad cop; you must be the good cop."

Milner slammed his hand on the desk. "Yo, McNally. You hear what I said?"

"You said you wanted a cup of coffee."

"Yeah. Yeah, I do."

McNally fished in his pocket, brought out some change, and put two quarters on the desk. "There's a shop in the lobby; we don't drink coffee in this operation. Caffeinism is one of the world's most insidious diseases."

Milner rolled his eyes. He walked over to the window. "Nice view, probably, when there's no snow. Can you see her place from here?"

McNally snorted. "Jesus."

Neuman pulled a cane chair up to McNally's desk. "Don't tell me, let me guess. Let me guess why you're pissed off. You're pissed off because you spent six months or whatever it was courting or whatever they call it these days Frances McAlistair and in all that time you never got her to take you as seriously as you would've liked to be taken and not only that but she not only said she didn't want to marry you, she said she didn't want to see you again, and then some guy you maybe didn't even know did a brodie off her terrace or maybe her roof and all of a sudden you're famous as Frances's boyfriend. It would piss me off too; it's like—I don't know—being told to stay out of the cookie jar, then having your brother break it and having people point a finger at you as being the one with the sweet tooth. Except your brother's not dead, of course. If you know what I'm saying."

Milner, still at the window, shook his head and sighed through his nose. Neuman couldn't blame him.

McNally, who had been staring at Neuman, softened his look. "Exactly. That's exactly what it's been like. She rejected me, Ives died, I'm hooked up with her again. Except that she won't return my calls. And it's because I'm hooked up with her that you're here. I'm a suspect."

"Well, not a *sus*pect, Mr. McNally, because nobody's said there was a crime committed. You're just someone we want to talk to to try to, you know, figure out exactly what happened. So you think Ives was what to her—a lover, a very good friend, just a roll in the hay, what?"

McNally laughed a laugh that was deep and good-humored enough but that also had a touch of mountain-and-people-dismantler in it. "Don't you guys know even that little about her? Frances doesn't roll in the hay. Frances is abstinent."

"You want to explain that?" Neuman said. "I mean, I know what it means, abstinent, but, you know, what do you mean? What I mean is, how do you know? I mean, I know how you know in, you know, your case, but how do you know in, you know, other cases?"

Milner turned and stared.

McNally laughed. "What's your name?"

"Neuman. Lieutenant Jacob Neuman. This is my, uh, partner, Lieutenant Milner. *David* Milner."

"Have you guys talked to the others?" McNally said.

"What fucking others, McNally?" Milner was back at the desk. "Everybody acts like we've got all fucking day, we don't have all fucking day, if you want to know if we've talked to the *others*, the fuck don't you say other *whats*— other assholes, other retards, other mountainfuckingeers, other whatever the fuck it is you're talking about, just so we could save a little time, you understand what I'm saying, or what?"

Neuman got up. "Excuse me." He went to Milner and touched his arm. "Uh, Lieu—"

Milner whirled on him. "Keep your hands off me, you asshole, Neuman, you're as bad as the rest of them, you and your fucking *chit*chat, just ask him if he tossed Ives off the fucking terrace or not and we'll get the fuck out of here."

Neuman pointed a finger in Milner's face. "You listen to me, you goddamn crooked motherfucking incompetent moron asshole screw-loose bastard greaseball. You don't like the way I do something, you put a sock on it until we're where we can talk about it, don't show me up in front of *any*body, you hear what I'm saying? You show me up again, forget about what I said about putting a bullet in your kneecap—you show me up again I'll put a bullet in your gut and I'll make sure I do it so you don't die, you'll just fucking *leak* for the rest of your fucking life."

McNally, leaning back in his chair, eyes moving like a spectator at a tennis match, raised a hand tentatively. "May I, uh, say something?"

They glared at him.

"I just wanted to say, other *guys*. I wondered if you'd talked to the other *guys* Frances is known to go out with. 'Escorts'—that's gossip columnistese for us. I've never been fond of it. I suppose I don't have to read what they write, do I? Nobody's ever put a gun to my head and said I must.

"Joe Briles is the only one of them I know. Eric Freedman, the painter, is another one, and another is Paul North, the race driver who used to be an actor. I don't know Briles well. We're both members of the Vertical Club; he plays tennis, I run and pump iron, so our paths cross only in the locker room. I got stuck over there in a rainstorm once and couldn't get a cab; he had his limo—he's some kind of textile importer, or maybe it's exporter, I'm not real hip to business—and he offered me a lift.

"We talked about Frances. It was impossible not to; I can't talk about importing *or* exporting and he can't talk about publishing or mountaineering and each of us wanted to know if she was sleeping with the other; there was no way to find out but ask, so I asked. He looked relieved that I had because he clearly had wanted to too.

"He said no. I said me neither. I wasn't glad, exactly,

to hear it, and he didn't look as though he was, either. The expression on his face—and on mine too, I suspect—was one that asked: Why the hell not? This is a good-looking guy, in good shape, good-humored, obviously doing pretty well, maybe even very well. What the hell does she want if a guy like this isn't enough for her? Somehow I think it was easier for us to ask the question about the other than to ask it about ourselves."

McNally panned a finger back and forth between them. "Are you guys okay? I mean, I don't know what was going on before, but—"

"We don't like each other," Milner said.

Neuman grunted.

McNally looked from one of them to the other a few times, then decided that the gap wasn't bridgeable—not by him. "All I'm saying about Frances is that her abstinence is the biggest mystery about her. I don't even think that's the right word for it: It's not just that she won't sleep with men; it's that she . . . well, that she can't. I don't mean that she's not physically able to—that she's frigid or deformed or whatever. And I can't stress enough that I don't mean she's a lesbian. There're several gay women on my staff—Missy's one—and I think I understand something about how their minds work, and how they work is nothing like how Frances's works. She's a straight woman—a sensual, sexual heterosexual, who just happens to not have sex. Why? Or why not? That's the question."

"You're asking us?" Milner said.

McNally laughed. "Jesus, you guys are something. Do you do this sort of thing often?"

"We don't work together often," Neuman said. "We're two guys who just happen to be working together because of a computer. A computer *pro*gram."

"I see."

"Maybe Frances just happens to not have sex," Milner said, "because she's got AIDS."

"That would be an easy answer," McNally said. "But it's a sort of modern answer. By that I mean I think Frances's—again, abstinence is not the best word— Frances's abstinence is something she's . . . she's *had* for

a long time. *And*—and this is the really important thing—I
think it's something she'd have and would continue to have
even if she met someone she was crazy about. It's not just
what she is, it's who she is. Am I making any sense?"

"So you think she's got AIDS?" Milner said.

"He just said he didn't think so," Neuman said.

"I didn't ask you."

"And I told you what he just said."

"Who the fuck cares what you did?"

"You ought to. It'd save a lot of wear and tear on your
brain."

"I got a brain, at least."

"Yeah, where you sit."

"Jesus, Noomz, don't you know any that're a little
older?"

"Don't call me Noomz."

"Kiss my ass."

"Hey, guys."

"Whore. You're a whore, Milner. A whore and a pimp
and a leech and a shakedown artist and not only that, you're
your own fucking bagman 'cause nobody else—nofuckingbody else—is sick enough or slimy enough or low enough to
do your dirty work for you, so you not only have to run the
pad, you have to carry the fucking bag yourself."

"Guys?"

"Fuck you, Noomz."

Neuman came out of the chair swinging at Milner, but
McNally somehow got up out of his chair in the interval
between the idea and the act and reached across the desk
and caught Neuman's wrist in his right hand and flipped it
back up into the small of his back. His left hand McNally
put on Milner's chest to warn him not to try to take
advantage of Neuman's disability. "Guys, you've got to work
this thing out."

Milner touched the knot of his tie. "Hey, McNally,
why don't you fuck off?" He went to the door. "You make a
move on me again, Noomz, you're history." He went out.

McNally let Neuman go. "You all right?"

Neuman rubbed some blood back into his wrist.
"Yeah. Sure."

"That was a good sign, you know?" McNally said.

"What was?"

"His leaving without saying he was going to ask for a transfer to another assignment, or get you transferred—or whatever the terminology is."

"Yeah, to you that's a good sign?"

McNally nodded. "It means he's willing to at least consider the possibility that there's something to your point of view."

"You're a weird fucking guy, McNally, you know that?"

McNally laughed and shrugged.

"So did you do it? Did you toss Ives off McAlistair's terrace?"

McNally shook his head firmly. "No."

"Know what he was doing up there?"

"No."

"Think any of these other guys—Briles, Freedman, the car racer—think any of them threw Ives off the terrace?"

"I'd be guessing, obviously."

"Guess."

McNally hesitated. Then:

"By the purest coincidence, one of the staff at the Vertical Club mentioned getting a note from Briles in Hong Kong. He's there on business and is staying longer than expected and wanted the tennis pro to know that he'd be unable to pick up some equipment he'd ordered. I also happen to know from reading the sports pages that Paul North is racing in South America at the moment. I think his latest race was in Buenos Aires. And Freedman, if I'm not mistaken, winters in Mexico or maybe it's *New* Mexico, but at any rate someplace other than here."

"So they didn't throw Ives off the terrace because they aren't here—is that what you're saying?"

"Yes."

"Well." Neuman backed toward the door. "Uh, thanks."

"I didn't hurt your arm, did I?" McNally said.

"Nope."

"I hope you guys work things out."

"Yeah."

"It's possible, isn't it, that Ives was a suicide, or fell accidentally? Someone didn't necessarily toss him off the terrace, to use your phrase, did they?"

"Not necessarily," Neuman said. "Nothing's ever necessarily." Neuman's Law.

"If you talk to Frances. . . . No, I suppose it wouldn't be appropriate for me to give you a message for her."

"No. No, it wouldn't."

"Well."

"Yeah."

"I'll be in town if there's any . . . if you need . . . I'm not going anywhere."

"You're not a suspect, McNally. I think we said that."

"You said I was someone you wanted to talk to."

"Yes. But . . ."

McNally laughed. "Yes?"

"Is there anybody who knows where you were when Ives died, anybody who knows where you were, say, from, oh, eleven P.M. to one A.M. after you had dinner with Frances McAlistair? You called her, just so you know what she told us, a little before eleven, said you wanted to come over and talk about some of the things that didn't get talked about at Mazza's. She said you couldn't come over, you say you didn't; what did you do and who knows about it, if anyone?"

"I did some work. Home work. Work is my sedative, my solace. No one can corroborate that, except that Missy knows it in the sense that a pile of stuff was on her desk when she came in the next morning. My doorman knows that after I got back I didn't leave the building. His name is Tom McNally—just like mine. I don't think he'd perjure himself on that account. He's quite surly, and quite conscientious; he knows who's in and who's out. Sometimes I think he knows with whom and doing what."

Neuman smiled. "Yeah, well. We'll probably send someone around to talk to him, just in case he looks at you funny."

"Thanks for the warning."

"Okay. Well. I guess I'll see you."

"So long, Lieutenant."

"So long."

"Good luck with your partner."

"Yeah."

Neuman's Law: A guy'll be nice to you, wish you luck
with your partner, manifest a general sensitivity and all
that, tell you, hey, go ahead and ask my doorman, old Tom
McNally, if it isn't the truth that I didn't go out of the house
again on the night in question, the night somebody threw
poor Charlie Ives off Frances McAlistair's terrace, and it'll
turn out that in fact it isn't the truth—or not exactly.

To wit: Milner having taken the car and himself having
nothing better to do and being right around the corner from
Sutton Place, Neuman walked over and found Tom Mc-
Nally the publisher and mountaineer's building and asked
the doorman when Tom McNally the doorman came on
duty.

"He's on duty and you're talking to him," the doorman
said, which Neuman knew anyway because his uniform
jacket said *Tom* in maroon stitching and his face said surly
and conscientious.

"Police," Neuman said, showing his gold shield and
knowing he hadn't had to say or show anything, that his
mufti said that he'd spent some time in uniforms, that his
face said cop. "On Tuesday, sometime around eleven or a
little later, did Tom McNally the tenant leave the building?"

"Can't say."

Neuman waggled his fingers. "Yeah, you can say. This
isn't a court or anything. It comes to that, you'll have a
chance to, you know, polish your story."

"I can't say," McNally the doorman said, "because
McNally comes and goes, except when he's got company,
by the service entrance."

"The service entrance."

"The service entrance."

"Which is where?"

"The basement."

"There's a service elevator?"

"There is. But he doesn't use it, he walks."

He would. "He walks to the basement, takes the service entrance out?"

"Correct."

Was there anything more to know? There was always something more to know, but you didn't always know what it was: Neuman's Law. "Any particular reason he does that?"

"I've never asked him. I assume because going down it's quicker and going up it's harder."

"Un hunh. And that's the kind of guy he is—always trying to, you know, save steps, shave seconds, and to build up stamina and stuff."

McNally the doorman said nothing. But then it hadn't been a question, had it?

"What kind of lock does it have, the service door?"

"A panic lock on the inside, a dead bolt on the outside."

Aha. "So he needs a key to come back in. You said comes and goes."

"That I did. He has a key."

"He has a key."

Again, nothing.

"How'd he get it? Does everybody have one?"

"Far as I know, he's the only tenant."

"But the landlord knows, or the super?"

"Can't say."

"But the point, anyway, is this." Let's hear it, Jake; this should be good. "The point is because he has a key he could come or go without your knowing it."

"That's what I said a while back, yes."

"So you did . . . Do you, uh, have a sense that he does come and go without your knowing it?"

McNally the doorman shook his head.

"He doesn't?"

"I didn't say that. I said I didn't have a sense that he does."

"Right. That is what you said. Well, uh, thanks."

McNally the doorman nodded.

"I'll see you around, I guess. Or maybe not."

McNally the doorman shrugged.

"So long."

"Aren't you forgetting something, officer?" McNally the doorman said.

Neuman checked for his hat, his scarf, his gloves. "Uh, I don't think so."

"Aren't you going to tell me not to mention to Mr. McNally that you were here checking on his alibi?"

"No, hey, no. We're not talking alibi here. I'm just asking a few questions. I told him I'd be by. If you see him, hey . . ."

"He's a generous man, Mr. McNally."

"I'm sure he is. He looks like the type."

"Not just at holidays, but all year round."

"Hey, there aren't too many people like that."

"He knows the dates of my children's birthdays."

"Oh, yeah? How many kids do you have?"

"Two. Kathleen and Robert."

"Kathleen and Robert. Nice names."

"The staff of a building like this develops a certain loyalty toward the tenants."

"I can see that."

"It wouldn't be fair for me *not* to tell Mr. McNally that you were here."

"Probably not, no."

"Good day then."

"Thanks. I mean, uh, yeah. So long."

Jesus. Neuman's Law: Never ask a doorman to look too closely at, forget about bite, the hand that feeds him.

9

Air Sax didn't know who to play. A little Kenny G., a little Junior Walker? He didn't know, he was so sick.

Five fucking measly yards he got for berking Michael Corry, whoever the fuck he is, turns out he's *some*body. Or was. Okay, he wasn't famous or anything, but he had his picture in the papers, and not only 'cause he got berked in the Eighty-sixth Street Sixplex in the middle of a Stallone flick with a bucket of popcorn over his head, 'cause he was, you know, like semi-well-known in his field.

Epidemiology.

Whatever the fuck that is.

Whatever it is, it pays good, pays a hell of a lot better than berking people, that's for fucking sure, 'cause when the cops went through his apartment, Corry's, looking for clues and shit on who mighta berked him, they found twenty fucking large in an Adidas bag in the back of a closet.

Epidemiology. That means he was like a skin doctor, right?

No wonder he didn't feel like playing nothing. No wonder he felt like shit. It reminded him of a scene in *The Muppet Movie*, the scene where Miss Piggy and Kermit meet up, start having this thing together, then she splits, after she splits, Kermit goes into this joint, there's a dog tending bar, he asks Kermit how's it going, Kermit says his trim split, the dog says he's been down that road himself, but now he's through with trim, the dog, these days he goes home after work, has a drink, eats some dinner, reads a book, takes himself for a walk, goes to bed. Him and Kermit sing "You Can't Live With 'Em, You Can't Live Without 'Em," Kermit splits, the dog says, "It ain't often you see a guy that green who's got the blues that bad."

Shit.

Twenty fucking large. Who has that kind of scratch lying around the house? Is that like, you know, what he makes a week, he didn't get a chance to get to the bank? Makes for doing what? Picking at people's pimples, moles, warts and shit? Shit.

So what's he gonna, chalk it up to experience? Right. *How do you do. Permit me to introduce myself. I thought perhaps you might need some berking done. My fee is twenty-five large, and while I know that perhaps sounds a trifle—how shall we say?—steep, you mustn't forget that I am possessed a that all-important ingredient experience. . . . References? Well, for one thing, I'm the guy who berked the epidemigeologist who had twenty large in a Adidas bag in his closet, and while you might could argue that's nothing to be proud a especially, I'd like to point out he did get berked, the epidemigeologist, there is no doubt that he bought it, which is what I was hired to do, berk him, and when it comes to getting a reputation, knocks as well as acolytes are part a the process.*

Right.

Shit.

He's sick is all, 'cause it was a beautiful idea putting things on the heads of the guys he berked. I mean, every fucking paper picked up on it, had it in the headline, the first paragraph. It was on the eleven o'clock news, WINS. The Popcorn Killer—shit like that. It was better than that—more, like, you know, poetic, but he can't remember it, he's so fucking sick. Next time he'da put something different on the head of the guy he berked and people woulda seen it and they'd, you know, know right away that he was the one that berked the guy.

What made him *really* sick is he thinks it's 'cause of the trim who paid him the five fucking measly yards to berk the epidemigeologist that the thing went down the way it did. He don't know why he thinks that, but he thinks it, and it makes him sick and he wishes he knew who the fuck to ask how to get in touch with the trim; all he's got is a phone number and it don't answer, the number, it's a pay phone, prob'bly.

Hey, he's got some free time on his hands, nobody's

got a epidemigeologist they need berked right this minute, why don't he go into all the pay phones around town till he finds the one with that number, then he just hangs out around the corner, turning blue on account of the cold, till some trim comes by and uses it, he'd know she's the trim who paid him five fucking measly yards to berk the fucking epidemigeologist with twenty fucking large in an Adidas bag in his closet, he can ask her the fuck kind of way is that to do business.

Sick. It ain't often you see a guy that blue on account of the cold who on account of he's sick is that green.

10

No action for the local teams in the National Hockey League last night. Too much action for the local NBA teams, which is why the Knicks lost to Chicago by nineteen and the Nets lost to Atlanta by twelve. The National Weather Service forecast: Clear and cold, with the high today around twenty, the low tonight around ten. Right now it's eleven degrees in the Big Popsicle, and those northeasterly winds make it feel like . . . Bella Coola, British Columbia.

Newly wed, and already Neuman and *David* Milner had split up—Neuman slogging over to the *Herald* to talk to Charles Ives's bosses, peers, rivals, whatever, *David* headed Neuman knew not where and didn't give a fuck—to Moe Ginsburg, probably, to get a free suit, or Katz's for a salami, or Crazy Eddie for a VCR.

It was better thus ("an afuckingward-winning idea," *David* had called it), given the weather, given their *thing*, their animosity, their profound mutual disrespect and their contempt for each other's morals and methods.

And yet Neuman could entertain the possibility that he maybe, just maybe, would choose *David* over Roy Fields. Or maybe not: maybe he simply *wished* Fields on *David*, for they were birds of a vainglorious feather.

"Chuck Ives was one of the last of the old-time newsmen," Fields was saying, sitting deep in his big leather chair, his head back and an eye on the empyrean. "Sure, he was only forty-six, but like Phil here, and unlike Karen"—Fields flourished a hand at Karen Auburn, dressed in suit and tie too, like Fields and Quinlan and Neuman and Federici, but being blond as could be and configured like a goddess (and her tie being a floppy bow and all of theirs

78

ordinary four-in-hands), unlike all of them—"Chuck was pre-automation. That made him an old-timer. He still took notes on folded copy paper instead of a notebook, still wrote his pieces on a typewriter." (Fields would have decried the practice, Quinlan thought, had he known about it at the time, but by this time it was part of the instantaneous legend, to be sung about, forte.)

"Chuck would've been the first to see that his death was what's known in this business as a *good* story, which is to say that it's not every day that one of the most popular columnists of one of the country's biggest dailies—Chuck had his picture on the delivery trucks; his stuff sold papers—falls to his death from the penthouse apartment of a controversial and charismatic United States attorney.

"Funerals, memorials, the launching of official investigations—with all due respect, detectives, they happen all the time; they have a way of dragging a good story right off the front page with the weight of their predictability, their lack of, well, sex appeal. What did Chuck use to call those second-day stories, Phil? Chuck was a student, detectives, of some of the shortcomings and deficiencies—particularly when it came to language—of the newspaper business; he kept us honest. What did he call them, Phil?"

Quinlan wondered by what alchemy Ives had been transmuted from a ballbreaker to an ombudsman—and Fields from a hands-off publisher to one steeped in printer's ink and rue. "Sifting-through-the—"

"*Sift*ing-through-the-rubble stories. From the practice, detectives, committed in particular by the wire services—Chuck broke in at UPI and was therefore entitled—the practice of far too often beginning follow-up stories on plane crashes, train wrecks, building collapses and other catastrophes something like . . . What was that one, Phil? The one in that piece Chuck wrote for *CJR*—the *Columbia Journalism Review*, detectives—that said it all so perfectly?"

And how Ives had got from being something of a catastrophe himself to someone who said things perfectly. "'Rescue workers sifted through the rubble of New York's daily newspapers'—"

"'—through the rubble of New York's daily newspa-

pers yesterday, searching for clues to their banality.'"
Fields feigned surprise that he had had a Xerox of the piece
on his desk all along, and he held it at arm's length as he
read from it, as if it were being forced on him: "'They found
clichés, commonplaces and platitudes, larded with photographs of celebrity breasts accompanied by lists of the
breasts' owners' favorite things—Fergie or Di, Balducci's or
Zabar's, Steve's or Ben and Jerry's, the Boss or John Cougar
Mellencamp, Nell's or Nick's—and their recipes for roast
caramelized veal and curried tofu on pita bread, but
nothing that could accurately, or even charitably, be described as news.'"

Fields put his head back and bellowed once. "Brilliant.
It's a difficult balance to strike, detectives, between enter-
taining and informing, and Chuck wasn't afraid to point out
that we sometimes fell short. Even so, I think Chuck
would've recognized the problems we're having following
up on his, uh, misfortune. I'm concerned that we may have
to resort to what Chuck—again in one of his pieces—once
referred to as the John Garfield approach: a reference to a
perhaps apocryphal but often-repeated anecdote about a
newspaper of another generation whose readers couldn't
get enough of news of the famous actor's heart attack,
suffered while in the, uh, saddle . . . something they
couldn't just up and say in those days; confronted with the
necessity of putting out yet another edition and not having
a shred that was new enough to put into a screaming
one-hundred-forty-four-point headline, an alert editor sug-
gested to his colleagues that the head should be: John
Garfield Still Dead.

"I mean," Fields said, "you guys just don't have
anything, do you? We run Charles-Ives-still-dead bullshit
or we don't run anything at all." Fields shot his cuffs,
entwined his fingers. "I know you're here to ask us
questions, detectives, but my question to you is what've
you guys got, and if you don't have anything, why the hell
not?"

Neuman didn't answer right away; he was working on
Neuman's Law of Laws: Confronted with the stark naked
undeniability of death, people did what they could—
everything they could—to demonstrate that they were

alive and kicking. Fields would've juggled if he could have, or done handstands or swallowed swords, or all of the above all at once; he would've painted a landscape or baked a cake or washed the windows in the Empire State Building; he would've raced in a triathlon, transposed some of the *Well-Tempered Clavier* for the banjo, learned Urdu; built a gazebo, taken apart a transmission, taught an old dog new tricks, beaten a dead horse into the ground with a grindstone, sold some oceanfront property in Arizona. Fields would have, if he could have, shoveled away every flake of snow. Since he couldn't, he talked.

"These things take time, Mr. Fields," Neuman said. Neuman the Wise, Neuman the Profound, Neuman the Eloquent. Neuman the Shmuck You Should've Said Something Longer Because Now Fields Was Going to Start in Again.

Fields didn't start in again, and he didn't rub his hands together, exactly, but his face got gleeful. "Phil, why don't you tell the detectives what *we* know?"

Quinlan tried to sit up higher in a chair intended to keep subalterns lower than the boss. "Ives did a magazine cover story on McAlistair last November. It said in essence that a year from then she was likely to be a political force to be reckoned with both on a state level and nationally. It was a good piece, an unusual piece—almost an essay, rather than an objective piece of reporting. That was okay with us; we liked the writing a lot; we don't get enough good writing i—" Quinlan stopped in midpreposition, for Fields was reading again, from another Xerox, the piece in question:

" 'A woman of forty-six but looking ten years younger, wearing a gray linen suit, a white silk blouse, gold on her ears and at her throat, her auburn hair cut to look tousled, her skin as white as cream, Frances McAlistair shakes a visitor's hand a little longer than necessary, a manifestation—literally—of her welcome. Her hand is big, her fingers long and spare, her grip expert. That is the right word, for the visitor's hand in hers is like a tool in a craftsman's. She is, after all, a public figure, and the visitor, a reporter, is useful.'

"Beautiful stuff, detectives. We don't have many people who can write like that. Listen: 'The visitor had once

interviewed a Nobel laureate whose thick rectangular
glasses seemed to help him see not only better but more.
Frances McAlistair's glasses make her *seem* to be seeing.
She wears them like safety goggles, as proof against entreaties. When she's at ease, they are parked up in her hair,
or dangle by an earpiece from her pursed lips, or are
discarded altogether on her desk. But confronted by a
stranger, a petition, a tough question, and on they go; she
seats them carefully with her fingertips against the temples,
like a racer—'"

"Fields?" Neuman said.

Fields lowered the Xerox and raised his eyebrows.

"It's two degrees outside, and two feet of snow, the
wind makes it feel like Canada someplace, it took us
forty-five minutes to get here from East Five-two. You guys
can stay here all day; when this is all over, we've got to go
outside again, go somewhere else. You really think we've
got nothing to do but sit here and listen to you read this
shit? You got something on McAlistair, give us what you
got. Miss Auburn, you must've been invited to sit in
because you have something to say about all this. Spill it,
will you?"

Karen Auburn looked up from her alligator shoes and
looked to Quinlan and Fields for permission. Quinlan was
counting the snowflakes; Fields made a gesture that could
mean anything at all. "I was on assignment in New Orleans
in mid-September, and I ran into Charles Ives. Not 'ran
into,' exactly; I spotted him in a bar in the French Quarter.
I didn't talk to him. I was . . . I was surprised to see him
there because I was under the impression he was working
on the McAlistair piece in New York. And I was surprised
because I know something about McAlistair and there's
nothing about New Orleans in what I know."

She's going to do it too, Neuman thought. Should he
shoot her between the eyes, or should he just let her
ramble, let her live?

"When I called the national desk later that day to file
my story, I mentioned that I'd seen Ives. *They* were
surprised to hear that—anyone on a special assignment like
Ives's reports to them—since he hadn't told them he was
going out of town, since he hadn't used the news assistant

on the desk who handles such things to make plane or hotel reservations, since he hadn't put in for an advance against expenses.

"If Ives wasn't in New Orleans on the McAlistair story, was he there on personal business? Not that anyone knew of. Was he taking some vacation time, some comp time, before starting a push to finish his piece? Again, not that anyone was aware.

"I called the desk of the hotel whose bar I'd seen him at; he wasn't registered there—not under his own name, at any rate. I called some other hotels in the Quarter. Nothing. I called every hotel in New Orleans he was likely to stay at. I called every airline that flies there. Nothing. Finally, I called Phil—"

"Why?" Neuman said.

Karen Auburn's eyes narrowed. "Phil Quinlan. This gentleman here."

"I didn't say who. I said why."

Karen Auburn looked at Quinlan, but he didn't look at her, as if *he* didn't know why. "Phil's the executive editor," Karen Auburn said.

"And Ives was a colleague, a fellow reporter. Why rat on him?"

"I don't think—"

"Sure it is. A colleague's doing something the boss doesn't know about, you tell the boss, you're ratting. Whatever you call it, that's what it is."

"Ives was . . ."

"Was what?" Neuman said. "If he was flying under and registered under an aka, then he couldn't very well be spending the paper's money, since the paper wouldn't issue a ticket to a reporter under an aka unless there were circumstances that a lot of people would know about, right? Okay, maybe he was cheating the paper out of a little time, flying down south when he should've been working, but that's none of your business, is it? Why didn't you just wait till you saw him again—down there or up here—and ask him what the hell was going on, was he getting it on with some Cajun queen, or what?"

"I don't really—"

"Yeah, I think you do," Neuman said. "I think you all

do—all three of you. You said you know something about McAlistair, Miss Auburn; you know something about her because Foley Square's your beat. Foley Square's your beat, you probably would've liked a shot at writing the story about her that Ives got to write. A story like that, that says the person it's about is going to be a heavyweight, politically speaking, on a national basis as well as state-wide, seems to me—who I admit don't know anything about the newspaper business—seems to me it would make the person who wrote it a sort of heavyweight too.

"You said you didn't talk to Ives when you spotted him in New Orleans, Miss Auburn; you started to say why, but you didn't finish. I'll finish: You didn't talk to him 'cause you were pissed off at him. Am I right or am I right?"

Karen Auburn looked at Fields, who had taken up a snowflake count too, then back at Neuman. "You're right. My beat *is* Foley Square. I did want to do the McAlistair piece, and, well, as a sop I was sent to New Orleans to cover a Caribbean Basin economic conference. Not my beat and not a big story, but the point was that I have a good time: one afternoon briefing a day on things no one was going to read about anyway, which meant I could party late and sleep late."

Speaking of parties, Neuman wanted to ask, which one of these guys are you sleeping with that they should be so concerned about your being upset that you didn't get an assignment that they'd send you someplace exotic where you could party late *and* sleep late? Then he looked again and knew that the answer was that she was sleeping with both of them, but that neither of them knew that, each of them thought he was *the one*, only Karen Auburn knew that neither was—and now Neuman did, Neuman the Wise, the Profound, the Eloquent. "Look, this is real interesting, but the fact is I'm running out of time, I've got other people to talk to, other places to be. Somebody tell me, as briefly as possible: What was Ives doing in New Orleans and would Frances McAlistair push him off her balcony for it, 'cause that's really what you're saying, isn't it—that he was down there finding out something she would rather he didn't, something I gather he didn't put in this magazine piece he wrote about her, something he was—what?—blackmailing her with, he tried to up the ante, she pushed him off her balcony? That is what you're saying happened, aren't you? Not you, Miss Auburn—you Quinlan, you Fields. Aren't you?"

Fields cleared his throat, but Karen Auburn kept on talking. "We confronted Ives when he got back from New Orleans—Phil and I and Joe Reese, the managing editor. He wouldn't say what he was doing there. He didn't deny that he was there—he couldn't—and he didn't try to say that he was there for personal reasons, or whatever. He wouldn't say anything at all. But we're sure the trip had something to do with McAlistair. Can I tell you one more story, Lieutenant? I'll keep it brief."

Neuman shrugged and looked at Federici. "I don't know; I guess so. How about it, Detective? You got time to listen to another story?"

Steve Federici just shrugged and tried not to smile, to giggle, to leap into the air and kick his heels and scream and yell. He had all the time in the world, he wanted to giggle and leap and kick and scream and yell, because he was in unseemly love. Unseemly because he was eight months pregnant; unseemly because the woman he was in love with wasn't his wife, who was eight months pregnant too; unseemly because the woman he was in love with was a newspaper reporter writing about the investigation he had pulled—a career-making investigation, some of the guys back at the precinct were saying, involving a fed and all, and if things were unseemly now it was nothing to how unseemly they were going to get if it got out that his career got made by a newspaper reporter he was in love with, if that's how it turned out, if that's what happened, hey, he knew it was too early to tell, but what a body Karen Auburn had—a centerfold body, a body that was always in motion: a little shiver of the shoulders here, a little shimmy of the hips there, a lot of slip-sliding of clothing, hissing of stockings, tossing of hair, jangle of jewelry, bracelets, whatever. Breasts, legs, ankles, collarbone, wrists—she had everything, she had it all.

Especially, though Federici hadn't even glimpsed it but was certain it was there, Karen Auburn had underwear. Underwear: the onetime Italian Scallion's favorite thing, the thing he liked better than his mother's lasagne, better than Jennifer's (his *wife* Jennifer's, his *preg*nant wife Jennifer's) tabouleh or pilaf (his wife being a health food nut), better than any food, any pastime, any diversion, anything at all—notwithstanding that Jennifer, his *wife* Jennifer, his *preg*nant wife Jennifer, wouldn't *wear* underwear. Oh, she wore under*pants*—cotton ones she got at Lamston's, three for $4.99—and *his* undershirts, which gave some support to her heavying breasts . . . but she wouldn't wear *under*wear, especially when he called it lingerie, which Jennifer said was like calling a bedroom a *boudoir*, it was treating women like whores, plainly and simply.

Federici told Jennifer she would feel different after she had the baby, after she had her body back. That was a mistake, because she said she didn't feel the baby was taking *over* her body, *he* was the one who was trying to take over her body, with his goddamn Frederick's of Hollywood negligees, which was an insult to his intelligence and his taste, because first of all, negligees, peignoirs, baby dolls, mules, fuck-me pumps—all that shit was too obvious, too cheap, didn't do a thing for him; and second of all, what he knew about lingerie he knew because he was a subscriber to the Victoria's Secret catalogue, which Jennifer knew full well because for a while he'd had it mailed to the house, until she came down on him about it; then he'd had it mailed to the precinct, but so many guys would scope it that it would be tattered and torn, with pages ripped out and other pages, he was sure, semen stained, by the time it found its way into his mailbox; so he'd rented a box at one of those mail-drop places near the precinct. Nineteen bucks a year, which seemed a hell of a lot to pay for a harmless diversion, especially when you included the five bucks it cost for the seven issues of the catalogue. Nineteen bucks plus five bucks equaled twenty-four bucks, divided by seven equaled $3.42 an issue, which was almost the cost of an issue of *Playboy* or *Penthouse*, which he thought somehow proved his point. Or did it prove Jennifer's? Karen Auburn, he was sure, would understand, Karen Auburn who was saying:

"Eight years ago this coming summer, Ives covered a

murder. He was working on the city desk at the time. A man named Donald Yost—a small-time actor—came home from a movie with his wife to find a man—an ex-con—burglarizing his loft. Yost grabbed a kitchen knife; there was a struggle; Yost was shot and killed and the intruder fatally stabbed; he died the next day. Yost's wife was the only witness.

"Ives got involved with Pamela Yost—romantically involved. In not very long, he discovered that she'd lied—that the intruder wasn't an intruder at all, but someone both she and her husband had known; *she'd* known him intimately. It was sordid; it was chic; it had orgies and pornographic movies and blackmail and another murder—the murder of a woman reporter for this newspaper. If Ives had told the police what he was finding out, she arguably might be alive today."

Arguably. Neuman always had to think for a minute about what people meant whenever they said arguably. Bernstein, the shrink he didn't call a shrink, said arguably a lot. Neuman would say something like *Klinger's an asshole and Easterly's beyond the motherfucking pale* and Bernstein would say *Arguably.* There were two sides to every story was what it meant, he guessed; there was no accounting for tastes; you never knew how things were going to turn out no matter how smart you were; or something: Neuman's Law.

So what Karen Auburn was saying—and saying and saying—was that if Ives had told the cops Pamela Yost had fucked the guy who killed her husband—and who her husband killed—then the woman reporter might still be alive today . . . unless she got hit by a bus or eaten by a shark or she stepped on a third rail or fell or jumped—or was he pushed—off a penthouse or got thrown down on by someone who strangled his wife, then raped her, then convinced anybody who would listen that he'd been on his way to Valley Stream while his wife was being choked and violated, then for some reason thought the jig was up.

"We think something like that happened here," Karen Auburn was saying. "We think Ives got involved with McAlistair—romantically involved."

"Oh, yeah, what makes you think that?" Neuman said.

Neuman the Master at getting people to spill their guts out, to tell him what they had to tell him, what he had to know to do his job, then getting out the door and on his way to other important matters. Like the way he'd gotten *David* to tell him just what it was he kept saying over and over he knew about Ives. The asshole. The inarguable asshole. *David*, not Ives.

"Lieutenant." Fields again, back from oblivion. (Where Quinlan, from the look of him, had now gone. Which meant what? Neuman was damned if he knew.) "Lieutenant, all we're asking is that you consider the possibility that Chuck Ives was murdered because he knew something that if it had been made public would have scuttled Frances McAlistair's political ambitions. I can see by your expression that you're about to inquire why, if he knew such a something, he didn't make it public when he had the chance, when he had the forum, when he could have had the paper's legal and moral support—"

"In fact," Neuman said, "what I'm about to inquire is you must be nuts, right, if you think I can run an investigation in the direction you're saying I should run it in with the only suspicional thing that Ives took a trip without telling you. If and when you've got something I can look at or listen to—notebooks, tape recordings, photographs, videotapes, eyewitnesses, whatever—then I'll be happy to look at them or listen to them; otherwise, you're wasting our time. You have our numbers, you know how to reach us, anything occurs to you that you forgot to tell us, let us know. Detective Federici, let's go."

Federici got up slowly, as if his back were killing him, as if he might never be straight again if Karen Auburn didn't put her healing hands on him, didn't give him her chiropractor's phone number, her massage therapist's, her yoga instructor's, her herbalist's, her Alexander technician's, her shiatsuist's, her own. She didn't even look at him, but then she hadn't all the time they'd been there.

"Miss Auburn?"

"You startled me."

"Sorry," Neuman said. "I saw you go in there, I've been waiting for you. I've got one more question."

Karen Auburn jerked a thumb at the women's bathroom door. "Shall we? It's empty."

Neuman smiled and shook his head. "Your beat's Foley Square, you've watched Frances McAlistair's moves, you've heard whatever stories you've heard, you're smart: Do you think she was sleeping with Ives? I know you said you thought the two of them were 'romantically involved,' but what I want to know is do you think she was sleeping with him. Before you answer, let me tell you something you don't need to know how I know, something you'll forget I told you, something if it turns up in your paper, if it ever gets out I told you, I'll be real unhappy about it, I'm liable to do something like, oh, let the air out of your tires or something. None of them were sleeping with her, McAlistair, none of the guys she, you know, went around with."

Karen Auburn nodded. "I'm not surprised. I've watched her moves. No, I don't think Ives was sleeping with her."

"Now this is sort of a personal question," Neuman said, "and you don't have to answer it if you don't want to, but there aren't many women cops and none that I can think of offhand that I'd ask this question of and I suppose I could ask my wife but I don't like to mix business and personal, if you know what I'm saying. The question is, if you weren't, you know, sleeping with any of the men you hung around with, what might be some of the reasons you weren't?"

Karen Auburn folded her arms under her breasts. "AIDS, herpes, vaginal warts—anything that's sexually transmitted. I'm not a doctor." She shrugged. "Homosexuality, frigidity, fear of intimacy. I'm not a psychologist, either. I don't mind saying that I'm sexually active, Lieutenant, and it's hard for me to imagine someone who's not physically or mentally ill who's not."

"Is it also hard to imagine telling people that that's how physically or mentally ill you were?"

"Yes."

"So hard that you might not tell?"

"Yes."

"So hard—"

"So hard I'd kill someone to keep *them* from telling?

Yes. But that's a very abstract answer, Lieutenant. It's hard
for me to imagine killing anyone for anything—except
bicycle messengers for running red lights and cabdrivers for
not yielding to pedestrians. Of all the ways to kill someone,
I suppose pushing them off a terrace is the easiest to
imagine myself doing."

Neuman nodded. "So what're your plans, Miss Auburn? I mean, you're not going to just let this story die, are
you? You're not going to write one of those—what did
Fields call them?—sifting-through-the-rubble John Garfield stories, are you?"

She smiled. "If I can get to an airport, I'm going to
New Orleans, armed with a photograph of Charles Ives and
the names of some contacts in the New Orleans lesbian
community."

"Oh, yeah, and where does one get names like that,
just out of professional curiosity?"

"I got them from DeBree, the paper's gossip columnist."

"So in addition to being physically or mentally ill, you
include the possibility that she's, you know, gay?"

"Yes. We're talking about a woman who might one day
seek the presidency. The country is scarcely ready to grant
that aspiration to the straightest of straight women; it's not
about to throw its support to a dyke."

"It's probably not, no. Just one more question, Miss
Auburn, and thanks for standing here all this time to help
me out. Foley Square's your beat; who in Frances McAlistair's office doesn't like her?"

"I've never heard of anyone. I—I've never heard of
anyone."

"You started to say something else."

"It was going to sound catty."

"Hey, what the hell."

A pause. Then: "I have a personal theory that addictive
drugs are going to turn out to be a far bigger problem than
anyone right now can even imagine—that the kind of
corruption and deception and fraud that in the past has
been motivated by greed is in the future going to be
motivated by addiction. If I were looking for someone

inside a, say, federal prosecutor's office who might be trying to profit by the boss's downfall, I'd look, so to speak, in the bathrooms, in the toilet stalls; I'd look up people's noses and under their sleeves."

"So to speak," Neuman said. "But yeah, I get what you're saying. Well, thanks again for standing here like this, and, well, you know, have a good day."

"You're welcome, Lieutenant. Thanks for taking me into your confidence. . . . Your colleague Detective Federici, is he . . . God, I can't even say it. Single?"

"No, he's not. He's married and having a baby. A girl. They know these things in advance these days, somehow. They have tests and stuff, I guess. Too bad they don't have tests, you could give it to somebody, you'd know whether they were a crook. A truth serum or something."

She studied her alligator shoes again. "Or something. It's too bad they don't have tests, you could give them to somebody, you'd know if they were married or not. You wouldn't waste so much time fantasizing." She looked up and smiled at Neuman. "Or maybe I'm the test. If I'm attracted to a man, I can be sure he's married or gay."

"Speaking of which, back at the time you were just telling us about, the time of the Yost thing, Ives had a girlfriend who we're sort of looking for in case she was still in touch with him and knew about what he'd been doing. You don't happen to know anything about her, do you?"

Karen Auburn shook her head. "It was before my time here. You might ask Phil. Phil Quinlan. He and Ives were buddies when they started out. Then they fell out—over a woman, I think. Possibly the murdered reporter I mentioned; Phil won't talk about her, and in my experience women men won't talk about are women they've been involved with."

Neuman thought about telling her he'd guessed more about her experience than she might imagine. Instead he backed down the hall—the way he left lots of places these days. "Well, uh, so long. Have a good trip to, uh, you know, New Orleans."

She nodded. "If I find out anything interesting, I'll call you."

"Do that. Yeah, would you do that?"
"Sure."
"Thanks."
"No problem."
"Goodbye."
"Bye."
"Bye."
"Bye."

11

"To begin at the beginning, my first memory is of being licked in the face by a large black dog. I was three, and playing on the lawn of my parents' summer home in Southampton. It was at the end of a road called Wyandanch—pronounced Wyan dance by natives, and named after a chief of the Montauk Indians. The dog must've been a neighbor's, because we had cats—three Abyssinians— and a Shetland pony.

"My mother's father, George Clifford, built the house. He had invented a drill-bit holder—not the bit itself, mind you, but just the clamp that holds it—that to this day is indispensable to oil exploration, and was able to retire at a very young age to indulge in his true love—croquet. He was a national champion in the thirties.

"My mother's mother, Prudence Seale Clifford, died when Mother was twelve and her brother, Archer, ten. Tuberculosis. They were raised by a nanny. Grandpa George died the year before I was born; he left the house to Mother and another house, in Maine, to Uncle Archer. Archer was something of a vagabond, however, a prototypical beatnik, and wasn't interested in owning more than he could carry on his back. He sold the Maine house for a fraction of its value and went to England to join the RAF. He was killed in the war; the plane on which he was a navigator was lost on a mission over Bulgaria."

"Some navigator," Kate Naismith said.

"But this is all before the beginning, Mr. Ives."

"It adds texture. Too many profiles jump from the cradle to college commencement."

Kate hit Rewind briefly, then released it and listened again to Charles Ives's voice on the tape.

"*It adds texture. Too many profiles jump from the cradle to college commencement.*"

"Hello, Charles," Kate said. "Mr. Ives."

"*What was it like, being very rich?*"

"Really, Charles. How gauche."

"*It's a fair question. . . . That I was privileged was an inescapable fact. Father, however, had been born poor and never forgot it. He involved himself with poor people on a daily basis. He was a doctor, as I know you know. When Father asked Grandpa George for Mother's hand, Grandpa asked Father by what disease, in his opinion, was the world most threatened. Grandpa's next question, Father always said, was going to be, 'Well, if you're the fine doctor my daughter tells me you are, why haven't you found a cure for it, and if you're a man who can be defeated by a mere microbe, how can you expect me to give you a hand up the ladder by which you presume to ascend to the status of* my *son-in-law?'*"

"*Father's answer was 'Injustice'—*"

"Bravo," Kate said.

"*There was nothing Grandpa George could do but give them his blessing.*"

Kate stopped the tape and turned off the deck and the amplifier and shut her eyes and sighed. She opened her eyes and got up out of the bentwood rocker and went into the kitchen and looked out the window at the storm: Snow like rent gauze wrapped the streetlamp at Park and Newark; a yuppie couple, matched attaché cases held up like shields, bucked the gusting wind, heading for the yuppie dorms on Willow. *Home is the hunter, home from the hill, and the broker home from the Street.*

Kate put the kettle on and pressed the eject button of the Sanyo on top of the refrigerator to see what cassette was inside: Don Henley, *Building the Perfect Beast.* She'd been playing "Boys of Summer" a lot lately, hopefully; she took the Henley out and put in Prince and rewound by sight to the head of "Purple Rain" and played it softly for a change, dancing a slow dance with her shadow.

The kettle whistled just at the fade-out. Kate took the top off and steamed the inside of the teapot for a moment— the way Charles had taught her, Charles who would have been on her case for letting the water reach a boil because boiling water shocked the leaves. Or something. She turned off the flame and spooned some Earl Grey leaves into the pot and poured hot water over them, asking their forgiveness as she did. She covered the pot. She sluiced the water around awhile, then poured it through a bamboo strainer into a Hadley mug. She went back to the living room and turned on the amplifier and the deck and started the tape and sat in the rocker and listened.

"*Father meant it, though, when he cited injustice, and while he didn't marry Mother for her money, he certainly knew the money would make it easier for him to attain his goal of giving poor people what he called equal care for equal illness. He moved his practice to Park Avenue because the address gave him the clout to be associated with Lenox Hill Hospital—and because there's another part of Park Avenue: in the* barrio. *Father made house calls in Harlem every working day of his life. . . .*

"*Southampton Father suffered. He hated pretense. Not that he didn't love the house and the ocean. He was an accomplished small-boat sailor—something called a Finn— and especially loved to go iceboating in the winter, on Mecox Bay, in Water Mill. I still have a little house there—in Father's memory, as it were. I only wish I had more time to spend in it. I once spent a whole spring and summer, in seventy-two. It was one of the pleasantest times of my life. . . . Seventy-two. God. What a long time ago.*"

There was a knock on a door and at first Kate thought it was on hers, but she didn't live in that kind of apartment; her front door was on the street level and the apartment was on the second floor, up a long, narrow staircase, and sometimes Tim materialized in the living room without her having heard him come in the door. (The same thing happened to him with her sometimes, but Kate didn't count those times, for Tim was a casualty of rock and roll, deaf in one ear from ten years of playing too loud too often for too long. And she didn't count those times because they didn't scare some years out of Tim the way they scared them out of her. Especially lately. Especially now.)

The knock, Kate realized, was on the tape, and it was followed by a man's voice saying he was sorry to interrupt again, but it was the something-something matter, something Kate couldn't make out, and by Frances McAlistair's saying *she* was sorry for the interruption and suggesting perhaps they should have dinner together, *"if you're free."*

"I am, actually. Yes. Sure. That'd be nice."

"Oh, Charles," Kate said. "Won't you ever just take a pass?"

"Is five-thirty too early?"

"Five-thirty's fine."

"Five-thirty's fine," Kate singsonged and then was sorry she had. The dead are not mocked.

"If we could just go on for a minute here, I think you answered a question I've had."

"Oh?"

The phone rang. Kate's phone.

She stopped the tape and let it ring. And let it ring and let it ring and let it ring. On the twenty-second ring, she answered it. "Leave me alone, you son-of-a-bitch."

He hung up. Or she.

Kate flicked the plunger to get a dial tone and dialed the number she'd written on the pad by the phone the day before.

A man answered after two rings and said, "Talk to me."

Kate hung up. Stage fright.

She took a deep breath, dialed the number again right away and got a busy signal. She went into the kitchen and rewound the tape and played "Purple Rain" again and looked out the window as she listened. No one passed during the song, and when it was over she went back to the living room and dialed the number again.

"Talk to me."

"Is . . . Is Lieutenant Milner there?"

"Who's this?"

"My name won't mean anything to him."

"Hey, you never know. He knows thousands of people. Millions."

"That's what I mean. I mean, it's been years since I knew him."

"You know Milner?"

"Well, no. That's just it. I don't *know* him. I mean, it's

been years, and, well, he won't remember my name after all this time."

"Kate?"

She nearly hung up.

"Kate?"

"Lieutenant Milner?"

"Kate Naismith, right?"

"How did you know?"

"I've been thinking about you."

"You have?"

"Sure. Charlie Ives and all."

"Oh. Yeah. Sure. Charles."

"That's why you're calling, isn't it?"

"Is it?"

"Eight years, Kate. Eight years this summer, if summer ever comes, since we palled around together, you and me and Charlie and the rest of them. So what's up? You feeling blue?"

"About Charles?"

"Sure. Why not. I mean, somebody dies, people figure bygones're bygones."

"I haven't seen Charles since that summer, Lieutenant."

"Dave. I knew you were pretty ticked off at him, him running after that Yost woman and all, but I didn't know if you'd made up or anything. *Pam*ela Yost—was that her name? I couldn't decide if it was Pamela or Paula. I had somebody pull the file, but I haven't looked at it yet."

If I just keep talking to him like this, the phone will never ring again. "Pamela. Dave?"

"Yeah, Kate?"

"I wrote Charles a letter saying I never wanted to see him again and that I was leaving town if not for good at least for more than a little while. I stayed away only a couple of months, as it turned out; I missed the goddamn ugly, crowded, noisy, noisome place—"

Milner laughed.

"—and I just couldn't see myself liking being a somewhat bigger fish—I was a teacher; I don't know if you knew that; a high-school French teacher—in the smaller academic pond of a place like Portland or Seattle or Denver or

Albuquerque. Those were the places I visited. As it turned out, I gave all that up. *J'ai renoncé à tout ça*. I own a shop in TriBeCa—a lingerie shop, of all things—and I live in Hoboken, of all places, in a building that used to be a pickle factory, with a man fourteen years younger than I who plays bass in a New Wave band called None Is the Number, which is a line from Dylan's 'A Hard Rain's A-Gonna Fall': black is the color and none is the number.'

"They—the band—are having their quarter hour of fame by dint of never having been seen by their fans; they come onstage with all the lights out and play from behind black Japanese screens. It's impressive, in a weird sort of way. None Is the Number is a terrible name, though. People think it's Nun—n-u-n—Is the Number and they don't know what that means, or they think it's *One* Is the Number and that makes them think of an Al Kooper song called 'One Is the *Lone*liest Number,' or they think None Is is all one word—n-u-n-i-s or n-u-n-i-z or n-u-n-e-s—"

"Kate?"

"—and they don't know what that means, either. A friend of mine—one of those people who listens to WBAI all the time and knows one Central American country from another and pronounces Nicaragua knee-hah-rrrrrah-wha; I know a bunch of them, for some reason—said that if it was spelled n-u-n with a tilde e-s, it should be pronounced Noon-nyez the Number, then *she* asked me what *that* meant.

"I think they should call the band Kate Naismith. 'Kate Naismith's at Maxwell's tonight.' Wouldn't that sound great? Everybody knows Kate Naismith's one word. Maxwell's is a club in Hoboken.

"Hoboken, Dave. Can you imagine that? I was born in Philadelphia and my great fear as a teenager was that I'd wind up a secretary, living in New Jersey. I went through a year of what a friend of mine calls Jersey Denial Syndrome. Then one day last summer I woke up and not only faced up to the fact that I was living in Jersey, I took a train to Asbury Park. I actively wanted to go to Asbury Park. It was an amazing experience, Dave. I saw Madame Marie's. I saw the Stone Pony. I saw the Casino. I couldn't find the

Kokomo. You don't know what I'm talking about, do you, Dave?

"You wouldn't recognize me. Remember I used to have hair down to my ass? Well, I cut it all off; it's kind of punk now—very short on the sides and combed straight forward on top. I've changed in other ways too, Dave. I used to think it couldn't be any good if it wasn't in black and white and a foreign language. Now I think it can't be any good if it doesn't have hard bodies and loud music. My favorite movies—along with the John Candy parts of *Splash*—are *Flashdance* and *Purple Rain*. They make you laugh, they make you cry, they turn you on, they make you want to dance: What more can you ask of anything or anyone? When I heard Charles was dead, I opened my window and played 'Purple Rain'—the song—twenty-one times in a row, full blast. The hell with the snow; full fucking honors. When I finally stopped, one of my neighbors opened his window and applauded. Oh, Dave. Dave, Dave, Dave."

"Talk to me, Kate," Milner said.

"Charles sent me some tapes—an interview he did with Frances McAlistair. And someone's been calling me, ten or fifteen times a day, letting the phone ring until I finally have to answer it or go nuts, then just hanging up. Why don't I get a machine? I hate machines. Why don't I take my phone off the hook? I get business calls at home. I don't know why, but I think there's a connection. The calls didn't start till after the tapes came. There was just a note saying please hold on to these. I don't know why Charles sent them. I'm frightened, Dave. My boyfriend's out of town on a gig and I'm all alone."

"Could you read the postmark, Kate?"

"Friday. The package—a shoebox with brown paper— was mailed last Friday, from New York. Friday, Saturday, Sunday, Monday, Tuesday—five days before Charles died. I thought . . . well, it doesn't matter what I thought."

"Thought what, Kate?"

"I thought it was a Valentine's present—candy or something. I don't eat candy, but when I saw Charles's return address, I thought . . . I guess I missed him."

"Did you save the wrapping paper by any chance, Kate?"

"No. I'm sorry."

"Yeah, well. Why would you, right? I mean, you didn't know the calls were going to start or anything."

"Nikes. The box was from Nike running shoes." Kate laughed. "I remember your saying once, eight years ago, that amateurs always try to show how cooperative they're being by remembering details that didn't have anything to do with anything."

"You never know," Milner said. "If Charlie didn't have any Nike running shoes, then the box might mean he didn't send the tapes. On the other hand, one of his neighbors might've thrown out the box; Charlie might've thought it'd be handy to mail something in someday, he might've taken it out of the garbage can."

"You believe me then? About the calls?"

"Course I believe you, Kate. How many tapes are there altogether?"

"Six. Six ninety-minute cassettes."

"You play 'em at all, Kate?"

"I played the beginning of the one marked number one. It's dated last August."

"I remember August. Vaguely. Anything interesting?"

"No. Yes. I don't know. What happened to Charles? I mean, I know what *hap*pened, but . . . You're a homicide detective: Was he murdered?"

"Anytime anyone goes off a building, Kate, and there's no note or anything, we take a hard look at it."

"Charles was . . . *fond* of her, of Frances McAlistair. I can tell just by listening to the little of the tapes I've listened to. Was there something going on between them?"

"We asked around the building, talked to neighbors, porters, doormen, the whole bit. Charlie'd been up at her place a few times, McAlistair's place. Nobody'd ever caught them, you know, doing it in the elevator or anything—she's the U.S. Attorney for the Southern District of New York; U.S. Attorneys for the Southern District of New York don't do it in elevators."

"PDA," Kate said. "That's what we used to call it— public display of affection. Nice girls didn't do PDA."

"She's a nice girl, Frances," Milner said. "Tough but nice."

"What do these tapes mean, Dave? Did Charles find out something damning? Is it possible she killed him to keep him from making it public?"

"Where're you now, Kate? In Hoboken?"

"You think it is possible, or you'd've said no. Yes, I'm in Hoboken."

"The tapes there too?"

"Yes."

"You going to be all right there? You got somebody who can stay with you?"

"I'll be all right. If I really thought I was in danger I could hardly ask somebody to stay with me, so I guess I'm not really in danger."

"If you hadn't seen Charlie for eight years, how'd he know where you lived?"

"It was what he was good at—finding people. He used to say he could find anyone in the world if he put his mind to it. It was a threat, sort of; he was saying that if he put his mind to it, he could find—I don't know—Anouk Aimée, and make her fall in love with him. He's good at that too—*was* good at that: making women fall in love with him."

"You say your shop's in TriBeCa, Kate? Why not bring the tapes there, we'll come down, my partner and I."

"It's at West Broadway and Thomas. It's called Le Peau Douce."

"The, uh, soft skin, right?" Milner said.

"I didn't know you knew French, Dave."

"*Mais oui.*"

Kate laughed. "I don't remember your having a partner."

"Yeah, well, I got one now. A ballbreaker. Listen to this, Kate; you'll get a kick out of this. Right next door to the precinct we work out of there's this health club; on account of the snow, they're letting us sleep there. So when somebody needs some time in the rack, it's impossible to get home, they go over there. They have a sauna, pool, weights, Nautilus, all that. Noomz—that's my partner—

uses the NordicTrack, one of those cross-country skiing machines—"

"Noomz?"

"His name's Neuman. I call him Noomz. Noomz says his doctor told him to lose weight but not to run or anything because he's too heavy, he'll throw his back out. He also says if the snow keeps up, he'll buy a pair of cross-country skis, he'll be the only cop in town knows how to use them. What's he gonna, chase the bad guys through the streets on them, or what? You'll love Noomz, Kate. I may have to come without him, though, since at the moment I don't know where the fuck he is, pardon my French. He doesn't talk to me much, except to tell me how he's going to put a bullet in my kneecap if I don't straighten up and fly right, how much he hates my guts."

"I'll bring the tapes tomorrow, Dave," Kate said.

"Good. That'd be the soonest we could get there, anyway."

"Tomorrow's Valentine's Day."

"Is it? Hunh."

"Happy Valentine's Day, Dave."

"Happy Valentine's Day to you, Kate."

12

A little Milns Neuman could've stood right now, after an hour of DeBree, who along with the talking thing everyone else had was your basic nonstop bullshit artist.

DeBree had been sitting in the lobby of the health club, drinking a carrot juice and reading a complimentary copy of *Whole Life Times*. He got out of the deep chair a lot more easily than Neuman expected—than Neuman could have himself. He extended a hand but kept his eyes on Gary, the aerobics instructor who'd gone to fetch Neuman off the NordicTrack. "Long before there was a joke about it," DeBree said, "I declined on principle to belong to any club that would have me as a, uh, *mem*ber, but I can see that in the case of this establishment there might be distinct advantages. As you are Lieutenant Jacob Neuman and as I am DeBree, we should have a talk."

"Yeah?" Neuman said.

"Yeah," DeBree said. "About Charles Ives, *requiescat*."

"We've done some interviews at the paper. We'll be doing some more, maybe next week, when we can spare the manpower. This weather, we've got guys—Ah, never mind."

DeBree swelled up a little. "Do you know who I *am*, Lieutenant?"

"You stick your nose in other people's business, their private lives," Neuman said, backing away again, as usual. He'd done only two kilometers on the NordicTrack; he liked to do three. .

DeBree laughed appreciatively. "Well said, Jake. May I call you Jake? We're contemporaries, you and I, veterans

of not dissimilar wars, recipients of as many blows in the
lists of life, comrades, one might even say—"

"So I'll see you over at the paper, maybe next week."
Neuman made it through the door. He was on the skis and
striding when DeBree came in, his Timberlands leaving wet
waffle prints behind him.

"All right, talk," Neuman said.

"Are you going to keep doing that?" DeBree said

What, exactly, he was doing, Neuman wasn't sure.
Never having skied, cross country or cross town, he had no
idea how much the machine was like the real thing, if at all.
He did know it wasn't as cold as the real thing, and that he
therefore had no intention of ever finding out just how
much like the real thing the machine was. But even so, he
occasionally fantasized that he was doing the real thing and
imagined that he discovered that the real thing wasn't that
cold after all, once you got used to it. He occasionally
fantasized that he was the guy in one of those Molson's
commercials where the guy with the growly voice says it's
a beer brewed for people for who racing a team of huskies
five hundred miles over snow and ice and frozen tundra and
stuff is their idea of walking the dog. He *always* imagined
himself winning, even though he wouldn't have a team of
huskies, it would be just him and his skis. "Yup."

DeBree made a sniffle of displeasure, but talked: "It
was last September fifth. I remember it as though it were
yesterday. I popped round to Chas's office—he had a little
cubicle in the rear of Special Features, back by the
so-called Drama Department—to update him, as we say in
the scrivening racket, on my efforts to find out what
Frances McAlistair had done with a part of a year of her life
that Chas had noticed was, so to speak, unaccounted for. It
was a lacuna big enough to drive a truck through, had
anyone cared to take note of it, which apparently no one
ever had; Chas had remarked on it simply from going
through the clips—a discontinuity, a little glitch that kept
things from adding perfectly up.

"Chas was listening to a tape of what I surmised was his
first interview with F. McA. 'To begin at the beginning'—I
can *hear* her talking, it's extraordinary; Chas had his back to
the door and was unaware that I was, er, uh, overhearing—

'To begin at the beginning, my first memory is of being licked in the face by a large black dog.'"

DeBree leaned toward Neuman and whispered. "I won't tell you what *my* first memory of being licked is, Lieutenant, or by whom.

"Chas saw me, and asked me, rather brusquely, I thought, what I wanted. I said I didn't *want* anything, I was simply there to tell him that I'd perused my files, as I had said I would, in search of info, data, facts, whatever, on the particular chunk of time in question, and, not surprisingly, had come up empty. I said I'd been trying to tell him that for several days, but he'd inexplicably disappeared. 'Where *were* you, Chas?' I demanded. 'I asked all over the office, and no one seemed to know.'"

Neuman took a towel off the hip rest and rubbed his face. "He was in New Orleans."

DeBree did a little stagger backward. "You astonish me, Jake. But then I should've known a man like you would be on the cutting edge."

Neuman stopped skiing. "Doing what in New Orleans I don't know. Do you know?"

"Are you going to continue your self-abuse?" DeBree said.

Neuman looked at the odometer: 2.2 k. What the hell. "No."

"A carrot juice?"

Neuman shrugged. "Sure."

They went out to the lobby and sat on stools at the juice bar. To the blonde behind the counter, DeBree said, "Robin, darling"—her name was on a badge on her chest saying *Hi, I'm your nutritional counselor*—"a coupla carrots, straight up, if you would be so kind."

Robin brought two tiny paper cups and two cocktail napkins with the club logo.

"Cheers," DeBree said, holding his cup aloft. "To nutrition, to counseling, to breasts and buttocks like Robin's, to men like us, cognoscenti of all of the above and more."

"Yeah," Neuman said, draining his cup.

DeBree didn't drink; he set his cup down and went on. "Chas fast-forwarded through his tape a tad and played

F. McA. talking about her father—about his especially
loving to go iceboating in the winter, on Mecox Bay, in
Water Mill. She still has a little house there—in her father's
memory, as it were. She only wishes she had more time to
spend in it. She once spent a whole spring and summer, in
seventy-two. It was one of the pleasantest times of her life.

"Chas said she might've just answered a question he'd
had—*videlicet:* What was she doing between the end of
nineteen seventy-one, when she left the public defender's
office in Oakland, and late seventy-two, when she joined
the Manhattan D.A.'s office?

"F. McA. said that in January of seventy-two her father
died. She'd already given notice that she was leaving the
P.D.'s office—because of burnout, the money and a failure
to be totally charmed by California and Californians. Her
father's death—on her birthday—caused her to accelerate
things somewhat. After a period of mourning and assuring
herself that her mother was in reasonable spirits, she went
out to Water Mill. It was late February or early March, and
she intended to stay a week at most, and wound up staying
till after Thanksgiving. She did some writing—a memoir,
she guessed you'd call it—about her time in the Peace
Corps and VISTA. She never finished the book, if that's
what it was. It was still too close to a time that she was
too naive *at* the time to really understand. Maybe one
day. . . .

"Chas stopped the tape there," DeBree said. "He told
me he'd gone out to Southampton. He'd wanted to see the
house on whose lawn the dog licked F. McA.'s face and to
talk to people who'd known her father, and he'd driven over
to Water Mill and found her house. The summer tenants
had gone, but a neighbor directed Chas to the real estate
agent, who had an office in Easthampton. She told Chas
that for all of seventy-two and part of seventy-three, the
house was rented by a painter named Hugh Spencer.

"I said I'd never heard of him.

"Chas said the art critics had told him Spencer sells,
that his work was decorative.

"I said decorative was a lucrative thing to be.

"Chas said Spencer still lived on the East End, that
he'd bought his own house, in Wainscott. Chas drove over.

Spencer was in. He told Chas that the time he'd spent in the Water Mill house had been the most productive of his career. He'd painted a canvas a week. In the more than a year, he'd been away from the house for more than a few days only twice—once to visit his mother in Florida, once to go to a friend's funeral in Vermont. He'd never in his life—other than on television and in the papers—laid eyes on Frances McAlistair."

Neuman waited for a while, but that seemed to be the end of it, whatever *it* was. "How do you remember all this stuff?"

"Re*member*? I don't know that I do re*member*, Jake. Memory creates, distorts and erases; it doesn't re*member*. I don't know that I re*member* a single thing, but that certainly was the gist of it."

"So what was she doing in seventy-two?" Neuman said.

"Isn't it obvious?"

"Not to me, no."

"She was having an affair."

"Ives told you that?"

"Indeed."

"Did he tell you who with?"

"Indeed."

"You going to tell me?"

"I think not."

"I think I'll run you in for obstruction."

DeBree wrung his hands. "How delicious. Just like in the movies."

"Yeah, well."

"Would I be sent to someplace like Rikers Island?"

"Not *like* it. It."

DeBree toyed with his cup for a while. "It would be pointless to tell you his name."

"Yeah, well, let me be the judge of that."

"Everything you say is so crashingly predictable, Lieutenant."

Neuman rubbed his first two fingers across his thumb. "Gimme."

DeBree shook his head. "Can't."

"You're not afraid of the guy, are you?"

"Not in the least. He's dead."

"Dead?"

"Once again, Lieutenant—crashingly predictable. '*Dead?*'"

"So you're saying that since the guy's dead, he couldn't've pushed Ives?"

"Did somebody *push* him, Lieutenant?"

"Is that what you're saying, DeBree?"

"Yes. Yes, that's what I'm saying."

Again, the brushing of the fingers. "Gimme. Or I guarantee you a night at the very least in the Tombs if not in Rikers."

DeBree played with the cup some more. "How's about I whisper it in your ear?"

"Gimme."

Debree leaned over. He smelled of a subtle scent. He sat back. "I can't"

"Write it down."

"How absurd."

"Write it down, goddamn it."

DeBree took a pen from his pocket and printed block capitals on his napkin. He put the napkin on the table face down and turned in his chair so that three quarters of his back was to the napkin.

Neuman turned the napkin over and read:

AL COBLEN

"Who?"

"Jake, really. The *writer*. Police Procedurals. Dick *Rich*ards."

"Who's that?" Neuman said.

DeBree slumped. "Al Coblen wrote twelve brilliant suspense novels featuring a New York City homicide detective lieutenant named Dick Richards. Each book had the name of a month in the title: *January is for Dying; Next February First; A Mantra for March; April's Fool; Depraved May*—from Eliot's 'The Waste Land,' a less-well-known coinage than his 'April is the cruelest,' by now wearisome truism; *June Brides; A Cold Day in July; An Aversion to August; A September to Forget; October 12, 1492; Never Wear a Bikini in November; December to a Degree.*

"There was considerable speculation, as the series neared its conclusion, about what the clever Al would do for his next trick. Not surprisingly, perhaps, he died—in one of those one-car auto accidents that no one ever just calls a suicide but that couldn't really have been anything but. Al lost it on Route 114 between Sag Harbor and Easthampton. He had a house on Shelter Island, which is just a skip and a jump away from Water Mill. He also had a place in New Orleans—he was a native of Louisiana; a hamlet or maybe it's a town, it sounds like a wide place in the road, called Thibodaux—and during that year that Frances wanted people to think she was in Water Mill they spent a good deal of time together there. Al's wife . . . I haven't said he was married, but that's the whole point, married with two bouncing boys, who—God—must be in their mid-twenties by now, full-rigged yuppies . . . Al's wife was keeping the home fires burning at yet another of their homes, on Perry Street in the West Village."

Neuman folded the napkin into smaller and smaller squares, then unfolded it and read the name again. "How do you know all this?"

"Chas told me some of it, some of it I knew. I was a fan, after all, of Al's books, and I was in those days as I am now in the rumor racket."

"So that's Frances McAlistair's dirty little secret."

"That's it."

Neuman shook his head.

"What?"

"Nothing."

"No, really, Jake, tell me. You can trust me to keep a secret. I'm a gossip columnist."

Neuman laughed.

DeBree pouted. "I'm quite serious. Perhaps in your day you've been singed if not burned by one of my colleagues, but the fact is that hardly ever does any of us write something that the party in question doesn't *want* written. They tell me them*selves* half the time, for fear no one else will think it worth telling—'DeBree, darling, there's a *dev*astatingly attractive young professional at the Racquet Club who has high hopes for my backhand'— which hardly makes it gossip at all.

"I've never hurt anyone. Never. And I know things,

believe you me, I know things that would curl your toes. But they're safe with me, secrets. I'm a repository, a mother confessor, of that which the average human being hasn't the fortitude to keep mum about. It's a burden, it takes effort, practice, calisthenics—I *e*xercise so that I can bear the secrets I know and take on new ones. But you must try to do that in your line of work—stretch yourself."

"Who else knows this?" Neuman said.

"Just the two of us, Jake," DeBree said.

"And McAlistair."

"And McAlistair, *naturellement*."

"And Ives knew, don't forget."

"I can't forget Ives. Poor Chas."

"And McAlistair knew Ives knew."

"Yes."

"Does she know you know?"

"No."

"Why did Ives tell you?"

"He wanted my advice on whether he should print it or not."

"And you told him no?"

"I told him that at this point in McAlistair's career, it would merely be hurtful—to McAlistair, to Coblen's wife, to Coblen's children. In the future, I told him, it would be that much farther in the past and that much more irrelevant."

"You didn't tell him that because you were, you know, professionally jealous that he'd found out something a guy like you should've known?"

DeBree bowed. "A good thought, Jake. But no."

Neuman rolled the napkin into a cylinder and unrolled it.

DeBree drank his carrot juice and signaled to Robin for a check.

"I'll get it," Neuman said. "I got a tab."

"I'm touched, Jake."

"Yeah."

DeBree stood. "I guess I'll be going then."

"Yeah."

"You know where to find me if you need me."

"Yeah."

"Happy Valentine's Day."

"Is that what it is?"

"Tomorrow."

"Hunh. Thanks."

"Don't mention it."

"Hi, Maria."

"Hello, Jacob."

"Happy Valentine's Day."

"Valentine's Day is tomorrow."

"Yeah, well, what I'm saying is I'm sorry I'm not home, babe. It's just with the weather . . ."

"How are things with Milner?"

"We're working separate. It seems to be the way to do it"

"Are you making any progress on your case?"

"I don't know. I don't know if there is a case. It's weird. People talk to me for hours, and at the end of it I don't know any more than I did at the start. Or maybe I do. Maybe I just can't see the pattern yet. If there is one. I don't know. For there to be a pattern, there's got to be a case, and for there to be a case, there's got to be a pattern." Neuman's Law.

"I wish this weather would end. I am starting to go crazy."

"You have enough food and stuff?"

"Yes. We were smart to believe those forecasts and do that extra shopping. Are you still sleeping at the health club?"

"Yeah. Working out too, on the skiing machine."

"You may need skis, if we are ever to see each other again. Do you think you'll be home this weekend? You could take the train and walk from the station."

"I'll try. It depends. I'd like to wrap this case up, if it is a case."

"We could have a delayed Valentine's celebration."

"I'm sorry I'm not home, babe. I love you."

"I love you too, Jacob"

"I should be going, I guess."

"Call again soon."

"I will. Happy Valentine's Day, Maria."

"Happy Valentine's Day, Jacob."

13

_____

San Antonio over the Nets, Sixers over the Knicks, Rangers over Vancouver, Islanders over the Capitals, the Red Wings over the Devils. The forecast from the National Weather Service: Periods of light snow today, accompanied by strong, gusty winds, temperatures getting only into the low teens. Accumulations of one to three inches. Clearing tonight, turning much colder, with temperatures zero to five below in the city and in the minus teens in the suburbs. In Central Park, it's twelve degrees, and with those strong, gust winds, it feels like . . . Cow Head, Newfoundland. Happy Valentine's Day, everybody.

"Happy Valentine's Day, Artie," Air Sax said, and put his MAC-10 on full automatic. Freddy Faso, who Air Sax did points with and loved like a brother, and the other two shooters did the same. At a nod from Air Sax, they stepped to the railing of the running track that circled the floor of the Washington Heights Armory and opened fire on the crowd of fifty-odd men below.

It was a lot messier than Air Sax had daydreamed it would be. A lot of the fuckers just wouldn't die. In his daydreams, they died like movie stuntmen, doing wild backflips and crashing backward into things as they took point-blank bursts in the chest, Air Sax leading the way with not one MAC-10 but two, one on each hip, Stallone style.

Some of the fuckers, in his daydreams, got shot in the back as they registered the fuck was going down and tried to make it out the door; like movie stuntmen, they threw their hands in the air and went a few more steps until their knees gave out, and then they went flat on their fucking faces on the floor.

There was no blood in his daydreams.

The thing of it was, him and Freddy and the other shooters weren't *at* point-blank range, they were shooting from the fucking balcony, shooting *down*, which is hard to do even with a machine gun on full auto, and the fuckers were running in so many different directions it was hard to tell which ones you'd started to work on so you could finish them the fuck off and which ones somebody else was working on and which ones hadn't even got hit yet.

There was blood everywhere, on everyone, on everything—blood and pieces of the fuckers.

In his daydreams nobody didn't get hit, but in the fucking reality of it more than just a couple hadn't been hit yet and at least two of them had got out of the fucking door, which meant they could hang around, him and Freddy and the other shooters, about thirty more seconds, then they'd better get the fuck out of the door too or they might as well go straight to the joint, forget about reading rights and shit like that, about a trial, absofuckinglutely, Mr. Malcolm 52X Rasheed, sir, I will be your bride and the fuck does it matter if I get AIDS, what's important is that you get your fucking rocks off.

The fuck was Artie Roth?

In Air Sax's daydreams, Artie Roth died a Oscar-winning death, backing away as Air Sax Stallone, the king of the fucking berkers, came strutting toward him, his two MAC-10s breathing smoke and fire and shit, bandoboleros full of extra ammo across his chest, no shirt on or nothing, wearing a headband made out of a dead snake or something, maybe some trim in the background, a couple of blondes cheering him on, like. Twins, maybe—twin blondes with big tits and long legs and wearing just them string bikinis that work right up into their crotches so you can see their cracks and their clicks and everything.

In Air Sax's daydreams, Artie Roth backs away with his hands up in front of him, saying no no no no over and over and over, please Sax, no Sax, have a heart Sax, Sax I will pay you anything you ask, what does that scumbag Dead Eddie pay you, I will pay you double, triple, quad*ruble*,

work for me Sax or even better Sax I will work for you, you
will be king of the fucking hill Sax I will personally berk
Dead Eddie so he will not be pissed off and on your case for
turning sleaze, you can have my Allanté, my house in the
Catskills, my table at Dominick's, my *daughter*, I will give
you my daughter Sax, she has a passable bod and is not that
ugly and I will personally see to it that she has the finest
instruction available and learns to perform the best blow
jobs on earth and she can wear a bag over her head while
she does it and you can pretend it's Raquel Welch or trim
like that who's going down on youse, please Sax please, no
no no no.

In Air Sax's daydreams, Air Sax puts a couple of rounds
with the MAC-10s on semi in the floor in front of Artie and
Artie does a little dance and starts to just totally sweat now
and piss and shit in his pants and shake and cry and moan
and then in his daydreams Air Sax slings one of the
MAC-10s over his shoulder and takes his Beretta 9 outta his
pants and shoots off a piece of Artie's ear and then one of his
fingers and one of his toes and the twin blondes are fucking
cheering and they're ready to hump Air Sax right then and
there but he's still got work to do so they hump each other
and Air Sax watches them for a while and then goes back to
work on Artie, who's got his back up against the wall now,
is totally out of room, out of luck, out of fucking hope.

And just to make a long story short, Air Sax, in his
daydreams, tucks his Beretta 9 back in his pants and
unslings the MAC-10 and puts both of them on full auto and
proceeds to blow Artie Roth into bite-size pieces, blowing
his hands off first and then his arms below the elbow and
then the rest of his arms and then his legs below the knee
and then the rest of his legs and then the top of his head and
then the rest of his head and then dicing up what's left of
him and then slinging the MAC-10 over his shoulders and
easing away, like.

And the twin blondes are all over him by now, un-
zipping his pants—they're leather pants; did he say they
were leather pants?—and taking out his dork and taking
turns sucking it and they've got his pants off by now and he's
humping one of them while the other one's humping one of

the MAC-10s even though the barrel's still hotter than shit and on and on like that for two or three fucking hours.

And in the fucking reality of it, Air Sax didn't know where Artie Roth was. *And* he wasn't even supposed to be here, Air Sax; he'd only decided to come along with Freddy Faso and the other shooters he'd already hired because an extra gun couldn't hurt and because he wanted the practice because all of a sudden he was in demand, he was hired to berk somebody else.

Trim.

And hired by trim.

The same trim who hired him to berk the epidemigeologist, the one who said *Donald Dubro, please*, when she called him and who neglected to tell him the epidemigeologist he berked for five fucking measly yards had twenty fucking large in an Aididas bag in the back of a closet. And when Air Sax asked the trim how the fuck come she neglected to tell him that, she said asking questions was unprofessional, which made him feel like busting her in the chops for saying it to him in the snooty way she said it but at the same time made him think, *Hey, I'm a pro*, which was what he wanted to be when he started out, it was his ambition, like, and he'd, you know, accomplished it, so take fucking that, Dead Eddie, you fucking cheapskate.

Speaking of which, he told the trim that if she wanted him to berk anybody else she was going to have to pay a lot more than five fucking measly yards whether whoever it was she wanted berked had twenty fucking large in an Adidas bag in the back of a closet or not, that was not the point, the point was that—she'd said it herself—he was a pro, a pro's gotta eat, he's got expenses, he's gotta cover his ass, he said he'd do it for a grand, the trim said seven-fifty, he said fuck it, all right, who?

Katherine Naismith, she said. *She calls herself Kate. She lives in Hoboken.*

Whoa now, Air Sax said. Several things. First of all, he said, Katherine Naismith's trim, right? She said, *That's right, Donald*, in that snooty way, which he ignored and started to say in that case it's going to cost you more than seven-fifty, it's going to cost you more than a grand, even, it's gonna cost you fifteen hundred on account of Katherine Naismith's trim.

But he didn't say it on account of he knew she'd laugh at him or something, that she'd say in her snooty way what difference does that make, that she'd say if there really *was* a difference, she ought to pay him *less* to berk trim, trim being the weakest sex and all.

Second of all, which he *did* say, *he* was from the 'Boken. I mean, he didn't live there anymore, he lived in Brooklyn, but he was *born* in the 'Boken, he still *knew* people in the 'Boken, he couldn't walk around the 'Boken berking people, somebody'd make him. And she said, which he knew she'd say, *If you're* scared, *Mr. Dubro, I'll simply look elsewhere.* And he said he wasn't *scared*, he was just taking the, you know, necessary precautions, and she said she wasn't especially interested in what he did or how he did it, as long as he got the job done.

Then the trim told him the address of Katherine Naismith, 89 Park, for chrissake, right in the middle of the old neighborhood, the place that used to be a fucking pickle factory. He'd probably run into Paulie Della Croce on the PATH, into Jimmy Stewart—not *the* Jimmy Stewart, *Jimmy* Stewart—in the Spa or at the Clam Broth House, into Mavis, even, Mavis Avis they used a call her 'cause she tried harder—tried harder to get laid than any girl in Hudson County, than any *guy* for that matter—run into Mavis on the avenue. It's a good thing there's snow all over the floor, there won't be nobody walking on the avenue, maybe he can get in, berk Katherine who calls herself Kate Naismith, get out without nobody making him.

Which is a problem he'll come to when he crosses that bridge; first he's gotta find fucking Artie Roth.

And make sure some of these other fuckers who just won't die *do* die so it won't look like it was just Artie Roth they came to find, which is the whole fucking point of the idea that he had in the first place when Dead Eddie said he'd do any fucking thing to berk Artie Roth and Mary Elizabeth Indelicato said Frances McAlistair was working up a sting where Artie Roth and a bunch of other unsuspecting guys were going to get things in the mail saying they were finalists in this contest to win a week in the

Caribbean or someplace, like Club Med or something, and if they wanted to win they should show up at the Washington Heights Armory on the night of Saint Valentine's Day and partake of a drawing of the winner's name, at which point they would be busted, all of them, on account of they was all wanted on various kinds of federal warrants and subpoenas and shit that they had managed to avoid, why not berk him there?

And hey, whoa, you know what the newspapers'll prob'bly call it, Air Sax had said at the time, you know what it'll prob'bly say in the headlines? It'll prob'bly say, I mean, you know, like these guys was invited to the place thinking they was going on a, you know, a Club Med vacation, which he sang like the TV commercial, *Club Med vacashun, something, something, civilizashun,* it'll prob'bly say in the headlines, after a whole bunch of them get berked, it'll prob'bly say something about, you know, Club *Dead*.

And nobody didn't say nothing, but he could tell Dead Eddie especially thought Club Dead was pretty fucking funny and as a matter of fact a hell of a lot fucking funnier than what Dead Eddie'd been saying the newspapers'd call it, which was Saint Valentine's Day Massacre II, like *Jaws II* and *Rambo II* and *Care Bears II* and shit like that, but Dead Eddie wasn't going to say he thought Club Dead was pretty fucking funny, a hell of a lot fucking funnier than Saint Valentine's Day Massacre II, which any asshole coulda thought of, he wasn't going to say it in front of Mary Elizabeth, him having this thing about her, always wanting to get into her fucking drawers, thought it was pretty funny and wishing he'd said it 'cause if he'd said it maybe Mary Elizabeth woulda let him in her drawers for a change instead of telling him off, which is what she always did the rest of the time.

Club Dead. Hah.

He'd bet anything that's what the papers were going to call it—he'd been right about them calling him the Popcorn Killer, right? Right.

Or he woulda bet anything if he could find fucking Artie Roth, and there wasn't no more fucking time to look for Artie Roth on account of he could already hear the cop sirens even over the noise of the MAC-10s. It was time to pack it in, even if it was going to take the cops twice as long to get there on account of the snow all over the floor; it was time to get the fuck out of Dead Club before he became one of its members.

"Happy fucking Valentine's Day, suckers," Air Sax said, and emptied his clip.

14

_____

Have you wondered, Kate, why after all these years you're still carrying around Charles's keys?

Kate told herself to stop wondering.

Have you thought, Kate, that maybe hiding out at Charles's isn't the greatest idea in the world, that whoever wants those tapes of his—if that's what they want, if they want anything at all, if there is a they—might be at Charles's apartment when you get there, or might show up any old time at all, like when you're in the shower, maybe, lathering up like Janet Leigh?

Kate told herself to stop thinking. Stop thinking and open the door. It might not even open; after all these years, somebody might've changed the locks.

The lobby door opened.

Has it occurred to you, Kate—this is New York, after all; people read the obits and the death notices, they hang out around funeral parlors, they haunt graveyards, probably, trying to sniff out vacant apartments—that maybe Charles's place has been rented, or is being readied to be?

Kate reminded herself that, yes, it had occurred to her, so she had had one of the Peau Douce clerks telephone the management company, pretending to be a real estate agent and asking the status of the apartment. The manager had told her that the police had asked him to wait till he heard from them, in case they needed to search the apartment, before clearing it out and renting it.

Aren't you the least bit curious, Kate, about why Dave Milner never showed up at the shop the way he said he would? Do you think maybe that means he'd didn't believe your story, that he was just humoring you, just stringing

119

*you along until he could hang up on you without hurting
your feelings?*

Kate asked herself why Dave Milner should be the
least bit concerned about her feelings. He was a cop, for
Christ's sake; if he hadn't shown up it was because he was
out doing cop things, running down leads, tailing suspects,
putting the word out to snitches, nailing bad guys red-
handed—things he didn't have to check with her, a civilian,
for Christ's sake, before he did them, or even tell her that
that's what he was going to do, leave a message, ask for a
rain check.

Nervous, Kate?

No.

Edgy?

No!

I see.

You don't see a goddamn thing. Just shut up and open
the door.

Shouldn't we take the elevator up first?

You take the goddamn elevator. I'm going to walk.

*Out of breath, Kate? You've really got to work out
more. What happened to that Jane Fonda tape you bought?
I thought you were going to join Jack La Lanne.*

Open the door.

The top and bottom locks opened.

Kate pried her boots off, set them in the hall and went
in. Her hand went right for the light switch; she turned it
on.

Just like old times.

The apartment, on the fifth floor of a six-story tene-
ment building on West Tenth between Fifth and Sixth,
hadn't changed a bit in eight years. And it had changed a
great deal.

As she hadn't changed a bit, and as she had changed a
great deal.

As everyone and everything she knew hadn't changed
a bit, and as everyone and everything had changed a great
deal.

The front hallway was the same, lined with bookcases
brimful of books she'd mostly never heard of, for Charles

Ives was—had been—the kind of reader who read (he'd
once said—and said and said, for he'd liked the sound of it)
to a different drummer. And there were changes: There was
a new light fixture of Tiffany glass, which meant that Tiffany
glass had to have gone out of fashion from a time when it
was in fashion, otherwise Charles, who shopped to a
different drummer too, would not have bought it.

There was an umbrella stand that hadn't been there
before, either, and one of those big golf umbrellas that
Charles was—had been—fond of hating for all the sidewalk
they took up.

The umbrella stand made Kate think better of leaving
her boots outside, and she opened the door and retrieved
them and took the golf umbrella out of the stand and
arranged her boots so that they dripped into the stand.

She wondered if she should wipe up the drips that had
already dripped in the hallway, so that *they,* if there *was* a
they, wouldn't know she was inside. She told herself to stop
wondering.

She went into the living room.

It was the same—spare, warm, inviting. Same bentwood rocker, same loveseat, same rya rug, same Kovacs
lamps, same Danish not-so-modern-anymore record cabinet, same Wyeth print of a young man on a bicycle, same
Susan Crile still-life vase, Same Roger van der Weyden
portrait of a lady with a wimple, same framed letter from
Joan Crawford thanking Charles for writing a flattering
interview about her, same fanlight mirror.

New: a poster made from a huge enlargement of a
Robert Doisneau black-and-white photograph of a couple
kissing on a Paris street; a poster from a retrospective at the
Whitney of works by John Singer Sargent.

The stero and tuner and tape deck were different—
high tech, black. The most recently-played records and
tapes were different too: no Dylan, no Dead, no Stones, no
Vivaldi or Boccherini or Beethoven; instead, Sting, Buck-
wheat Zydeco, Bananarama, Jackie Wilson, Satie, Orff,
Brahms. The evolution of a taste. From what to what?

The bedroom was the same—same brass bed, same
Mexican rug, same rolltop desk, same framed photographs

of Charles's favorite authors: Paul Scott, John Le Carré, John Fowles, James Agee, T. H. White, Gavin Maxwell.

"They're all English," Kate had once said.

"Not Agee."

"He might as well have been. His stuff's unreadable."

"What have you read?"

"Nothing."

Charles had laughed.

"What do you make of it?"

"Of your inability to read Agee?"

"Of your Anglophilia."

"I don't think an Anglophile's what I am. I don't have a particular desire to go to England. There are plenty of English writers I don't like, or have no curiosity about. I think the thing *these* writers have in common, other than their Englishness, is a kind of solitariness. White lived on an island, Maxwell on a remote, rugged coast. Fowles and Le Carré live by the sea too, I think. In his imagination, at least, Scott lived in India—and not in big cities, either; in Mayapore and especially in Pankot and Mirat."

"Wherever they are."

"They're fictional, I think, but fictional or not, they're in the mountains."

"Well, what are you doing here then, Charles—at sea *level* but hardly by the sea."

"Waiting, I guess."

"For your ship to come in?"

"For the rest of the crew."

"Meaning what—that you're looking for a mate? You who cherish solitariness?"

"I said I admire solitaries. I'm not sure I can be one."

"You've certainly done a good job of keeping me from moving in."

"Don't be silly, Kate. You wouldn't move in if I asked you."

"Try me."

"Move in."

"No."

They had laughed.

"But not because *I* don't want to," she had said. "Because *you* don't really want me."

And on and on, for years and years, arguing about the semantics of their arguments, arguing about whether what they were doing really *was* arguing, until—

Kate startled at a noise from the living room. Snow against the window, naturally. She wondered why she hadn't been more frightened by the sound.

She told herself not to wonder.

She wondered whom Charles had been fucking lately, and she went to his desk and turned through his address book. She was still listed in it—or rather, another incarnation of her was—the one that had lived on Grove Street and had wanted to marry Charles Ives and have at least one child.

There were names Kate recognized of people Charles had worked with, people she'd met at parties in the days when they'd gone to parties together because that's what people one of whom at least wanted to get married and have at least one child did.

There were names of people she didn't recognize, which annoyed her. What did he mean, meeting new people without her leave, and who *were* they, anyway? Who, especially, were these men? Who were—she was flipping backward—John Vermulen, Dan Tucker, Thomas Sorrels, Don Staroba, Jeff Saunders, Jim Prager, Nick Millford, Ken Karl, Brian Harvey, Harold Gilmore, Phil Feldman, Les Dillen, Michael Corry, Joe Blomberg, David Alonzo?

Who these men were was of more than academic interest, for in the days when they'd gone to parties together, the people Charles had met had tended to be—had almost exclusively been—women, for, as he put it—had put it—he liked women, he found them more interesting than men. Men could talk about only things—facts, data, stats; women had . . .

"Cunts?" Kate had said, and Charles had smiled and taken her by the hand, probably, and held her hand against his cheek and kissed her fingertips in a way that was—had been—intended to tell her that she was more than a cunt to him, that she was a—

The phone rang, and Kate backed into a corner and clasped her hands in front of her.

"No."

And rang.

"No, please, no. It's the wrong number."

And rang.

"Oh, God."

And rang.

"He's *dead*, for Christ's sake."

And rang.

"Oh, Charles."

And rang.

"No."

And rang and rang and rang and rang and rang and rang.

"No. No, no, no, no, no, no, no."

Karen Auburn rode the PATH for the first time in her life and found it not half bad, not bad at all.

Real life had a way of impressing Karen Auburn with its not-half-badness, with its . . . livableness, if there was such a word. It wasn't an impression she often got, for real life wasn't something she often experienced. Karen Auburn lived the high life, in the fast lane, on the cutting edge. She had an apartment in a building on Third Avenue that though it seemed to have sprung up overnight boasted in its advertising of its old-world charm and elegance; a summer house on Dune Road in Westhampton that by virtue of being on the wrong side of the road, the bay side, could actually be used most of the summer, unlike its more prestigious neighbors, whose views of the ocean included view of waves lapping at the pilings they perched on; a face known at Harry Cipriani, Indochine, Restaurant, 103 Second, Ernie's, and so on, and soon to be known—sure to be known—at the hot spots that would inevitably replace them as they had replaced hot spots like . . . ; stuff from Charivari 57, If, Fred Leighton at Trump Tower, Comme des Garcons, Artwear, Martha, Ibiza, Dianne B, Cyxtyz, Hermès, Missoni, Kaufman's Surplus and so on; and six lovers—at work, Roy Fields and Phil Quinlan; on Tuesday nights, when his wife believed him to be participating in a men-only therapy group, a writer of romance novels published under women's names; at nearly dawn, sometimes, after night games, on the mornings of weekend day games, when he was in town, when his sport was in season, an important member of the New York Mets; a semi-well-known movie actor and a television producer, both residents of Los Angeles, neither especially bicoastal.

More real life intruded when Karen climbed up the stairs from the Hoboken terminus of the PATH and confronted the taxi drivers, who looked like members of the guerrilla forces in some banana-republic civil war—fighters for this cause or that who hadn't seen a woman who wasn't decrepit or pregnant or nursing in months, had maybe never seen a svelte blonde in a Patricia Underwood fur trooper's hat, a short fur Azzedine Alaïa jacket, Thierry Mugler leather pants, Maud Frizon furlined boots—and whose cars looked like hell.

"Uptown?" the driver chieftain said.

"Eighty-nine Park," Karen Auburn said.

The driver turned away.

"Uptown?" a second driver said.

"I don't live in Hoboken. Where is Eighty-nine Park?"

"Uptown?"

It was a question, but maybe it had also been the answer. "Yes."

The driver walked back to the shelter of the PATH station.

"Shit." Karen Auburn thought about going back into the station and getting back on the PATH and going back to Manhattan. But she wanted to meet this old girlfriend of Charles Ives's, to see if maybe she knew why Ives had been in New Orleans, where Karen would be bound if the snow ever stopped, if the airports ever opened, if the trains ever ran again. Until such time, she might as well seek second-hand information.

Karen Auburn started walking, leaning into the snow and the wind, wondering what was so bad about Uptown that the taxi drivers didn't want to go there. Or was it that they went *only* Uptown? She would never know.

15

_The local NBA teams had the night off last night, and the
local hockey teams wish they'd had. The Rangers lost to the
Flyers, the Islanders were edged by the Kings, and the
Devils were burned up by the Flames, eleven—count
'em—to one. The National Weather Service forecast:
Cloudy and cold, with a chance of snow late this afternoon
or early this evening. No guesstimate yet on possible
accumulations. The high today will be around twenty, the
low tonight around ten; tomorrow should be more of the
same, also with a chance of a late-afternoon snowfall. Right
now it's twelve degrees in Central Park. The wind's from the
northeast at fifteen miles an hour, which makes it feel
like . . . Pelican Narrows, Saskatchewan._

CLUB DEAD was the headline in the _Daily News_,
white letters over a full-page photograph, made from the
running track, of the floor of the armory, five of the nine
victims visible, in poses like those children strike when
playing dead.

The _Post_'s headline was MOB REVENGE IN CLUB
DEAD RUBOUT.

Newsday said: CLUB DEAD FED FOULUP.

The _Herald_, mindful, presumably, of its vendetta (its
leaders' vendetta) against Frances McAlistair, used quota-
tion marks to soften the blow: JUSTICE DEPT. OKAYED
'CLUB DEAD' CAPER.

The _Times_ (which, Charles Ives had once written in
one of his irreverent pieces for the _Columbia Journalism
Review_, "whenever the opportunity presents itself, takes
stories that should be made nimble love to and instead
mauls them to death with its ponderous, serious, analytical,

126

historical, tragical, factual, objective, academic hand") reported: NINE DIE IN ARMORY SHOOTING.

Police Commissioner Franklin Montgomery spread
the papers out in front of him on his desk, studied each one
with some detachment and some interest, sat back in his
big leather chair and grasped his hands behind his neck.
"You've had fourteen hours, Inspector Klinger. What've
you got?"

Chief Inspector Lou Klinger stepped an inch or two
out of the arc of men, with the odd woman in attendance in
the second rank, facing the commissioner's desk. "Nine
dead, seventeen wounded, three critical. Four, possibly
five shooters. MAC-10s converted to full auto. Silenced.
Four weapons were ditched right outside the armory.
They're from an army supply depot hijacking in May of last
year. There was talk on the street at the time that the
hijacking was political—Weathermen, FALN, something
like that. The survivors who'll talk, though, are talking mob
hit—"

"Excuse me, Inspector." The commissioner sat forward
and rested his elbows on the desk. "I've read all this in the
papers. What have you got that the papers *haven't* got?"

"At this point, Commissioner?" Klinger said.

"At this point, Inspector."

Klinger shook his head. "We don't have any names,
Commissioner. We have one very tentative ID from one
witness, who said that one of the shooters—they were
wearing masks, Commissioner—had a build like a known
mob torpedo named Freddy Faso. We're looking for Faso
now. With the weather, sir, it's slow going."

"This thing went *down* in spite of the weather,"
Montgomery said. "The weather's no excuse."

"No, sir. I mean, yes, sir. From the look of it, sir, from
the way the shooters got clean away from the scene—they
couldn't have used cars, sir; it was too big a risk—from the
look of it, they had safe escape routes set up, maybe even
safe houses, bars, restaurants."

"Canvass them."

"We are, sir. They're quite a few."

"But not an infinitude, Inspector."

"No, sir. It's the cold and flu season, sir. Manpower's below nominal."

"It's the cold and flu season for the shooters too, Inspector. They had adequate manpower."

"Yes, sir."

"Where's McAlistair?" Montgomery said.

Bill Dolan lifted a hand. "Uh, sir."

"You're not McAlistair," Montgomery said.

"Uh, no. No, I'm not, Mr. Commissioner. I'm William Dolan, sir, the U.S. attorney's—"

"I know who you are, Dolan, for Christ's sake. Does it actually surprise you that the police commissioner of the city of New York would know who you are?" Montgomery pushed his phone toward Dolan. "Call her. Get her over here."

"Commissioner Montgomery?" A bustle, a hubbub, a parting of the rear ranks.

"Who're you?" And another question on Montgomery's face: Don't I know you from somewhere?

"This is Ms. Indelicato," Dolan said. "In Ms. McAllistair's absence—"

"*Absence?*" Montgomery said. "My people have to clean up a mess McAlistair made in a building on a street that's within the limits of this city and that therefore comes under my jurisdiction, and you're telling me she's *ab*sent? I want to know if she was intending to let my people know this little gathering was taking place, and you're telling me she's *ab*sent? I know she was going to arrest people; what I don't know and want to know is who was going to do the arresting if she wasn't intending to let my people know this little gathering was taking place, and you're telling me she's *ab*sent?"

"Ms. McAlistair's on her way to Washington to report to the head of the Criminal Division," Mary Elizabeth said. "I'm not her ranking deputy—Mr. Dolan is—but I had direct responsibility for the planning of the sting operation."

Montgomery sat back in his chair. "Did you now?"

Mary Elizabeth didn't read from the clipboard she held in her hand; she looked right at Montgomery. "To prevent leaks, we chose to limit the number of law enforcement agencies involved in the operation. The alleged crimes were crimes under federal jurisdiction, so local police were not deemed necessary to the arrest process. There were agents—trained at using firearms—from the FBI, ATF, the DEA, Customs and INS—agents in sufficient numbers to cope with the anticipated number of respondents who were likely, if armed, to be armed only with sidearms. The agents were not, we fully admit, adequate to cope with four, possibly five shooters with automatic machine guns.

"Transportation had been laid on by the army, which was happy to loan us three two-and-a-half-ton trucks, that would have been more than adequate for the anticipated number of prisoners and that—as was demonstrated when they were used to transport the wounded to hospitals— were supremely capable of coping with the weather."

Montgomery snorted. "So you're saying what, Counselor—that because the deuce-and-a-halfs and their drivers got the poor fuckers who were all shot up to the hospital you were justified in your harebrained scheme?"

Dolan came to Mary Elizabeth's rescue. "You asked for a briefing on the arrest arrangements, and Ms. Indelicato's given you one. The philosophy behind the operation was Ms. McAlistair's; she's authorized me to say that she takes full responsibility for it; if you wish to discuss its merits, you should discuss them with her."

"*Merits?*" Montgomery said. "*Merits?* There wasn't more than one merit; there were no merits. None. Nada. Zip. Zilch. Zero."

"I appreciate your opinion, Commissioner," Mary Elizabeth said. "Let me remind you that you're not my boss."

"And let me remind *you* of something," Montgomery said. "Let me remind you that *your* boss is a material witness in a suspicious death by unnatural causes—"

"That's irrelevant to our business here," Mary Elizabeth said.

"Is it? I really don't think so. I think we're talking about an indifference to and contempt for police standards and methods."

"If you'll excuse me," Mary Elizabeth said, "I have work to do." But before she stepped back into a seam in the crowd, Mary Elizabeth took her glasses off and put them up in her hair. Not an unveiling, exactly, not that moment when the traveling salesman removes the librarian's glasses and says, *Why, you're . . . you're beautiful*. But it wasn't her face that was being disguised; it was her voice. Not altogether disguised—some of its uniqueness had shown through like a face behind a veil—for she wanted to tweak at the police commissioner's uncertainty; she wanted him to be nagged by the conviction—well, by the suspicion, the possibility, the notion—that he had heard her voice before.

16

"Jake." Tim McIver stood in a far corner of Klinger's office, taking up as little space as he could. He looked guilty nonetheless, as if he'd been thinking insurgent thoughts.

"Tim."

"Dave, long time."

"Tim." Milner stooped to look in the kneehole of the desk. "Where's the Klings?"

McIver laughed nervously. "The inspector went to the head. He'll be back in a minute."

They nodded. They put their hands in their pockets. They shifted their feet.

McIver cleared his throat. "I guess you heard, Nate and I pulled the armory thing."

"We heard, yeah," Neuman said.

"The feds fuck up, and we have to straighten it the fuck out."

"It's tough," Milner said.

McIver tipped his hat back on his head. The last of the fedora wearers. "Klinger says he wants you guys kept abreast on account of the one you pulled, the brodie off McAlistair's terrace. Do me a favor, will you? Keep your-*selves* abreast. I mean, don't take that the wrong way or anything; it's just that Nate and I have enough to do without trying to remember whether or not you guys're abreast or not. So, you know, call *us*."

"Sure thing, Timmy," Neuman said.

"Anything you want to know about what we got, Timmy?" Milner said.

Neuman looked at Milner: Was he making fun of him by mimicking his using the diminutive? Or was he . . . what? He didn't know what, so he didn't know if. Did he?

McIver tipped his hat forward. "I guess I should know everything you got."

Neuman nodded and looked at Milner.

Milner nodded and looked at Neuman.

Neuman had to laugh.

Milner did too.

"What?" McIver said.

Neuman shrugged. "We got shit."

Milner laughed. "Less than shit."

McIver laughed. "That's funny."

"It is funny," Neuman said.

Milner said, "Yeah, it is."

McIver touched his hat brim. "I meant . . . I mean . . . I thought you guys didn't exactly, you know, get along."

"We don't," Neuman said.

"I can't stand the motherfucker," Milner said.

"Hey," Neuman said.

"Hey, yourself," Milner said. "I'm kidding. See how I'm smiling. See these teeth?"

"If I were you, I'd be worried about maybe losing those teeth. If I were you—"

Milner put a hand out. "Jake. Chill out."

"I don't want to chill out. You chill out. Don't tell me to chill out."

"Chill out, Jake."

"Yeah, Jake," McIver said. "Chill out."

"I hate when people say chill out. It makes me cold. I don't like it."

"Fuck what you like," Milner said.

Neuman put his hand inside his coat. "You want that kneecap?"

"You go for your piece, Noomz, it'll be the last move you make."

"Don't call me Noomz."

McIver straightened his hat. "Hey, guys."

"Fuck you, Timmy," Neuman said.

"Take a walk, Timmy," Milner said.

"Don't call him Timmy," Neuman said. "I've worked with him plenty of times, I can call him Timmy. You call him Tim. You call him Lieu*te*nant. He's got years on you."

"Fuck you."

"Hey."

"Don't push me, motherfucker."

"Cocksucker."

"Guys."

"Asshole."

"Scumbag."

"*Guys.*"

"You should've seen *David* with Frances McAlistair, Timmy. He was scared out of his fucking mind. He could barely talk to her. Not that he stopped talking, not *David*— you should hear this son-of-a-bitch talk, Timmy."

"Hey, you don't go telling nobody what happens on a job, you got that straight? Nobody, you got it? *No*body, you dig?"

"Talk, talk, talk."

"Hey!"

McIver took his hat off and put it on Klinger's desk. "I'm going to shoot somebody."

"Stay out of it, Timmy," Milner said.

"Don't call me Timmy."

"Stay out of it, McIver, you asshole."

"Fuck you, Dave. *David.*"

Milner slapped at McIver. "Hey, watch it."

"Hey, don't touch him, Milner." Neuman shoved Milner.

"Kiss my ass." Milner shoved Neuman back.

Neuman reached to get a headlock on Milner, but Milner was too tall. Neuman punched at the side of his head.

Milner blocked the punch and got a headlock on Neuman.

McIver beat on Milner's shoulder. "Let him go, you stupid fuck. You're bigger than he is."

Milner took a backhand swipe at McIver.

McIver got a headlock on Milner.

They swayed this way and that across the floor, bumping into things, knocking things off the desk and off the tables along the wall, knocking over chairs.

Klinger opened the door. "What the fuck?"

They let go of each other and shrugged and pulled their clothing straight and brushed their hair smooth with their hands, like teenagers caught necking.

Klinger went to his desk and sat and flipped through a stack of messages. He looked up. "Well?"

Neuman looked at Milner, then at Klinger.

Milner looked at Neuman, then at Klinger.

"Us first?" they said together.

"You first," Klinger said.

Neuman looked at Milner. "You want to start, Dave?"

"You start, Jake."

McIver stared.

Neuman went first: "There's a year missing from Frances McAlistair's life, a year when she says she was living in a house out in Suffolk County, writing a book, an autobiography, a memoir, whatever, but she was actually doing something else, because someone else was living in that house, someone Ives found, an artist, a painter, he did his painting in the house, he hardly went out for more than a year.

"Karen Auburn, who covers Foley Square for Ives's paper, ran into Ives in New Orleans in the middle of September. He was there at his own expense under an aka, doing what, he wouldn't say, but because he wouldn't say—and because he was under an aka and paying his own bills—she and Fields, Ives's publisher, and Quinlan, his top editor, figured it had something to do with McAlistair.

"It doesn't follow automatically, I know, that his being under an aka and paying his own way means it had something to do with McAlistair, but they told this story about something Ives did once, Auburn and Fields and Quinlan, something about getting involved with a woman he was writing about, something Dave here already knows. You want to tell it, Dave—about Ives and this woman eight years ago?"

"You go ahead and tell it, Jake," Milner said.

McIver, who had retrieved his hat before Klinger could say anything about its being on his desk, put it on and curled the brim and shook his head in bewilderment at their sudden détente. Was it just the presence of brass or had their clumsy kermis cleared the air?

"Ives covered a murder that Dave'd pulled," Neuman said. "A guy came home and surprised a burglar in his house. They had a fight, the guy got stabbed, the burglar got shot, they both died, the guy's wife watched the whole thing. Ives started, you know, screwing around with the wife. Then he found out that her story wasn't legit, that the burglar was someone she and her husband both knew, someone she'd been screwing herself once upon a time.

"Another *Herald* reporter, who was also working on the story, for reasons I don't exactly understand—maybe Dave remembers—got herself killed because Ives didn't tell us, tell the cops, tell Dave, what he was finding out about the wife. The point is Auburn and Fields and Quinlan think Ives did the same thing here—that he was, you know, screwing around with McAlistair, that he found out something about her, that he didn't tell anybody—that that's the kind of guy he was, he did stuff like that to, you know, control women.

"The sort of catch is, Tom McNally, the one of the guys McAlistair used to, you know, *date* who might've been a candidate to be somebody who would've thrown Ives off the roof, because he was the only one who was in town at the time and because he's about six five, two fifty, McNally says he wasn't screwing McAlistair—he McNally—and he doesn't think any of the others were, either.

"Karen Auburn, who's smart, thinks so too—thinks Ives and McAlistair weren't, you know, screwing. I asked her why not—why wouldn't a woman as good-looking, energetic, healthy, all that, as McAlistair have a, you know, a sex life. She said AIDS would be a reason, or some other physical thing, or something emotional, or being, you know, gay, or just being afraid of, you know, intimacy. She said if she had any of those things—she herself, she Auburn—and if she was also thinking about a political career, yes, she might kill somebody who threatened to tell the rest of the world. . . .

"That's one version. The other version's DeBree's version, the gossip columnist for the *Herald*. DeBree says Ives told him that during the missing year, McAlistair was having an affair with a writer named Al Coblen—"

"Al *Coblen?*" McIver couldn't help himself. "Who wrote the Dick Richards novels?"

"I think so," Neuman said. "I mean, I think that was the name DeBree said. Dick Richards? Yeah, that sounds right. You've read them, I guess, hunh, Timmy? I never did."

"I've read them *twice,*" McIver said.

"Hunh." Neuman looked at Milner and smiled. Milner winked at Neuman. McIver looked from Neuman to Milner and back at Neuman, shook his head and looked down at his stomach.

"Would you please continue, Lieutenant Neuman?" Klinger said.

"Uh, right. Sure. Okay. Yeah. Well. That's it, I guess. DeBree thinks McAlistair was having this affair with Al Coblen, who was married at the time but his wife and kids were in the city and he was out on Shelter Island at the same time McAlistair was saying she was in her house in Water Mill, which is right close by. Coblen was born in Louisiana and also had a place near New Orleans where he and McAlistair supposedly spent some time, which is supposedly what Ives went down to New Orleans to check up on. Coblen's dead—in a car crash, right, Timmy?"

McIver nodded mournfully, as if it had happened just the day before.

Neuman shrugged. "I guess that's it. Except that McNally, the guy McAlistair used to date who could've thrown Ives off the roof because he was in town and because he's about six five, two fifty, McNally told me his doorman could verify that he was home went Ives did his brodie, but what the doorman said was he *couldn't* verify it because McNally has a habit of coming and going by way of the service entrance. I don't know whether McNally told me to ask the doorman for an alibi because he's got nothing to hide or because it's some kind of smoke screen, but it needs some clearing up. *That's* it."

Klinger looked at Milner and raised his eyebrows.

Milner said, "Before I run this down, Inspector, I'd just like to say what an excellent briefing that was on the part of Lieutenant Neuman. Clear, direct, to the point, no wasted words."

Neuman shuffled. He thought he'd wasted ten or fifteen thousand words.

McIver stared. He thought so too.

Klinger said, "Get on with it, Milner."

Neuman had to smile. No more Dave; *David*.

Milner got on with it: "Around the time Ives was screwing the wife of the DOA who Jake, who Lieutenant Neuman just mentioned, he also had a steady girlfriend named Kate Naismith. I met her at the time and liked her and I guess she remembered me, because she called me the other day, after reading in the paper, I guess, that I pulled Ives's case.

"She said Ives sent her some audiotapes—maybe a copy, maybe the originals—of an interview he did with Frances McAlistair. Six ninety-minute cassettes. The package was a shoebox with brown wrapping paper, mailed the Friday before Ives did his brodie, with a note saying please hold on to these.

"Since she got the package, someone's been calling her ten or fifteen times a day, letting the phone ring for however long it takes till she has to answer it or go nuts. No one says anything when she does. Kate thinks there's a connection. She's only listened to part of one tape, and couldn't say anything about the content. Kate lives in Hoboken, so I asked her to bring the tapes to a store she owns in TriBeCa. I got jammed up, so I haven't called her."

"That's it?" Klinger said.

"That's all I've got," Milner said.

"I just remembered something." Neuman flipped through his notebook. "We're still doing interviews at McAlistair's building and around the paper, still getting dribs and drabs from Crime Scene. One thing I just got before I came over here—sorry I forgot to mention this to you, Dave—is Crime Scene ran down the keys on Ives's key ring, none of them is to McAlistair's building or her apartment, so how he got in is a bigger mystery than it was, since she says she didn't let him in. Sorry, Dave, I didn't mention that to you."

Milner's wave said it was okay, hey, Milner was jammed up too, he knew. McIver's stare said Neuman had already *said* he was sorry, enough was enough.

Klinger put his fingertips together and sighed through them at the top of his desk. "Lieutenant McIver, did you tell Lieutenants Milner and Neuman about the connection between your DOA and their DOA?"

"Uh, no, sir," McIver said. "I didn't get a chance, sir. I forgot, sir."

Klinger slammed his hand down on the desk. "Well, tell them, for crying out loud."

"Yes, sir. Uh . . ." McIver turned toward Neuman and Milner but kept his eyes on the floor. "Before we pulled this armory thing, Nate and I pulled a thing at a sixplex theater on East Eight-six. A guy got whacked with a nine-millimeter Walther. A minor mob hit, it looked like, but the DOA turned out not to be mob, he was just a guy. An epi—epidemilio—Shit, I can never say it—"

"Epidemiologist," Klinger said.

"Thank you, sir. A guy who tracks contagious diseases, Jake. Dave. The thing of it is, he's a guy who made about fifty grand a year doing research for a medical think tank over by Bellevue and he had twenty grand in untraceable bills in a gym bag in his closet. He also had your DOA's name and phone number on a slip of paper in his wallet and your DOA's name in his datebook. They met for lunch at Rusty's last September."

"Can we get a look at that datebook, Timmy?" Neuman said.

"I'll tell Property. But don't lose it, will you? It's evidence."

Klinger's phone rang. "Yeah? . . . Send them in."

After a beat, the door opened and James Jones came in, followed by Matt McGovern followed by Steve Federici, looking like death.

"Detectives," Klinger said.

"We'd like to talk to Lieutenant Neuman, sir," Jones said.

"Talk," Klinger said.

"What's up, Jonesy?" Neuman said.

"Here, Lieutenant?" Jones said.

"Sure," Neuman said.

"There was a call for you from the Hoboken police,"

Jones said. "One of their DOAs had your business card on her, one of the reporters you talked to, Karen Auburn."

It took Neuman a moment to sort out subject and predicate, but when he had, he realized that there was nothing wrong with the way Jones had said it in the first place; he'd said it chronologically, that's all. It took him a moment, too, because it had never been fun and never would be to hear that someone you'd developed some kind of, oh, rapport with, some kind of understanding, someone you'd talked to about some sort of intimate things, things like sex and death—to hear that someone like that was a DOA. Dead. Whacked, probably, since you didn't get too many people in your line of work who die of natural causes, in their sleep, peacefully.

And the thing was, it was people like Karen Auburn, people you developed some kind of rapport with, who more often than not got whacked, died peacelessly, if there was such a word; the other people, the people you had no rapport with, the people you couldn't stand the sight of and would've paid a lot of money never to see again, the people you didn't talk about intimate things with, you just talked dirty—those people were invincible, immortal, omnifuck-ingpresent: Neuman's Law. "Yeah. What else?"

"She was shot in the back of the head, sir, a pro job. A nine-millimeter, it looks like, but their Crime Scene's still working on it; the body'd been lying there for twenty-four hours, maybe. The cold kept it, you know, preserved, but it's still tough getting good forensics. Especially in Jersey."

"Don't tell me, let me guess." Milner had his notebook out and was paging back through it. "She was found in or near Eighty-nine Park Avenue or Park Street or Park something, yes?"

Jones got out his notebook and paged through it. "In a lot next to Eighty-nine Park Avenue, yeah. Their Crime Scene thinks she bought it in the doorway of Eighty-nine Park, like when she was ringing the bell or something, she was dragged into the vacant lot, dumped under some junk, like, kind of covered over with a canvas thing, a tarp."

"Don't tell me, let me guess, Dave," Neuman said. "Eighty-nine Park Avenue is where Kate—uh, Naismith was it?—lives. Am I right or am I right?"

"Right as rain, Jake," Milner said.

McIver shook his head again.

Milner put his notebook away. "You all right, Feds?"

It was a moment before Federici realized Milner was talking to him; for a moment he thought some feds had come into the room—some assholes from the FBI, ATF, Treasury, the C fucking IA maybe. And no, he wasn't all right, thanks. The fuck could he be all right when the woman with a centerfold body, a body that was always in motion, the woman who had it all—breasts, legs, ankles, collarbone, wrists, the woman with whom he had been in unseemly love, was dead, a bullet hole behind her left ear like some two-bit wise guy, not like somebody who dressed (he was sure of it, though he still hadn't seen it, would never see it now) in camisoles and tap pants and teddies and bustiers and thongs and . . . and . . . and. "I'm all right, yeah. It's just that we, you know, met her, talked to her"—smelled her, listened to the shivering of her shoulders, the shimmying of her hips, the slip-sliding of her clothing, the hissing of her stockings, the tossing of her hair, the jangling of jewelry, bracelets, whatever—"me and Lieutenant Neuman."

Milner looked at Federici like *So the fuck what?* then looked at Jones. "Ask Hoboken to send us the ballistics on that nine-millimeter, if that's what it is. Eight'll get you five that is what it is and that it's the same nine-millimeter that Timmy's DOA got whacked with."

"Who's Timmy?" Jones said.

"Lieutenant McIver here."

"Oh. Sorry, Lieutenant." Jones snapped his fingers. "*Your* DOA is the guy in the sixplex with the popcorn box on his head, right?"

McIver nodded.

"What's his name again?" Jones said.

"Corry. Michael Corry. He's a, uh, he's a scientist who tracks diseases."

"An epidemiologist?" Jones said.

McIver nodded.

"Dave" Neuman said.

"Yeah, Jake?" Milner said.

Jones, Federici and McGovern looked at one another, then at McIver, who avoided their looks by tipping his head back and rubbing his chin.

"Why did you say that—that you think the same nine-millimeter was used on Auburn and on this guy Corry?"

"You're the one who got me thinking along that line, Jake," Milner said. "You got me thinking along that line when you said you asked Karen Auburn why McAlistair wouldn't have a sex life and Auburn said some disease might be a reason. Maybe this guy Corry knew just what disease, exactly, and he got whacked for knowing. Maybe Karen Auburn was starting to find out what disease, exactly, and she got whacked for starting to know."

"Like maybe Ives fell or jumped or was he pushed for knowing."

Milner chuckled. "Yeah."

Neuman smiled. "Yeah."

Jones, Federici and McGovern looked at one another, then at McIver, who looked at them like the fuck were they looking at. They looked away.

Klinger sighed. "Everybody through?"

Everyone shrugged, shuffled, nodded, rolled their heads around on the ends of stiff necks.

"Yeah."

"Yeah, we're through, Inspector."

"Yeah."

"Yes, sir."

"Yeah."

Klinger stood. "Guess where I'm going while you guys are out playing in the snow? I'm going to City Hall to explain his honor the mayor how so much shit could go down in so little time in this weather." He left.

After a moment, Milner said, "Feds?"

Federici said, "Yeah?"

"Kate Naismith, who is the woman who lives at the address where Karen Auburn got whacked, owns a shop in TriBeCa—Le Peau Douce, a lingerie place at West Broadway and Thomas. I want you to go down there—"

"A *what*?" Federici said.

Milner narrowed his eyes. "What?"

"What kind of shop did you say she owns?"

"Watch my lips: lahn-zher-ray."

Federici had his notebook out. "Broadway and Thomas?"

"*West* Broadway and Thomas."

"West Broadway and Thomas."

"Le Peau Douce."

"Luh . . . Poh . . . Doose."

"Find her—" Milner said.

"Yeah."

"Make sure she's all right—"

"Yeah."

"Stay with her if—"

"Yeah."

"Let me finish, will you, Feds."

"Sorry, Lieutenant."

"Stay with her if necessary. Call in every couple of hours. . . . What're you waiting for?"

"That's it?"

"That's it."

Federici saluted, and left, double time.

Milner shrugged. "Must be the syzygy. I thought of telling Klinger to tell the mayor it was the syzygy, but his sense of humor needs a lube job."

"The what?" Neuman said.

"Syzygy. A rare alignment of the earth, sun and moon, resulting in increased tidal forces. In addition, the moon is in perigee, its closest point to the earth, which further emphasizes the effect of the tides. Tides throughout the world are averaging several feet above normal. Locally, the syzygy's coincided with a major storm, resulting in—well, all hell's breaking loose."

"How do you know all that stuff, Milns?" Neuman said.

Milner shrugged. "I figured, you bucking for Art Theft too, Noomz, I'd better start brushing up on other areas of knowledge."

Neuman laughed and threw a soft left hook at Milner's arm. "You stupid fuck."

Milner countered with a soft right uppercut. "You asshole."

They laughed and dropped their hands and walked out of the office with their arms around each other.

Jones and McGovern and McIver wouldn't look at one another.

17

___

*The Celtics trounced the Knicks last night, one forty-one to
one eleven. The Nets had a better time of it, beating the
Spurs. On the ice, it was the Rangers over Calgary and the
Devils over the Kings. National Weather Service forecast:
Cloudy, windy and cold. High today only in the high teens,
low tonight zero to five above, tomorrow more of the same,
except maybe a little colder and a little cloudier. Right
now in Central Park it's twelve degrees, but those west-
northwest winds make it* feel like . . . *Miscou Harbour,
New Brunswick.*

Dead Eddie Milano wanted one of those T-shirts that
said "Life's a Bitch and Then You Die," except he wanted
his to say "Your *Wife's* a Bitch and Then You Die," 'cause of
all the things that were going down—*coming* down around
him: the Valentine's Day thing, the thing with Mary Liz,
the tax thing his accountant said he wasn't gonna have to
worry about till next year, all of a sudden he's got a worry
about it *this* year, the weather. Of all those things, the
worst thing of all, hands down, top dog, numero uno, was
still Rosalie, shoulda been a professional wrestler, and his
fucking kid, who's gonna grow up to be a pansy faggot hairdresser.

What'd she do, Rosalie? Nothing, that's what. Nothing
but her usual bitching, whining, moaning, I need a new
microwave, I need a new dress, new shoes, a new hat,
boots for the kid (*Boots?* What kinda boots? Pansy faggot
hairdresser boots?), I don't want a watch this show, it's time
to watch that show, talk nice to Mama, Eddie, let Mama
read the paper, Eddie, Mama makes the best lasagne in a
world, don't she, Eddie, tell Mama, Eddie, scratch my

back, Eddie, hold my hand, Eddie, how come you never kiss me anymore, Eddie, you never want to go bouncy-bouncy anymore, Eddie, I remember when you wanted to go bouncy-bouncy all the time, you going bouncy-bouncy with some chippy on the side, Eddie, I'll rip her eyes out, I'll bite her tits off, yaddada yaddada yaddadafuckingya till there was nothing he could do except go outta the house, take a walk in the middle of a blizzard, the fucking upshot being Artie Roth's sidemen instead of freezing to death from sitting outside Dead Eddie's building all fucking night got Dead Eddie handed to them on a platter, practically, muscled him in the back of a Delta 88, the fucking upshot being he is about to get rubbed out and dumped in the Gowanus Canal.

Your wife is a bitch and your life is a bitch, and then you fucking die.

Him. The woist hombre.

Shit.

Life is such a bitch he don't even know where to start.

The tax thing he don't even understand, so forget about that, that's why he hires the accountant, to worry about these things, *not* to fuck up by telling him he's not going to have to worry about it, then all of a sudden telling him he *is* going to have to worry about it, about American suppository receipts or some fucking thing.

The thing with Mary Liz he understands all too fucking well, he don't need an accountant to explain it to him, he don't need no road map, it is as clear as the hair on Rosalie's back. She is quitting her job, Mary Liz, he is never going to see her again.

"Quitting?" he said to her. "Fuck you mean, quitting?"

"You owe me half a week's tips off the credit card receipts, but I didn't get around to chipping in for coffee and juice for the month and for Val's birthday present, so we'll call it even."

"Mary *Liz*."

"Oh, Eddie, you knew it wouldn't last forever."

"Right. So what'd it, last six months?"

"Seven. Seven and a half."

"Big fucking deal. It's like yesterday you came here, you didn't know shit, I had a get Val and them to teach you how to talk dirty, *I* practically had a teach you how to hold the phone. Today you're going a do what? Hey, whoa, wait a fucking minute. You're not thinking a starting your own service, are you?"

"I'd rather not work tonight, Eddie, unless it gets real busy."

"You are."

"Val's here and Diane's on the way. They can use the tips."

"You *are*."

"Don't forget you'll have to get someone else to proofread the ad."

"You fucking are. You're thinking a starting your own service."

"Val can probably do it. You should pay her a little extra, though."

"So what're you, saying I been stiffing you 'cause I didn't pay you a little extra to proofread the fucking ad?"

"I didn't mind, Eddie. I have two jobs. Val has one job and two kids, so pay her a little extra."

"Shit. I teach you how to hold the fucking phone, practically, and you go and start your own service."

"Eddie?"

"Yeah?"

"Don't say it again, okay?"

"Well, why're you leaving then?"

"It's not safe."

"Fuck's not safe about it? You can't fucking get AIDS over the fucking phone." Dead Eddie had laughed.

Mary Elizabeth hadn't. "The cops smell an inside job, Eddie. I should've quit months ago."

He'd laughed again. "The fuck'm I, going a suspect you a being the one working both sides a the fence?"

"You *know* I'm working both sides of the fence, Eddie. The suspicion's going to come from the other side."

"That's what I'm saying." Wasn't it?

"What is?"

What was? "Well . . ."

"I'll give you a little going-away present, Eddie," Mary Liz had said.

A blow job? "Yeah? What?"

"The real name of a client."

"A client a who?"

"You."

"What client?"

"He calls himself Bill. He prepays by money order. He's a masochist—golden showers, coprophilia, getting walked on with spiked heels, that sort of thing."

Whatever the fuck coprophilia was—wanting to poke somebody dressed like a cop, probably, wearing a motorcycle hat, handcuffs, a nightstick, all that shit—Dead Eddie didn't want to know about it. Golden showers, he knew what they were; spiked heels, he knew what they were too: He'd never told nobody this, *no*body, but Rosalie had a pair of spiked heels, she liked to walk around in front of him with nothing but them on and a silk scarf she held between her legs like it was a towel she was drying herself off with, she'd pull it back and forth so it rubbed against her, you know, snatch, she'd moan and shit and ask if she could walk on his chest, he'd say fuck no, he wasn't no weirdo, so she'd ask him to pinch her nipples, pinch them harder and harder and harder, he wouldn't pinch them that hard, he wasn't no fucking weirdo like the guys who talked to his girls on the phone.

He didn't want to know about it 'cause he didn't want to think about Mary Liz telling a guy over the phone she was going to piss on him, take a crap on him, dress up in spiked heels and a cop uniform and walk all over him, whoever he was. "I don't wanna know about it."

She shrugged. "Suit yourself."

Why the fuck hadn't he just listened to who the fuck it was? He listened to who the fuck it was, he coulda been holding a card in his hand when Artie Roth's sidemen muscled him in the back of a Delta 88, instead of holding a limp dick. His own.

Your wife is a bitch and your life is a bitch, and then you fucking die.

Except Dead Eddie was pretty sure—even though they had him down on the floor of the car with his face in the carpet of the floor and one of the sidemen's feet on his neck—pretty sure they weren't headed to Brooklyn, they were headed uptown, which could mean they were going to dump him in the river by the boat basin, it wouldn't have been the first time, or in Riverside Park, or up under the el tracks around a Hundred Twenty-fifth Street, it wouldn't have been the first time for any of those places, either.

Except they were going west now, Dead Eddie was pretty sure, slipping and sliding and slurping west down a one-way street on account of he couldn't hear no cars slipping and sliding and slurping in the other direction.

And then all of a sudden real fast they were there and one of the sidemen had Dead Eddie by the back of the neck and hauled him up off the floor of the Delta 88 and through the door of this warehouse, like, in the Twenties it looked like, over by the river, just from the glimpse Dead Eddie had of the sky and the other buildings and shit.

And then they were in this elevator the size of a fucking room going up and up and up, the sidemen standing behind Dead Eddie where he couldn't get a good look at their faces and where they could sap him he made any moves they didn't like and shit, the sideman driving the elevator standing with his back to Dead Eddie so Dead Eddie can't see *his* face, a *Daily News* rolled up in his back pocket with another one of those headlines saying Club Dead this or Club Dead that, Dead Eddie didn't know Club Dead what, 'cause he hadn't even had a chance to look at the paper on account of Rosalie, his pansy faggot kid, drove him out of the fucking house into the fucking street.

Your wife is a bitch and your life is a bitch and your kid is on the road to being a pansy faggot hairdresser, and then you fucking die.

And then there was Artie Roth waiting for the elevator door to open and when it did he walked right up to Dead Eddie and brought his knee up in his crotch. "You insubstantial twit."

"Uhhhhhhh," Dead Eddie said.

"Have you ever heard of visualization, Eddie?"

"Ahhhhhh."

"The concept that one can accomplish a task, effectuate it, actualize it by seeing it accomplished, effectuated, actualized in one's mind's eye beforehand?"

"Oooooooh."

Artie Roth hit Dead Eddie in the solar plexus. "I didn't think you had."

"Unh unh unh unh unh unh."

"You inconsequential aberration."

"Unh unh unh."

"What I'm suggesting, Eddie, is that it behooved you to attempt to visualize me dead before sending your sidemen out to attempt to make my death a reality. You would have noted, I submit, the impossibility of such visualization and would have obviated the ensuing fiasco."

"Unh. Unh. Unh. Unh."

"More to the point, Eddie, it behooved you to attempt to visualize me in the armory *at all*, visualize me having fallen for the feds' pathetic ruse. You can't kill a man, Eddie, who isn't present, and if you'd made even the most enfeebled pass at imagining me there, you'd have become cognizant of that impossibility. And, Eddie, don't send your own flunkies on a job you don't want your fingerprints all over. People made Air Sax every which way but Thursday."

Air Sax? Air Sax wasn't supposed to have been on the fucking job. The fuck was he doing on the fucking job, he wasn't supposed to have been on it?

"And did you know, Eddie—a lot of people do, but I bet you didn't—did you know Air Sax is letting himself out as an independent contractor, available for small-time hits and who knows what the fuck else? You can't let your flunkies go indie on you like that, Eddie. It's not good business. As business, it sucks."

Air Sax? The fuck was Air Sax doing doing small-time hits? Doing them when? Doing them on whose time? All the things that were coming down around him . . . the Valentine's Day thing, Mary Liz quitting her job, starting her own service, probably, the thing with the American suppository receipts, the fucking weather, Rosalie's usual bitching, whining, moaning, taking a fucking walk in the middle of a fucking blizzard, handing himself on a platter to Artie Roth's sidemen, practically, Artie Roth slapping him around like he was a fucking kid or something—somebody's nephew, somebody's wife's cousin ready to run numbers, get coffee, learn the ropes—instead of the woist hombre, which was what he was, or used to be, anyway, humiliating him and shit . . . all those things, and on top of it he finds out fucking Air Sax is doing an indie. "Unh. Unh. Unh. Unh."

Artie Roth put thumb and forefinger against Dead Eddie the onetime woist hombre's cheeks and squeezed.

"Aheeoohoohooooh."

And squeezed. "We used to play a game when I was a child, Eddie—my brothers and sisters and I and our Uncle George, our father's brother, our favorite uncle."

"Ah ah ah ah ah ah. Ow ow ow ow ow ow."

"He'd hold us like this, then command us to 'Say Doreen'—the name of a cousin once removed on my father's side."

"Unh unh unh. Ow ow ow."

"It's difficult, when the cheeks are being held in such a way as to prohibit the formation of the alveolar *D*. Try it, Eddie. Say Doreen."

"Or ee."

"You see? Now, Eddie, try saying the name of the individual who informed you—or rather *mis*informed you—as to my attendance at the, uh, what was it called? Vacation giveaway."

"Ah oh oh."

"Sorry, Eddie. I didn't get it. Say it again."

"Ah oh oh. *Ow!*"

"It's interesting, isn't it, Eddie, how one can understand a sequence of sounds to be a sentence even if the words themselves can't be comprehended? For example, I have no doubt that what you're endeavoring to say is 'I don't know,' meaning that you don't know, or so you would have me believe, the name of the individual who misinformed you as to my attendance at the vacation giveaway. Isn't that so?"

"Es. *Ow!*"

"It's the wrong answer, Eddie. Doesn't even a brain as ill adapted to a life dependent on wit and guile as yours is have the ability to grasp that elementary fact?"

"Ih oo. Ah oh oh."

"It's true? You don't know?"

"Es. *Ow!*"

"You dumb fuck, Eddie. You stupid dumb fucking wop asshole."

"Mmmmmmmmmwaaaaaaaagh."

"Okay, Eddie, one more chance. One. More. Chance. Or what, you ask? Or we take a walk down to the end of the room, Eddie. Hard as it may be to believe given its current condition, this warehouse was once a jewel in New York's mercantile crown, a point of disembarkation for cargo from the great merchant ships that plied the Atlantic, and at the end of the room is a door that opens directly onto the Hudson River. I'm sure you're aware, Eddie, that the Hudson is frozen over these days. Well, not entirely frozen over. Right around the shoreline there are what I believe are called *leads*, fissures or cracks in the ice. It's about a fifteen-foot drop to the water, Eddie, so you'll be conscious when you go in. I have no idea what the water temperature is—it must be at least thirty-two, mustn't it, if there's ice?—and no idea how long a man can live in water of that temperature, or what happens to your body after it goes under, or what kind of condition your body'll be in when it turns up, if it turns up, next spring, or whenever, so this will be in the nature of a scientific experiment, won't it? The Coast Guard, or some such agency, would probably be interested in the data—"

"Ah ot a ahuhee."

"What was that, Eddie?"

"Ah ot a ahuhee."

"'I've got a family'?"

"Es."

"A wife and lovely young son, isn't it?"

A bitch shoulda been a professional wrestler and kid gonna be a pansy faggot hairdresser. "Es."

"Pity."

"Ah ee."

"Mr. Roth to you, you wop nonentity."

"Ih er Oth."

"Fuck you, Eddie."

"Ees, Ih er Oth."

"Eddie, Eddie, Eddie."

The fuck was he going through this for? She was quitting her job, Mary Liz, she didn't ever want to see him again, she was starting her own service, probably, fuck him, so fuck her, right? "Air ee uh *ih* ah eth Ih el in *ah* oh."

Artie Roth pulled Eddie's face up close to his. "I didn't get that, Eddie. Say it again."

"Air ee uh *ih* ah eth Ih el ih *ah* oh."

"Is that the name, Artie?"

"Es."

"The name of the individual who misinformed you as to my attendance at the vacation giveaway?"

"Es."

"Say it again, Eddie."

"Air ee uh *ih* ah eth Ih el ih *ah* oh."

Artie Roth let go of Dead Eddie's cheeks. "Say it again, Eddie."

Eddie rubbed his face. "Ow. Oh. Ah. Shit, Artie."

"Say it again."

"Mary. Elizabeth. Indelicato."

Artie Roth shook his head sadly. "That's the right answer, Eddie, but what a cheap scumbag you are for giving it to me." He put a hand on Eddie's shoulder. "Still, Eddie, I should express my gratitude to you. You exterminated Arnie Ames, the maggot, not to mention Nicky Bleeshka, Howie Canell, and Charlie the Chimp Intilli, each of whom at one time or another suffered from the delusion that he might one day be *primus inter pares* on the West Side of Manhattan—a delusion you, too, have been burdened with.

"And, Eddie, I should tell you a little secret. You told me one. I'll tell you one. I'll tell you who told me the vacation giveaway was a no-no, Eddie, a setup. Saint Valentine's Day for Christ's sake, of course some weasel of a wise guy would try to etch his name in the annals of the underworld by replicating the notorious massacre. Even so, Eddie, I was the beneficiary of a warning to give the vacation giveaway a wide berth. And the individual, Eddie, who gave me that warning is the same individual who misinformed you as to my attendance at the vacation giveaway, misinformed you at my behest, since it seemed a rare opportunity to eliminate Arnie Ames, Nicky Bleeshka, Howie Canell, Charlie the Chimp Intilli and any other, uh, bystanders. The name is Mary Elizabeth Indelicato, who is a clever young woman, Eddie, working more sides of the street than the street has sides, and all because of a cocaine habit you could drive a dump truck up to. Ciao, Eddie."

"Wait, Artie. Please. For the love of God, please wait."

"Wait for what, Eddie?"

"Listen. Just listen, will you?"

"Listen to what, Eddie?"

"I got this service, you know? This phone service? This phone sex service."

Artie Roth laughed. The laugh of a man who knows your wife is a bitch and your life is a bitch, and you're about to fucking die. "Have you been listening, Eddie? That you're about to offer me the names of your clients, especially that of Police Commissioner Franklin Montgomery, when I just told you about my relationship with Mary Liz, indicated to me that you haven't been listening. You don't have shit to sell me, Eddie. You really don't. You don't have shit. You just *are* shit."

And Artie Roth turned and walked the length of the warehouse. Having no interest at all in what the water temperature was or in how long a man could live in water of that temperature, or in what happened to Dead Eddie's body after it went under, or in what kind of condition it would be when it turned up, if it turned up, next spring, or whenever—having no interest at all in scientific experiments, he didn't look back as two of his sidemen lifted Dead Eddie, the onetime woist hombre, by the armpits, carried him to the door and dropped him into the Hudson River.

18

Midtown:

"Hey, Noomz, look in the trunk of the car."

Neuman stopped on his way around to the driver's side and popped open the trunk. Inside were a pair of cross-country skis and boots. "Holy shit."

"You're a nine and a half, right?" Milner said.

"How'd you know that?" Neuman said.

Milner smiled and got in the passenger's door.

Neuman shut the trunk and got in the car and put the key in the ignition. "Sure you don't want to drive?"

"Nah, you drive."

Neuman started the engine and let it warm. "What I heard about you, Milns, is you never let anyone else drive. Ever."

Milner shrugged. "What I heard about you, Noomz, is *don't* ever let you drive. Never."

"Where'd you hear that?"

"What does it matter? It's bullshit, right?"

"I'm a fair driver. Not great. Fair."

Milner wiped fog off the windshield with the back of his hand. "I once read a poll where people rated themselves as drivers. Some incredible fucking percentage rated themselves excellent, which you don't have to be on the road for more than about two minutes to know is a crock of shit. So I like hearing you say you're fair. It probably means you're better than average."

Neuman cleared his windshield with the palm of a ragg mitten. "I can't keep those skis, Dave."

"Why not?"

"Well, I mean, you got them as a freebie, right? A handout, right? Some sporting-goods guy gave them to you

154

or something, right, to look the other way about trucks unloading in front of his store or something, right?"

Milner touched his chest. "You cause me grievous pain, Noomz. First of all, I'm a homicide dick; what fuck do I give where trucks unload? Second of all, would I give my partner a gift that would embarrass him, compromise him, make him culpable, even?"

"So where'd you get them?"

"Herman's. They're having an end-of-season sale. We should be so fucking lucky that the season's ending."

"You *bought* them?"

"Yeah, I bought them."

"With, you know, money?"

"Matter of fact, yeah. Cash money."

"They're for you then, right? They just happen to be nine and halfs."

"They're for you, Jake. That's why they're nine and a halfs."

Neuman gripped the steering wheel as if he wouldn't be dislodged. "I can't take them."

"Why not?"

"I don't know."

"They're to cement our partnership."

"Cement?" Neuman said.

Milner shrugged. "Whatever."

They laughed.

"Also it's thanks for not saying anything in front of the Klings about my walking out of McNally's office."

Neuman put the car in gear and went up the ramp to the street. He turned out of the driveway and headed west. "I didn't get you anything."

"Hey, it's better to give than receive. But I got my eye on that hat of yours."

Neuman looked in the mirror at his ragg-wool watch cap. "This hat?"

"Yeah."

"*This* hat?"

"It's warm, isn't it?"

"Yeah, it's warm, but everybody's always on me about how stupid it looks."

"If it's warm," Milner said, "what difference does it make how it looks?"

Neuman turned south and drove for a while. "You want this hat?"

"Not *that* hat. A hat like it."

He drove a while longer. "So what's this about you bucking for Art Theft?"

Milner laughed. "I've been meaning to ask you the same thing."

"You really bucking for it?"

"I don't know. It'd be kind of slow, don't you think?"

"*Kind* of?"

Milner laughed.

"And what's this about your having a wife named Maria from Venezuela or someplace?"

"Venezuela, yeah. Your wife's Maria too, right, from Puerto Rico, right?"

"*Si*," Neuman said.

Milner laughed. "That's about all the Spanish I know too. I know *Coño de tu madre* and I know *Yo no soy marinero, soy capitán*."

Neuman laughed. "That's from that song a couple of years ago, isn't it? I got good and sick of that song. You've got a daughter too, right? An adopted daughter."

"Carmen," Milner said. "She'll be twelve in May, if there ever is a May."

"What's that like?" Neuman said. "Having an eleven-year-old girl around the house."

"It's not *like* anything," Milner said.

Neuman laughed.

Milner turned sidesaddle on the seat. "So what've we go here, Noomz? I mean, if we really believe McAlistair's story, then we've got a suicide and that's all. I've been thinking about why would a guy go to somebody else's house to commit suicide, and I thought of two reasons: one is, he doesn't live on a high enough floor himself, assuming doing a brodie's the option he's selected; the other is, he wants it in the record books that he was that tight with the individual whose floor he did a brodie off.

"Last summer—remember summer?—I read this book. Maria read it, my wife, she liked it, so I read it too.

It was called *Dawn's Husband*. I forget who wrote it, but it was about this guy, a plain ordinary businessman, who meets this movie actress. They're at JFK waiting for a plane that's delayed because of a snowstorm in the Midwest and they strike up a conversation and then they go for coffee and then they gave a drink and then they have dinner and they finally go to a motel.

"In the morning the guy gets on the plane that's finally come but she's already missed the thing she was supposed to go to—she was going to be on Johnny Carson or something—so she gets on a different plane to go somewhere else. They kiss goodbye and all and he's got her number and she's got his, and he's really hoping that they can get together again and we're rooting for him 'cause he's a really nice funny pleasant enjoyable guy, he knows a lot about a lot of different things, he's nice-looking, dresses nice, he's a good athlete, plays in some Y basketball league, his team won the championship, he scored thirty-two points or something, but he's modest about it, she had to pry it out of him.

"Her plane crashes, she dies, the guy reads the obits in the papers, they talk about her old boyfriends, they say lately she'd been on her own pretty much and happy to be that way, he tries to tell his friends, the people he works with, he was, you know, her lover. They say yeah, sure, have another, have two.

"He finds out they're having a memorial service, all kinds of celebrities're going to be there, some of the old boyfriends, a couple of who're movie stars too, plus politicians, writers, painters, the whole bit. She's sort of like a Jane Fonda type, this woman; she's more than just an actress—she's got her fingers in all kinds of different pies. Come to think of it, she's sort of like a Frances McAlistair type , and that reminds me of something I've been meaning to say to you, Jake. You were right: That time we went up to her place, I was pretty nervous."

Neuman shrugged. "Hey, me too. It just, you know, came out different."

"I don't know. I thought I made us look kind of bad. Our team, I mean. And cops in general."

"I don't think so," Neuman said. "And anyway, so what if you did?"

"Meaning you think I made us look bad?" Milner said.

"Maybe," Neuman said. "I mean, *kind* of bad, not *real* bad."

Milner leaned over to see Neuman's face. "You putting me on, or what? I can't tell."

Neuman laughed. "Hey, Dave, relax. You were nervous, you were nervous. It's no big deal."

"So you don't think I made us look bad?"

"No."

"Really?"

"Well . . ."

"What?"

"You didn't make us look too good when you started that fight in front of McNally."

"Me? You started that fight."

"I did?"

"Yeah. Don't you remember?"

"No. What was the fight about?"

"I don't remember."

Neuman laughed. "Tell me the rest of the story."

Milner faced front. "So he goes to the funeral home, the guy, he can't get in, he doesn't have an invitation, nobody knows who he is, he tries to tell them he's a friend of the deceased, they say take a hike, buddy, this is a big-time wake, the plebes'll get their chance to pay their respects later today, the line's already forming around the corner, the end of it's in about Yonkers.

"He goes nuts, finally, the guy, he can't get anybody to believe he had this connection with her. Hell, it was more than a connection, it was the real thing. Okay, it was a one-night stand, but a one-night stand was one night longer than any stand she'd had with anybody else lately. He goes nuts, he flies down to Atlanta, which is where the airline she flew her last flight on has its headquarters, buys a piece at a pawn shop, goes to the office of the president of the airline, whacks him. He's a kind of Chuck Yeager type, the president, so his murder gets a lot of press coverage. The guy turns around at his arraignment, he yells to the reporters the reason he did it is to avenge his girlfriend's death.

"Still nobody really believes him, but he gets his mug in the papers, on the tube, for a couple of days, he refuses to cop to an insanity plea, so he goes off to the joint to make license plates, he's not cut out for the place, all kinds of horrible things happen to him which I'll spare you the details of, finally he gets in a fight with a guy he knows'll kill him, being in for killing several people already. It was a better book than I'm making it sound."

"But you think Ives was the same kind of guy as the guy in the book," Neuman said.

"You got it, Noomz. I think he had this thing for McAlistair, she liked him okay but wasn't going to make the kind of commitment he wanted, he had to do something that would, you know, connect them up in the public's mind, so he slipped into her apartment, either before she got there or after, went out on the terrace, did his brodie. Fact we didn't find a key doesn't mean shit. He might not've had it with his other keys, he might've had it in his pocket or in his hand, even, he might've thrown it over the side as an act of, you know, defiance, he might've dropped it on the way down, it'll turn up in the spring, if there ever is a spring.

"You drive pretty good, Noomz. Careful, in control, not going to break any speed records, but good."

"Thanks," Neuman said.

"You're welcome."

"I hear you see Bernstein," Neuman said.

"Fuck's that supposed to mean?" Milner said.

"Hey, Dave, relax. I'm making conversation. You and I've got these things in common: we're both bucking for Art Theft."

They both laughed.

"We've both got Hispanic wives named Maria. We both see Bernstein."

"You see Bernstein?" Milner said. Once a week?"

"Twice a month."

"I see him once a week."

"I know."

"What do you mean, you *know*? It's supposed to be

privileged. I'll bust Bernstein's chops the next time I see him."

"He didn't tell me. Klinger told me."

"I'll bust *his* chops. I don't care if he is brass."

"Bernstein's going to have his hands full when he finds out we've got a relationship that's cemented yet," Neuman said.

Milner laughed. "I didn't say we were cemented. I said the skis were cement; we've still got to see if the cement holds." He pointed out the window. "We're here. Shit, it's one way against us; I didn't even think of that. Don't go all the way around the block, just park right here; we'll walk. Hell, we'll take the skis, try them out. I mean, that machine you work out on, it's supposed to be just like cross-country skiing, right?

"Let's walk," Neuman said. "I'd hate to leave you in my dust, so to speak."

"Your cement, you mean," Milner said.

19

Downtown:

Lee Coblen laughed. "*Frances* McAlistair?"

Neuman's law: People who knew perfectly well whom you were talking about when you casually laid on them the name of someone who was sleeping with their spouse, or embezzling their money, or sneaking into their garden at night and snipping the rosemary, always—*always*—said *Frances* McAlistair, or whatever it was, leaning on the given name, to buy themselves a little time mostly, but also in the hope that they really *would* have misheard you, that you had actually said *Nancy* McAlistair or *Fanny* McAlistair or *Gladys* McAlistair or whatever, which would be a different matter altogether.

Neuman had to smile when he remembered how he'd said *Dave* Milner when Klinger informed him that his new partner not only had a Hispanic wife named Maria but also was taking an art history course in anticipation of applying for a transfer to Art Theft. And he had to smile when he remembered how their *thing*, their deep-seated animosity, underlain by profound mutual disrespect and contempt for each other's morals and methods and reinforced by occasional but highly fraught confrontations over a considerable period of time, seemed to have been turned into a deep-seated admiration, underlain by profound mutual respect and regard for each other's morals and methods, on the strength of one half-assed wrestling match and a couple of semi-shouting matches over a couple of days.

Maybe all you had to do to see what an asshole you were was to act like an asshole: Neuman's Law.

"Doesn't ring a bell, Mrs. Coblen?" Milner said.

"Who told you she and Al had an affair?" Lee Coblen said.

"Meaning they did?"

She laughed. A nice laugh. A genuine laugh. The laugh of someone whose dead husband's books were still in print, still serving as the basis for movie and television adaptations, still raking in the pazoozas, still paying the freight for this Chelsea town house, for the house on Shelter Island, for the Benz she'd just gotten a phone call from a mechanic about, a mechanic unlike any mechanic Neuman had ever talked to, one who'd explained things and answered questions and explained some more things and had told her, from the sound of it, when she'd asked, how much it would cost; of someone, her husband being dead, who wasn't likely to be made too jealous by the news that he'd had an affair a decade and a half ago; of someone who'd probably heard other rumors of other affairs, and who'd maybe been the subject of a few of them herself, since she was straight and tight and hard and when she laughed she sounded like Lauren Bacall. "Absolutely not."

"Why do you say that?"

"Because you say seventy-two. You did say seventy-two?"

"The spring and summer, in particular. In Louisiana, some of it. You were in New York while your husband was down there working on a book. What was the name of the town, Lieutenant Neuman?"

"Thibodaux," Lee Coblen said before Neuman could.

Neuman said, "Right," and felt like a fool, for he knew already that though right it might be, it was wrong.

Lee Coblen shook her head. "We spent the last half of seventy-one and the first half of seventy-two in Los Angeles. We had a house in Nichols Canyon. All of us. Al, the boys and I. Al was writing a script for *Depraved May*. The producers changed the name to *In the Bloody, Bloody Month of May* and changed virtually everything Al wrote too, but we got beautiful tans and powerful shoulders from all the swimming we did. Powerful thighs too, Al and I; we fucked a lot—more than we ever did back east. It was an idyllic time in a marriage that had its share of shitty times, and I resent the bitch's saying she was balling my husband during that time, because it undermines what we had together."

They believed her, Neuman and Milner said with glances—the glances of men whose admiration is so deep-seated and so underlain by profound mutual respect and regard for each other's morals and methods that they don't even have to talk to each other.

"I'm sorry," Neuman said.

"Me too," Milner said. "We're sorry."

"Cops," Lee Coblen said. "Someone always said that in Al's books—with disgust, contempt, exasperation. *Spat* was the verb Al always used. '"Cops," the writer's widow spat.' I never liked it. It always sounded false to me obligatory, a cliché. The thing about clichés, of course, is that they're true."

"We'll let ourselves out," Neuman said.

"Thanks for your time," Milner said.

"Cops." She didn't spit it, just kind of puffed it out, like when a piece of hair or something sticks to your tongue and it's annoying as hell but not so annoying that you can't get rid of it by blowing out a little poof of air, so that's what you do.

Poof.

Way, way crosstown, over in Hospital Land:

"I'm Dr. Pignatano. Are you the gold shields asking about Mike Corry?" He looked like Groucho Marx—lots of eyebrows, big nose, big mustache, big glasses. In the breast pocket of his white lab coat was a big cigar that he touched fractionally from time to time, the way a tourist touches his wallet.

"I'm Lieutenant Milner. This is Lieutenant Neuman. I won't beat around the bush with you. We don't know shit about Dr. Corry or this place or what he did here or anything at all. We're not even investigating his murder. But the name of a man whose death we are investigating turned up in Corry's appointment book—they had lunch together back in September—and Corry's name was in that man's address book. The death we're investigating could have something to do with Corry, although not necessarily with Corry's death. Are you still with me?"

Dr. Pignatano smiled. "That's a big ten-four."

Another glance between men whose admiration, respect and regard obviates speech. This one said, *Who is this wacko and why is he talking like a civilian's idea of how a cop talks?* "You told Detectives McIver and Bloomfield you had no explanation for the twenty thousand dollars they found in a suitcase in Corry's bedroom closet—"

"Nor," Dr. Pignatano said, "for the popcorn box the perp placed over the DOA's head after whacking him."

And another. "Right. But—"

Dr. Pignatano put a finger to his lips and rolled his eyes, Groucho style, at the nurse eavesdropping on them while pretending to file charts. He got in between Neuman and Milner and by the pressure of his hands on their shoulders invited them to walk with him away from the nurses' station. He opened a stairwell door and handed them through. He flipped up the tails of his lab coat and sat on the stairs, like a concert pianist, like Groucho. Then he played:

"Mike Corry was a nose-candy junkie. I didn't tell the other gold shields that because they didn't ask; all they wanted was hard copy on why Corry split his gig at this place; the stuff that really went down isn't in the hard copy, it's off the record, it's what his colleagues and his co-workers know.

"Little Red, Saint Hilda's and Hugh's, Andover, Princeton, Harvard Med, Mass Gen, Rockefeller Institute, this place—Mike Corry was a classic case of a dude educated to within an inch of his life, with virtually no experience of the real world. Whenever he ventured into it, the real world, he overdid. He didn't just date women; he got married—three times, the last time I counted, and he was only thirty-seven or thirty-eight. He didn't just exercise; he did triathlons—before the yuppies took to them because they liked the way they looked in Spandex. He didn't just make dinner; he was a gourmet cook—electric flour sifter, pasta machine, fish poacher—the kind of martinet asshole who practically chews your food for you, to make sure you don't mix taste sensations while his back's turned. He didn't just do half a gram of soda on a weekend every now and then; he free-based every day, sometimes twice a day, three times a day, and I wouldn't be surprised if he mainlined too, and if the autopsy didn't show any track marks it was because he was too good to leave track marks."

"They also might not've been looking for track marks," Neuman said. "Sometimes they only find what they're looking for—kind of like the rest of us."

Dr. Pignatano nodded. "I've seen a few cop flicks in my time, a few cop shows on the tube. I know what goes down."

"We could sort of tell you had like an inside knowledge," Milner said. "But what I'd like to know is what the fuck're you talking about, what's this got to do with anything? You saying Corry was dealing, that's where the twenty large came from?"

Neuman gave Milner a look that was more than a glance. There were some things they hadn't worked out yet, that would require more than a glance to work out, that would require talk, talk and more talk until they were sure that they *did* share a deep-seated admiration underlain by profound mutual respect and regard for each other's morals and methods. One of those things was who was going to be the good cop and who was going to be the bad cop, because notwithstanding that it had been done to death in movies and on TV (and in Al Coblen's books, probably; even McNally the mountaineer had made some crack about it, and he didn't look like a guy who watched a lot of television, what with climbing and dismantling mountains and all), it was essential to the effective functioning of a team of detectives that one of them be a good cop, Mr. Nice Guy, sympathetic, empathetic, understanding, helpful, caring, friendly and on and fucking on, and that the other be a bad cop, a tyrant, a sadist, blah blah blah, why was he going on like this, what did it matter, what had Klinger said.

Podell's come up with a program that matches detectives according to their skills, their backgrounds, their personalities, their off-duty interests. . . . We're not talking about a permanent matchup, Jake. We're doing this on a case-by-case basis. . . . So whenever this case was over—whatever this case was—he and Milner were going to be just a couple of lonely guys again, eating by themselves in greasy spoons, talking to themselves in squad cars whose heaters didn't work and whose radios got only the dispatcher of some taxi company a lot of foreigners worked for; they'd be daydreaming about what it would be like on Art Theft, sipping wine with gallery owners and collectors and famous painters, offering their arms to fashion models and movie starlets to help them through the mob of oglers who were keeping them from getting a good look at the Braques (was Braque a painter or a composer?), riding in limos and shit and talking on cellular phones to counterparts in Paris and London and Rome and Hong Kong, saying *Mais certainement, Henri*, and Tut, tut, Nigel, and *Prego, ciao, basta, Luigi*, and *Kung fu, Wu*.

Whoever was the good cop or the bad cop, Dr. Pignatano the cop show buff was off again: "Not dealing, because that involves an unpredictable demand, a floating permanent crap game where floating's the operative word. Mike didn't know anything about economics, but he knew a lot about addiction, and he knew that you can't count on an addict to be there in the long run.

"Be there in the long run. I never thought of it before, but that's the perfect description of the people Mike dealt with in his research. Mike was a specialist in the demographics of chronic diseases. Do you gentlemen understand the term?"

"Chronic is, uh," Neuman said.

"It's when you . . ." Milner said.

Another glance. Shrugs. Laughs.

"An acute disease, you either buy it or you get better," Dr. Pignatano said. "A chronic disease, you got it for months, years, for your whole life, if you're lucky."

Milner glanced at Neuman, who shrugged and said, "So, uh, AIDS, say, would be, uh . . ."

"Acute," Dr. Pignatano said.

"So Corry didn't, uh, track people with AIDS."

"Negative."

"So who did he track? I mean, you said he tracked chronic diseases. Any particular disease?"

"Any particular disease in, say, New Orleans?" Milner said.

Dr. Pignatano looked from Milner to Neuman and back at Milner. He smiled

Milner looked at Neuman, who smiled.

Milner smiled. "Yes? New Orleans is a yes?"

"A near yes," Dr. Pignatano said.

"Near? How near? Near to what?"

Dr. Pignatano touched his cigar, fingered his mustache, pushed his glasses up on his nose. "We're closing in on a privileged area. The best thing might be for me to take you down to the library and show you some of Dr. Corry's published works. I can appreciate that you gentlemen don't have a lot of time to hang around a library, and I'm not trying to toy with you. I'll take you directly to the document in question. I just want you to draw the conclusion yourself."

"Okay, that sounds good," Neuman said, "but just what conclusion is it we might be drawing? I mean, it's like what I said before about autopsies sometimes not finding what they're not looking for."

Dr. Pignatano nodded. "You mentioned AIDS. Look for a disease, like AIDS, but not acute—remember the difference?—that someone might pay money to have the condition kept a secret."

"And it's a disease that people get in Louisiana?" Milner said.

Dr. Pignatano smiled. "They can get it anywhere. One of the places it's treated with the greatest success is in Louisiana."

"Is this fun for you?" Neuman said. "Playing cop?"

Dr. Pignatano shrugged. "Kind of."

"Bingo," Milner said.

"What?" Neuman said.

"Carville."

"*Ice* cream?"

"Not Car*vel*. Car*ville*—v-i-l-l-e."

"What's that?"

"Not what; where."

"All right, where's that?"

"Louisiana."

"Couldn't you just say that, Milns?"

"I just did, Noomz."

Neuman sighed. "Is Carville near New Orleans?"

"I don't know where the fuck it is. It's in Louisiana, though."

"There might be a lot of places in Louisiana."

"Come on, Noomz. Jesus."

"I don't want to go off half-cocked, that's all."

"You want to go *home* sometime soon, don't you? We crack this case, we can take some time off, go home, get in the rack with the wives, shovel snow and shit."

"I thought we were looking at a suicide here."

"Yeah, well, what we might be looking at is maybe Ives committed suicide, but somebody whacked Corry. Unless you think Corry whacked himself, then put a box of popcorn on his head, then threw the piece under a chair, then somebody *found* the piece and used it to whack Karen Auburn, who just happened to be trying to find the New Orleans connection herself."

"No, I don't think that," Neuman said.

"Good," Milner said.

"So who's in Carville?" Neuman said.

"Not who. What."

"Okay. What? Don't break my balls, okay, Milns?"

"What's eating you, Noomz?"

"Don't start, all right?"

"Start what?"

"Calling me Noomz."

"You called me Milns."

"What's in Carville, Lieu*tenant Mil*ner?"

"A hospital. A U.S. Public Health Service hospital."

"Yeah. So?"

"So let's make a phone call."

"They might not tell us on the phone. It's like Piggy said; it's privileged."

"Who's Piggy?" Milner said.

"Pignatano."

Milner laughed. "You're a funny guy, Noomz. Nobody ever told me you were a funny guy. They told me you were an old fart who couldn't drive."

"Yeah, well. They told me you were an asshole and a con man and a grifter and an extortionist."

Milner laughed. "Yeah, well. It's not like our paths ever crossed or anything like that."

"The fuck're you talking about, Milns? Our paths crossed when you were in the Six and I was in the Nine—"

"You were in the Nine? I don't remember that."

"You don't remember that 'cause you never knew where the Six ended and the Nine started, so you were on the pad at places in the Nine you shouldn't've—"

"Hey. Neuman. I have never been on any pad in any precinct anywhere. You got that?"

Neuman shrugged. "Hey. You know. It's your word against theirs."

"Who's *they*, Neuman?"

"You know—cops."

"Cops. How'd Coblen's wife say it—*cops*? There're cops and there're cops. Sometimes with cops the only thing you can say about them is *cops*."

Neuman rolled a pencil back and forth in front of him. "Never been on a pad, hunh?"

"Never."

"Never scored a suit or a TV or a meal or—"

"A *meal*? You're on my case about a *meal*? You're saying you never scored a meal? Not once in—what?—twenty-eight, thirty years?"

"Thirty-five," Neuman said.

"Thirty-*five*?"

"Thirty-five."

"You've been a cop for thirty-*five* years?"

"Or thirty-six. Depending on how you count. I took that year off a couple of years ago after I found out my partner, Bobby Redfield, was going around killing people—people he and I were supposed to be finding the killers of."

"I remember that. That was tough, Jake. They called you Redford and Newman—Newman with a *W*; it used to piss me off, but I bet you guys were good."

"We were fair, yeah."

"I bet you were good. . . . Thirty-*six* years?"

"Depending on how you count."

"You've probably got a few things to teach me, then. I've only been a cop for thirty-one years. In August. If there ever is an August."

"Do me a favor, will you?"

"Anything, Noomz."

"Stop saying things like 'If there ever is an August.' It's depressing."

"It *is* depressing."

"I don't mean it's depressing that there might not be an August; it's depressing that you keep on saying it."

"When did I say it before?"

"You didn't say *that*. You said something like it."

Milner shook his head. "You'd think after thirty-five or thirty-six years you wouldn't be so touchy."

Neuman rolled his pencil back and forth some more. "How long you been seeing Bernstein?"

"About a year. How about you?"

"About a year and a half. Why'd you start going? Maria sort of pressured me into it, but I'm glad she did. But why'd you start?"

"My Maria sort of pressured me too. She said something like I should see a shrink or she was going to kill me. I think those were her words, more or less. I'm glad too."

"I don't call him a shrink," Neuman said. "I call him a—"

"Hey, spare me this, will you? What're you, working with Bernstein or something? Every week I have to listen to him tell me how I shouldn't call him a shrink."

"It's funny," Neuman said. "A month or six weeks before we got matched up, your name came up in a session with Bernstein. I hadn't thought about you in years."

"Hey, don't tell me about it if you don't want to," Milner said. "I mean, it's between you and him."

Neuman laughed. "He asked me what I didn't like in a cop, and I told him the things I thought I didn't like in you."

"'Thought'?"

"At the time, yeah. I mean, I didn't know you."

"You kind of did, though," Milner said. "I mean, we had more run-ins than just the time I was in the Six and you were in the Nine. I mean, I can remember three or four times. That time at Columbia, the time in Chinatown, the time in Rockefeller Center. I mean, shit, we hated to see each other coming."

"We had a deep-seated animosity, underlain by profound mutual disrepect and contempt for each other's morals and methods and reinforced by occasional but highly

fraught confrontations over a considerable period of time,"
Neuman said.

"That sounds like Bernstein talking," Milner said.

"It is."

"You seen him lately?"

"Not with all the snow."

"Me neither. I miss him."

"I miss him too."

"We should go see him together sometime."

Neuman laughed. "Right."

Milner shrugged. "We should."

"Word gets out, people'll think we're, you know."

"Fuck 'em. . . . So what're we doing here?"

"Louisiana."

"Louisiana. You want to call or should I?"

"You call," Neuman said. "I've got seniority."

"You're the old fart—that's for sure."

"You should see a shrink, Milns, 'cause you're a sick
guy."

"You, Noomz, should see a psychologist."

20

Fascinating, Kate Naismith thought, how she could see the whole goddamn thing. Who needed television, movies? Just press Play on the tape recorder and the button in her own mind marked Imagine.

Imagine her old lover Charles, for example, whom she knew like the back of her hand, right at the very beginning of this very first tape, saying he hasn't used his tape recorder in a while and to be sure the mike's working right could Franny McAlistair please say something. Before she can, he also thanks her for saying she'd read his work, which we in the listening audience haven't heard her say because she said it before the electronic or electrical or whatever the fuck it is reproduction of the conversation commenced.

Then Franny says he's welcome, and then there's a little fluttering noise like she's nervous and uncomfortable and she says, not hysterically or anything but like she wishes she were somewhere else, anywhere else, that she doesn't know what else to say.

Charles, great wit that he is—was—says, *"Just say, Testing, one, two, three, four,"* but she doesn't say that, she gets her composure back and says she also read his novel about Vietnam and liked it too. A perfect thing to say to a writer, to which Charles says a laconic but heartfelt thank you. (Kate had read Charles's novel about Vietnam but would never have given him the satisfaction of telling him she had, but that's another story.)

Then there's the moment that was hard to imagine, because the next thing is Charles's voice reading a list of authors and books, and what must've happened, Kate on long reflection had figured out, is that there was an interruption—Franny got a phone call or something and had to leave the room and she invited him to have a look at her books, they were books that would tell him something about her, which was what he was there for, wasn't he, to learn something about her for his profile.

"*Lots of books about women,*" Charles says to himself and to his tape recorder and reads off a whole great lot of them, and then there's the sound of a door opening and closing and Franny coming back and saying that she'd been gone more than the moment she'd obviously said she'd be gone and she was sorry and that the call—so it *was* a call—was from an old friend in Hawaii. They'd been trying to connect for days, but the six-hour, she thinks it is, time difference has been difficult to negotiate.

Got that? Hawaii. It's important.

Important because after Charles's voice reading the book titles and b*efore* the sound of the door opening and closing and Franny coming back there was a long pause. Kate imagined that during the pause Charles snooped around and picked things up and put them down and looked at pictures and things. Things like maybe, oh, a *map* that Franny had on the wall of her office. A map with a *pinhole* in it.

It all made sense when Kate went to the tape marked—where was it?—9 October, which was the affected way Charles wrote dates.

"*I understood that the last session would be* the *last,*" Franny said. "*I'm surprised to see you.*"

Charles said, "*I've been to Carville.*"

"Where?"

"*Frances, for Christ's sake. This map is hanging here for all to see.*"

See? Map.

"*No one's ever seen it before.*"

"*I saw it.*"

"*Carville's not even on the map. It's too goddamn small.*"

"*The pinhole's not small. You had a pin in the map— the map that was a present on your twelfth birthday, or whatever it was, and I saw it. I was, I submit, invited to see it.*"

See? Pinhole.

"Carville? Why?"

"Because I know."

"Know? You don't know *something like that*. Somebody tells you. Who?"

"You. The map. 'The Hale Mohalu matter.'"

"The what?"

"The first day I interviewed you, just after we'd started, Dolan interrupted and said there was someone on the phone—about 'the Hale Mohalu matter.'" (He means on the phone from Hawaii.) "Hale Mohalu is a hospital near Honolulu. Its patients were to be moved to a more modern hospital, but some of them stayed behind to protest the move. . . . I looked it up. It's a matter of record, as it's a matter of record that you're on the board of Hale Mohalu—"

"And on the board of all kinds of hospitals. My father was a doctor, don't forget. Hospitals interest me. I'm on the board of obstetric hospitals, but I'm not pregnant, of psychiatric hospitals, but I'm not crazy—"

"But you do have something in common with the patients at Hale Mohalu."

Kate imagined that he probably approaches her here, puts a hand out, tries a less aggressive approach than the one he's been using, less confrontational.

He said, "Frances," and she said, "Don't touch me!"

Then there's this weird thing where somebody comes crashing through the door—somebody Kate imagined had been listening outside, probably, as though he was ready for something bad to happen, somebody we will meet, as the playwrights say, as Bill.

"Really, Bill," Franny said, sounding amused, almost.

"You shouted," Bill said. "I'm sorry . . . I . . ."

"I may shout again, Bill. I may scream and rant and rave. And cry. I'm almost certain to cry. But that part of you that makes you so loyal, that enables you to see and hear and think for me . . . this time it's going to ignore everything: the tears and the shouts and the broken furniture—there's almost certain to be broken furniture—and when all this is over to forget that it happened."

"Frances—"

"*Please!*"

Kate could imagine Bill backing out the door, reluctantly but obediently because he is all the things Franny said he is and probably more that she hasn't even begun to imagine—or maybe she has a little bit, because the next voice is hers again, saying:

"*Poor Bill. He had such a bright future.*"

"*No one has to lose his future because of this.*"

"*Oh? Isn't it going to be in the paper?*"

"*I haven't written anything—*"

"*Or are you planning a TV special, à la Geraldo Rivera?*"

"*—and I'm not going to write anything—*"

"*Don't forget the lurid photographs.*"

"*—ever.*"

"*They'll have to fake the photographs of me. . . .*" Here Kate could imagine her holding out her hands and looking at them, turning them over and over, back and forth. "*I have only the faintest lesions. I wear hand makeup only in the winter, when they show up a little more.*"

"*You do have to worry about Karen Auburn. She spotted me in New Orleans.*"

"*New Orleans only, or does she know about Carville?*"

"*If she followed me there, she had to do it by boat.*"

"*You went by boat?*"

"*It wasn't only that I didn't want to be seen. I wanted to see it—as much as possible—the way it was first seen.*"

There's a pause here and the sound of moving about, and Kate could imagine Charles going to Franny's bookcase and reaching behind some other books and taking one out, because she sounded surprised, offended almost.

"*God, you* did *snoop.*"

"*It was hidden. It invites curiosity. . . .*" You imagine Charles reading this part: "'*In the early 1890s . . . the Louisiana Board of Control leased for five years these four hundred acres of land, once the fine Indian Camp plantation, with its antebellum mansion still standing but in a bad state of disrepair. . . . Inquiring neighbors were told the place was being prepared for an "ostrich farm—"'*"

"*Only we hid more than our heads,*" Franny said, and laughed a dry kind of laugh.

Your old lover Charles read on: "'*On the night of November 30, 1894, the first contingent of eight patients, who had been confined in the "pesthouse" in New Orleans, were put aboard a coal barge there (they were prohibited from traveling by steamer and train) and towed under cover of darkness up the Mississippi to the new location—*'"

"*Where did you find a coal barge?*" Franny said a little facetiously.

"*I chartered a small fishing boat.*"

Then almost nostalgically—and maybe she wasn't being facetious when she asked about the coal barge; maybe she was truly curious—Franny said, "*I went to Carville on the train. The City of New Orleans—before the song. I wanted to get there, but I wanted it to take as long as possible. . . . You asked what I was doing in seventy-two. You knew then, didn't you?*"

"*I knew you weren't in Water Mill. I'd met Hugh Spencer.*"

"*Who?*"

"*The man who rented your house.*"

"*Ah—the painter. God, you're a regular bloodhound. . . . I should make some more noise for Bill's sake. He'll be wondering why it's so quiet all of a sudden. Why is it so quiet? My whole life's come crashing down.*"

"*Frances, I'm no expert on medicine, but I spent enough time at Carville, talked to enough doctors and patients, to know that your condition is harmless.*"

"*Call it what people call it, Charles, not 'your condition,' and try saying that sentence again. All my eventual opponents need to know is that I was in any hospital for eight months. . . . The doctors didn't tell you I was there, did they?*"

"*No. They've sworn an oath.*"

"*So have I. To uphold the law. And I've broken it.*" Then, cunningly, she says, "*If they didn't tell you I was there, how can you be so sure I was?*"

"*Your picture was in the Star.*"

"*The what? Oh, God, of course, the hospital newspaper. I should've known better. How could I have known better? My picture with my real name?*"

"'Frances Clifford, captain of the women's volleyball team, receives a trophy on behalf of her teammates.'"

"Some pseudonym. My mother's maiden name. . . . So are you a blackmailer, Charles? Is that your scam?"

"Frances . . ."

"You said you aren't going to write anything."

"No. I didn't think for a minute about writing anything."

"And you haven't told anyone else."

"No."

"Then why, when you might have stopped yourself—when you found out I'd lied about Water Mill—did you pursue it? What did you want? Money? Power? You can't want sex—not with a—"

"I pursued it because I was afraid someone else would. I'm not the only reporter who's interested in your life. As you get closer to making a decision about your political future, there'll be more. This book, the map, your connection with Hale Mohalu, Water Mill—they're clues, blazes on your trail. Others will follow."

"I'll burn the book, tear up the map, resign from the board of Hale Mohalu."

"What about Hugh Spencer?"

"Who? Oh—the painter."

"And Karen Auburn. It may be a while before Karen figures things out. Her working premise is that you're gay. . . . But only a while. Karen's ambitious. You've got to tell people before she does."

"You're out of your mind."

"Because if she does, it'll be a scandal, while if you do, it'll be—"

"Foolhardy."

"I was going to say courageous. . . . Look, you aspire to high office. The public's earned the right to be skeptical about the morals of such aspirants."

"My 'condition' is a disease of the soul. In all your research, you must've read the Bible."

"The Bible's not a medical textbook. It uses your condition to mean any number of diseases."

"So you are an expert."

"It doesn't matter what disease you have—"

"*Charles, for God's sake. Half of my job is politics, the other half is negotiation. I shake hands for a living.*"

"*This isn't something between you and your doctor, Frances. You've given up most of your right to privacy. Maybe you haven't lied, because no one's ever asked you where you were in 1972. But I asked you, and you lied to me. And even if I hadn't asked you, there're lies of omission. . . . So tell the truth. Or rather, correct the omission. People may recoil from you at first, but they're not going to burn you at the stake. And keep on telling them, even if their backs are turned, their eyes averted. Tell them the facts, and eventually they'll turn and look at you and see that what you say is so.*"

"*Eventually.*"

"*Frances, you're a young woman. Maybe it'll take a little longer to get where you want to go, but in the meantime you can do a lot of enlightening. And gain a lot of respect. If Karen Auburn's the one who tells people, you won't be able to get anyone to listen. . . . I lied to you. I have told one person.*"

A gasp here, from Franny.

"*I want you to meet him. He's an expert on scandal.*"

"*I seem to be doing all right on my own.*"

"*Trust me. He'll know the best way to make this public.*"

Sardonically, she says, "*My fellow Americans, I am a—*"

But she can't get the word out, and Kate knew it was because Charles had kissed her, just like in the movies. There's some umming and aahing and rustling and smacking and then Franny's voice, a little breathless:

"*Am I your first, Charles? Your first—*"

Again, the word—*the word*—wasn't spoken, for he kissed her again. And again and again and again and again and again.

After listening to all this shit, imagining her brains out, what Kate still couldn't imagine was why the hell, if Charles was such a decent, upstanding guy, if he wasn't going to write any of this or anything, if he was in love with this woman, presumably—why the hell he had his goddamn

tape machine going all the time . . . without, it very
much looks like, mentioning it to her?

And when Kate got tired of that, she tried to imagine
something she could imagine, which was this:

Karen Auburn, who spotted her old lover Charles in
New Orleans, who if she followed him to Carville had to do
it by boat, whose working premise was that Franny was gay,
who was ambitious, who was going to cause a scandal—*that*
Karen Auburn was the same Karen Auburn who was shot in
the head in a "MOB-STYLE RUBOUT," the *Post* called it:
shot in the vestibule of 89 Park Avenue, Hoboken, New
Jersey, the police thought, and dragged to and dumped in
a vacant lot next door to 89 Park Avenue, Hoboken, New
Jersey, which just happened to be where Kate Naismith
lived, Kate Naismith who would've been the victim, she
imagined, if Karen Auburn hadn't died instead—died instead because for sure, for an absolute certainty, Karen
Auburn's killer thought Karen Auburn was Kate Naismith
because she was going into 89 Park Avenue, and the reason
Karen Auburn was going into 89 Park Avenue was that she
wanted to see if maybe Kate Naismith knew anything about
her old lover Charles's trip to Louisiana.

Easy to imagine that, but don't lose sight of the more
important fact here, the key, crucial, telling fact—namely
that the reason Karen Auburn was killed was that somebody
else was curious, too, about whether Kate Naismith knew
anything about her old lover Charles's trip to Louisiana;
somebody else *assumed*, too, that Kate Naismith knew
something about Charles's trip to Louisiana; somebody else
wanted to *kill* Kate Naismith to keep her from telling what
she knew about Charles's trip to Louisiana, never mind that
she didn't know *shit* about Charles's trip to Louisiana.

And that being the key, crucial, telling fact, Kate tried
not to imagine whether that somebody else, once they
found out they *didn't* kill Kate Naismith because Kate
Naismith hadn't been at 89 Park Avenue, Hoboken, New
Jersey, for a while, was going to start thinking about where
Kate Naismith might be and might even make the brilliant
deduction that maybe she'd held on to the keys of Charles's
apartment and that *that's* where she was right this minute.

Shit.

And that being so very possible to imagine, the question was this: Why didn't Kate call Dave Milner and remind him of their little conversation in which she mentioned that she was scared if not to death at least shitless and ask him if he couldn't please put his suspects, snitches and bad guys on hold please and get his ass over here please so she didn't have to huddle in the corner with the lights out too much longer please?

And that being the question, the answer was she didn't call Dave Milner because she wouldn't be able to keep from asking Dave Milner why he hadn't mentioned to her in their little conversation that a month to the day before Charles died (she knew from Charles's appointment book, which she found on his desk), Dave Milner had had a meeting (or had been scheduled to, anyway, which he still ought to have mentioned) at the Museum of Modern Art with her old lover Charles.

21

No local hockey or basketball action last night. The National Weather Service forecast: Clear and—what else is new?—cold. High today around ten degrees Fahrenheit, low tonight five to ten degrees below, high tomorrow only around five above. The temperature right now in Central Park is t-t-t-t-two, count 'em, two degrees above zero, and with the wind from the north at twelve miles an hour, it feels like . . . O'Leary, Prince Edward Island.

"Hoboken?" McGovern said.

"Don't argue with me, Matty, okay?" Federici said.

"If I didn't know you were born pregnant, Steve-O, I'd think you had the rag on, 'cause I'm not arguing with you, I'm asking you what you're doing."

"Every time I turn *around*, you ask me what I'm doing. I get in line for the tunnel to Jersey, you ask me what I'm doing. I change lanes 'cause the lane I'm in's jammed up, you ask me what I'm doing *and* tell me it's against the law. I know what the law is, I'm a cop. I make a right at the Hoboken sign, you ask me what I'm doing. I say I'm going to Hoboken, you say '*Ho*boken?' like it was fucking Tibet or something. Just give me a break, okay? Just lighten up."

"Born pregnant," McGovern said.

"And don't say that anymore, all right, Matty?"

After a while, McGovern said. "Can I ask you something, Steve-O?"

"No." Then: "What?"

"You ever been here before?"

"Hoboken?"

"Yeah, Hoboken."

"Yeah, I've been here before."

181

"So you know this isn't the main drag. This takes you out of town, toward the Lincoln Tunnel."

"I know that, yeah."

McGovern started to say something, then just sighed. "What?"

McGovern shook his head.

"What, goddamn it?"

McGovern karate-chopped the dashboard. "I just want to know where the fuck we're going, that's all."

Federici shook his head. "You with this job, Matty?"

McGovern flipped his hands. "What job? What job're we on? The Ives job? I haven't done any work on the Ives job since we went around McAlistair's building asking tenants if they saw anything. The Club Dead job? That's not our job, it's McIver's and Bloomfield's. The guy who got whacked in the sixplex? That's not our job, either, it's McIver's and Bloomfield's too; they're jammed up from here to Saint Patty's Day. The lady reporter who got whacked here in Hoboken? That's not our job, it's the Hoboken cops'. So what job? What"—*chop*—"fucking"—*chop*—"job?"—*chop*.

Federici nodded.

"What?" McGovern said. "What does *this* mean?" He nodded wildly. "Hunh? Hunh? What does it mean?"

"You're not with the job, that's what it means," Federici said. "You heard me on the phone with Crime Scene, right? You heard me tell you they said the nine-millimeter the guy in the sixplex was whacked with was the same nine-millimeter Karen was whacked with?"

"Karen? What's this Karen shit?"

"I told you: I met her, I talked to her"—smelled her, listened to the shivering of her shoulders, the shimmying of her hips, the slip-sliding of her clothing, the hissing of her stockings, the tossing of her hair, the jangling of her jewelry, bracelets, whatever; Karen with the breasts, legs, ankles, collarbone, wrists, everything—"me and Neuman. So what we're doing here, Matty," Federici said, "is we're going to talk to the witness who says she saw the guy who whacked Karen."

McGovern grabbed the door handle, as if he might bail out. "The *wit*ness? We can't talk to the *wit*ness. The cop who interviewed her, maybe—but not the *wit*ness. We're supposed to be doing one thing and one thing only, Steve-O; we're supposed to be finding this Kate Naismith broad, who what she's got to do with anything beats me. She was a girlfriend of Ives's or something. So big deal."

A *former* girlfriend of Ives's—who was dead, anyway, wasn't he?—and now, with Karen Auburn dead, the new unseemly love of Steve Federici, who bet Kate Naismith had breasts, legs, ankles, collarbone, wrists, everything, too. It sure looked that way in the picture of Kate Naismith her assistant had showed Federici when he and McGovern went down to Le Peau Douce, a photograph from a community newspaper accompanying a story about TriBe-Ca's ascent from light industriality to acronymity. The assistant—whose name was Flavia and who had breasts, legs, ankles, collarbone, wrists, everything, too, but was still just a kid really—the assistant had taken the picture down from a bulletin board behind the cash register and given it to Federici and he had slipped it under the rubber band that held subway maps even though they never rode the subways and highway maps even though they never went on highways and train schedules even though they never took trains and all kinds of other shit they didn't need to the sun visor, slipped it right in front where he could glance at it as he drove, as if while driving the streets, checking out the swaddled, shrouded, padded pedestrians, he would be able to make out Kate Naismith's breasts, legs, ankles, collarbone, wrists, her everything, under the layers of down or fur.

And underwear. Unseemly or not, he couldn't help loving a woman who clearly loved underwear so much that she didn't just wear it—he was sure she wore it, as he'd been sure Karen did, even though he hadn't even glimpsed it—she didn't just wear it; she *sold* it.

At a red light he couldn't run because there was a cab stopped in front of him and, because of the drifting snow, no room to pass, Federici wondered how Jennifer was—his wife Jennifer, his pregnant wife. Because of the snow and the job he'd pulled, he hadn't been home in four days and hadn't called in a day and a half. Was she still eight months pregnant? Of course she was; she'd been *born* pregnant.

Flavia. Flavia would be a nice name for their daughter: Flavia Federici. Except Jennifer would probably say, *Who's Flavia?* meaning she'd never heard the name, either, and would suspect it was the name of a woman he'd met in a bar somewhere—not that he hung out in bars anymore, not since he'd gotten married and pregnant.

"You've been here before," McGovern said, speaking of the devil. "Then you probably know we just left Hoboken, we're in Weehawken."

"The witness *works* in Weehawken, Matty. Get with the job."

"What fucking job?" McGovern said.

"You Mavis?" Federici said.

"Who're you?" Mavis said.

"We're cops."

"That ain't who you are, that's what you are. Who you are is assholes, 'cause this is a legitimate club and I do what it says, exotic dancing. I don't do blow jobs, hand jobs, you got no right coming in here asking for me in front of everybody, making me look bad with the customers, with the boss, with the other dancers."

McGovern whispered, "She may be a scag, Steve-O, but she's got that right."

Federici turned in his chair to watch a phthisic stripper grind to Dire Straits's "Money for Nothing." She had no breasts, no legs, no ankles, no collarbone, no wrists—no nothing. He turned back to Mavis. "You call this dump a club, Mavis? Can't you do better than this?"

Mavis opened her kimono. "See these tits? Guys draw the line at droopy tits. When your tits start drooping like this, you don't do better than this, you do this. It's kind of like you guys—you can't make an honest buck, so you're cops."

McGovern didn't stop watching the stripper. "You should be careful, Mabel, somebody might rearrange your face; you'll have to start a whole new career as a normal human being."

"Ma*vis*," Mavis said. "You stupid Mick."

Federici laughed.

McGovern said, "Ask her what you want to ask her, Steve-O, and let's get out of here."

"Not such a stupid mick," Mavis said. "A smart mick. You should listen to him, you stupid wop."

McGovern laughed.

"Mavis?" Federici said.

"Go ahead," Mavis said. "I can't wait to hear what's going to come out of your mouth."

"Just tell us about the guy who whacked the newspaper reporter, Mavis."

"You should know, Mabel," McGovern said, "that Steve-O here *met* this reporter, he talked to her, he had a thing for her, which is what we're here in Jersey, we're on a vendetta, like. You should also know that Steve-O here was born pregnant."

"You guys real cops, or am I dreaming I'm on some TV cop comedy show?" Mavis said.

"Just tell us about the guy who whacked the newspaper reporter, Mavis."

"You said that, sweetheart."

"I said it, but I didn't hear any answer."

"You said it, you didn't hear any answer, because I told you I didn't see anybody *whack* anybody."

"All right; you're going to get technical, Mavis, what *did* you see?"

Mavis took a handful of the lapels of her kimono. "I saw a guy I used to know walking near where she got whacked, the reporter, that's all."

"Tell us the rest," Federici said.

"I said that's all. You got trouble hearing? I saw him, that's all."

"Him being?"

"Him being what?"

"His *name*, Mavis."

". . . Donald."

"Donald what?"

"You Hoboken cops?"

"Donald what?"

"Dubro. I already told this to the Hoboken cops."

"When was the last time you saw Dubro, Mavis?"

"Ten, twelve years ago."

"A long time."

"I ain't missed him."

"He was a boyfriend, like, then?"

"I fucked him, if that's what you mean."

"But he wasn't walking around with his dick hanging out, was he, Mave—not with it so cold it feels like the fucking North Pole or something?"

"Prince Edmundland," Mavis said. "This morning they said it was so cold it *feels* like Prince Edmundland."

Federici said, "So since his dick wasn't hanging out, Dubro, how come you're so sure it *was* Dubro, Mavis?"

"'Cause he was playing the saxophone."

"Saxophone?"

Mavis giggled. "How did I know that if I said saxophone you'd say, 'Saxophone?'"

"I didn't say it like that. I didn't say *sax*ophone. I said saxophone."

"You said, 'Saxophone?'"

"Hey, Mavis," the stripper yelled. "I'm working."

Mavis gave her the finger. "Work this."

"Okay, Mavis," Federici said, "forget what I said and how I said it, just answer the question: Since his dick wasn't hanging out, how come you're so fucking sure it was Donald Dubro?"

"I told you, you stupid wop"—McGovern laughed—"he was playing the *sax*ophone. Not *playing* playing it, but pre*tend*ing to play it. It's what people used to call him—Air Sax. You know how people play, you know, air guitar? He plays air saxophone. I was coming down Newark Street on the way home from the PATH, I saw him standing in a doorway, bending over, leaning back, bobbing and weaving, like. First I thought he was a nut, a wino, a junkie, a weirdo, I stayed on the side of the street I was on even though the wind was blowing the snow right in my face, there wouldn't've been as much wind across the street where he was. I checked him out again when I got, you know, past him, to make sure he wasn't going to follow me or nothing, I had a better angle on him, I could see the reason he was bending over, leaning back, bobbing and weaving, wasn't 'cause he was a nut, a wino, a junkie, a weirdo, it was 'cause he was playing air sax."

McGovern looked at Federici. "Ring a bell?"

Federici looked at McGovern. "You too?"

McGovern nodded.

"Let's ride," Federici said. "Thanks, Mavis."

"Yeah."

"I mean it. It's a big help. You're an upstanding citizen."

"Yeah."

"I mean it."

"You *mean* it, you *mean* it. So what do you, want a blow job?"

"I wouldn't do that, Mavis," McGovern said. "He's pregnant."

James Jones knocked on a door on the tenth floor of the Hotel Paradise, two uniforms at his shoulder.

A man opened the door of the next room and looked out. One of the uniforms pointed his .45 at him and the man made a face like *Oops, wrong number*, and pulled his head back in and shut the door.

"Yeah?" a man said through the door.

"McDonald's delivery."

"I didn't order nothing."

"Room 1106. Delivery."

"This is 1006. There ain't no eleven."

"Well, it's paid for. You might as well take it."

"It's paid for?"

"It's paid for."

The door opened. "Well, shit . . . Oh shit oh Christ oh no oh fuck. Hey, that ain't fair, man."

"April fool, Freddy." Jones backed Faso into the room and closed the door, leaving the uniforms outside. "Why the fuck didn't you clear town?"

"I'm waiting for my old lady to get outta Rikers," Faso said. "We're going a Brazil."

"What's in Brazil?" Jones said.

"You're not," Faso said.

Jones laughed. "Work on your routine, you'll be the funniest guy in the joint."

"Who ratted on me?" Faso said.

"Nobody ratted on you, you scumbag. Somebody

made you, somebody you should've popped. You throw down on a roomful of guys like that, you got to pop all of them, or one of them's going to for dead certain make you."

"I give you something, you make a deal with me?"

"I don't make deals, Freddy, you know that. The D.A. makes the deals."

"You tell the D.A. I got something for him."

"Yeah? What?"

"Just tell him. I tell you, you'll go use it without making no deal."

"Hey, Freddy, watch my lips. I tell the D.A. you got something for him, you know what he's going to say? He's going to say, 'Yeah? What?' I'm going to have to come back to you, drag you out of your fucking cell, say, 'What, Freddy, do you got for the D.A.?' So save me a fucking trip up to Rikers, will you? Fucking place gives me the fucking creeps, I don't know why that is."

"'S'cause you know 'cept for the grace of God it could be you doing the points for being on the pad and shit, knocking guys a—Hey!"

"Aw, did I hit you, Freddy? Sorry, it slipped. I was aiming for that fly there. See it?"

Freddy Faso rubbed his face. "Tell the D.A. I know who berked the guy in the sixplex, the popcorn thing."

"Who berked the guy in the sixplex, the popcorn thing, was your buddy Air Sax," Jones said.

"Fuck do you know that?" Faso said.

"Fuck should I tell you, Freddy?"

"You're full a shit. You don't know it was Air Sax."

"I don't?"

"No. Ow!"

"Fucking fly won't hold the fuck still."

"Shit, man. That hurt."

"Then don't talk back to me, Freddy. Don't tell me something ain't so when it's a fucking fact that it's fucking so. A newspaper reporter got whacked over in Jersey with the same fucking piece used to whack the guy in the sixplex, we got a witness who says the guy who did the whacking over in Jersey was your friend fucking Air Sax. Unless fucking Air Sax's in the habit of loaning his fucking piece out, then fucking Air Sax whacked the fucking guy in the fucking sixplex."

"Fuck's the matter with you, man, saying fucking all a time?"

"I'm mad, that's what's the matter."

"Maybe it'll make you feel better," Faso said, "to know that okay, it was Air Sax did the berk in the sixplex. Who set it up was a piece a trim."

"Name of?" Jones said.

Faso said, "I don't know," and ducked. After a while, he looked up from under his arm.

Jones smiled sweetly. "Name of?"

"Read me my fucking rights, man," Faso said.

Jones rolled his eyes. "You have the right to remain a lowlife ratfuck scumbag. You have the right to remain silent. . . ."

22

So he berked the wrong trim, so fucking what? I mean, shit, he never even *seen* Katherine calls herself Kate Naismith in his life before he was hired to berk her. He never seen no picture, nothing. He kinda knew kinda what she looked like—she was kinda tall, kinda, you know, slim, had kinda short hair—and he knew where she lived, the 'Boken, 89 fucking Park. But that was fucking it.

I mean, shit. He took the PATH to the 'Boken, he went to 89 Park, he froze his ass off standing around for about four fucking hours, he tried playing—playing a little Toshiko Akiyoshi, a little George Coleman, a little Frank Wess, a little Willis (Gatortail) Jackson—but his fucking lips were fucking frozen, his fucking bladder almost fucking popped on account of he drank too much coffee to keep from freezing his ass *totally* off, he saw some trim who was kinda tall, kinda, you know, slim (or maybe she wasn't, he didn't know 'cause she was wearing a fucking, you know, fur jacket what with the fucking weather), who had kinda short hair (or maybe she didn't, he didn't know 'cause she was wearing a fucking fur hat, just like a lot a trim what with the fucking weather), he saw the trim going into 89 Park, going up the stairs. Nobody else lives on the second floor, he checked that out, just K. for Katherine calls herself Kate Naismith and T. for he didn't know what Bodwell, her roommate or boyfriend or whatever the fuck—who wouldn'ta thought she was the trim he was supposed to berk, who wouldn'ta berked her? Nofuckingbody, that's who.

Time for another fucking smoke.

Shit. Two years he quit smoking, two years of all kinds of shit, all kinds of grief—guys what welshed on debts, inside straights he didn't fill, ponies with legs that turned into rubber on the backstretch, hoops teams, footballs teams that didn't cover the spread, seventeens he hit and got dealt a five, fighters who all of a sudden forget their gloves ain't only to hit with they're to keep in front of their fucking faces to keep their jaws from getting clobbered, trim what wouldn't go down on him after telling him they loved him and shit and would do anything in the fucking world for him meaning they would spend his money and drink his booze and lie in his fucking bathtub for two fucking hours talking on the fucking telephone to their fucking sisters in fucking Iowa or something—all kinds of pains in the ass should oughta make a guy want to reach in his pocket, weasel a butt outta a pack, poke it in his face, light it the fuck up, take a drag, ooh, aah, that old nicotine whoopee rushola. But no, not him, not Air Sax, the king of the professional berkers. He toughed it out, showed some balls.

Till the day he found out he berked the wrong trim, like a lot of other guys before him for sure; still he felt like having a butt. A real butt. A Lucky. How fucking many did he have already?

One, two, three, four, five, six . . .

Anyway, the trim who hired him to berk Katherine calls herself Kate Naismith shoulda made sure he didn't go berking the wrong trim, the trim who says, *Donald Dubro, please,* every time she calls, the trim who said asking questions was unprofessional, which was the whole fucking point: He was a pro, and even pros make mistakes, berk the wrong trim from time to time.

. . . forty-seven, forty-eight, forty-nine, fifty, fifty-one, fifty-two. Fifty-two fucking butts of fifty-two Luckies. Shit. No wonder his throat feels like a fucking muffler should oughta get Midasized.

And two quarts of Johnnie Red don't make no fucking difference. Sorry—two *li*ters. Two fucking *li*ters of Johnnie Red don't make no fucking difference to how his throat feels, so let's open *li*ter number three, see if that makes a fucking difference.

The problem was when he ran outta *li*ters and butts he wasn't going to be able to get more *li*ters or more butts on account of number one he was fucking broke, he couldn't ask the trim who hired him to berk Kate Naismith for the second half of the seven fifty she owes him, and number two he can't leave this fucking sleazebag hotel on account of he's being looked for for berking the trim he berked, never mind that she happened to be the wrong trim. The fuck knew people got so hot and bothered when trim that worked for a newspaper got berked?

Karen Auburn. He never even heard of her, either, never even seen her, either, till he saw her picture in the fucking paper alongside a picture of him and a story saying somebody seen him hanging around 89 Park in the 'Boken. A *crummy* picture of him from 1974 it said underneath it, took when they processed him in the Rikers on a stolen-property rap which he'da beat if Kenny Palermo hadn't gone soft and rolled over for the fucking D.A. The only thing that ain't crummy about the picture is that it *is* from 1974 meaning he had long hair then, and was skinnier and, you know, younger, which'd make it hard for somebody to make him just on account of seeing the picture.

Hey! Here's a thought. All he's gotta do is drop a dime, 'cept now it's a quarter, and call 1-800-RATFUCK-SNITCH and get his hands on the reward being offered by the newspaper, the *Herald* or whatever the fuck, for information leading to the arrest and conviction of whoever berked Karen Auburn.

The way his luck's going, he probably ain't even eligible. Shit. He oughta be. Just 'cause *he's* who berked her shouldn't mean he ain't eligible. He should not only be eligible, he should get a bonus on account of he not only berked Karen Auburn and the epidemigeologist, he also berked a bunch of sleazoid assholes up at the armory in the Club Dead thing, which he was right about, wasn't he, the newspapers did call it Club Dead, not one fucking one of them called it Saint Valentine's Day Massacre II, so take that, Dead Eddie, you scumbag.

A double scumbag, 'cause for two days he's been calling Dead Eddie to ask him to help him get outta this sleazebag hotel, get to Mexico or somewhere or even the Catskills or somewhere where he could lay low till the heat wasn't so hot, and he ain't called him back, the double scumbag.

Or maybe he did call him back and he don't know it 'cause when they're not giving each other AIDS the people in this sleazebag're always hanging around the pay phone, dealing drugs and making calls to fucking Nickelragua and Africa, using stolen credit card numbers and if the phone rings they just answer it like it was their personal, private phone, and if he wasn't standing right there in front of them they just said he wasn't there and they hang up and don't take no message or nothing. So maybe Dead Eddie did call and one of the Nickelraguans or Africans didn't tell Air Sax about it.

Maybe that's him now, Dead Eddie, knocking on his door.

That or it's the cops on account of one of the Nickelraguans or Africans made him on account of the crummy picture of him in the paper and dropped a dime on him, 'cept now it's a quarter, and called 1-800-RATFUCK-SNITCH and his time is fucking up.

Well, fucking answer it, why don'tcha?

"Yeah?"

"Donald Dubro?"

"There ain't no . . . Holy shit! That you?"

"Open the door, Donald."

"You alone? How'd you find me?"

"Open the door, Donald."

Air Sax unhooked the chain and slipped the dead-bolt latch and opened the door. "How'd you—"

Find me. Holy shit. You're the trim who hired me to berk Katherine calls herself Kate Naismith? The trim who says, Donald Dubro, please, *every time she calls? The trim who neglected to tell me the epidemigeologist had twenty fucking large in the closet? The trim who when I asked her how the fuck come she neglected to tell me that said asking questions was unprofessional? You're her?*

Yeah, you're her, and that's a .38 Smith, ain't it, and the fuck did I open the door without getting my Walther? Now I not only berked the wrong trim, which any number of professionals coulda done and have, I let trim throw down on me, which not too many professionals or otherwise have done and lived to tell about it and I'm not gonna live I'm going to die and I only wish I coulda told somebody who you were before I did, 'cause they never woulda guessed you was a fat, bald guy.

23

*No local sports action again last night. The National
Weather Service forecast: Clear and cold today, tonight
and tomorrow. High today around twenty, low tonight five
to ten, high tomorrow again around twenty. The temperature right now in Central Park is eight degrees, and with
the wind from the north at fifteen miles an hour, it feels
like . . . Wabush, Labrador.*

Barefooted on a Saturday *chez lui*, wearing a formal
shirt open at the collar, with French cuffs flapping, faded
and tattered blue sweat pants with the ghost of a Bryn
Mawr logo on one thigh, DeBree settled himself on one
of the several dozen pillows that were the only things to
sit on in the living room of his Chelsea town house. Thick
drapes made it forever nighttime; the carpet was as lush
as a meadow; on the walls were larger-than-life oil portraits
of somebody's ancestors—not, said their emaciation,
DeBree's.

"I'm reminded, Jake," DeBree said, "by your ventur-
ing out in such cruel climatological conditions, of the joke
about one of the lesser-known members of King Arthur's
round table, a midget knight. Too diminutive to ride even
a pony, he had the ostler outfit him with a large dog—a dog
of indeterminate parentage, a dog that looked to be part
yak, part shag carpet and very, very small part dog. While
on a quest for the Holy Grail or the True Cross or an honest
man or a good cigar, the knight and his steed were caught
in a terrible storm. Thunder, lightning, wind and rain—the
whole nine yards.

"At one inn and post house after another, the knight
was turned back out into the tempest: full up, *complet*, no

195

vacancy. Finally, just when he was about to give up hope and try to make the best of it in a nearby copse, he came to an inn whose kindly keeper took pity on him. Alas, he had no rooms available, he said, but there was a bench by the fire in the main hall, where the knight was welcome to lie; his pitiful steed could curl up on the hearth. 'For I wouldn't,' the innkeeper asserted, 'put a knight out on a dog like this.'

". . . I see," DeBree said when Neuman wouldn't even smile. "Where's your partner, Jake? When am I—"

"You lied to me," Neuman said. "Frances McAlistair never had an affair with any mystery writer, Coblen, in 1972. In 1972, he was living in L.A., the mystery writer, Coblen, and she was in a hospital in Carville, Louisiana."

DeBree touched his fingertips to his lips. "*No.*"

Neuman reached behind him inside his suit coat and took out his cuffs. "What you're doing, asshole, is obstructing an investigation. They have jails for people who do that."

DeBree spread his hands concessively, then held them out, wrists touching. "Guilty. Lock me up."

Neuman put the cuffs away. "You said Ives told you about the writer, Coblen. But he didn't, did he? You made all that up, not Ives."

"Yes."

"Why? Did you think we wouldn't check it out?"

"I hoped you wouldn't. Why embarrass Coblen's widow with questions about something that's water under the bridge?"

"You didn't have any problem about embarrassing *me*, though, did you?"

DeBree shrugged. "You're thick-skinned."

Neuman kicked at a pillow.

"Now, now, Jake," DeBree said. "I can explain everything. If you'll just let me tell you a—"

Neuman waved his hands. "No. I don't want to listen to one of your stories. You can't tell short stories, you can only tell long stories. No. No, no, no."

DeBree folded his arms over his stomach, wrapping himself in silence.

Neuman groaned. "All right. But *very* short."

DeBree grinned and stretched and settled himself like a cat. "Last Monday, six P.M., I was at the office, my feet up on the desk, counting the dustballs in the corner, when the phone rang. Greta Garbo, I was absolutely certain, saying she didn't vant to be alone for von more—"

"You're doing it," Neuman said. "Last Monday, meaning the day before the day around midnight of which Ives did a brodie off Frances McAlistair's apartment house, correct?"

"Eminently correct *and* colorfully stated."

"Go on," Neuman said. "But cut the crap. Cut the eminentlys."

DeBree sniffed. "It was, in fact, Charles Ives calling. He was at Frances McAlistair's palatial Park Avenue penthouse, as the boys in the city room can never forbear writing. Could I come over right away, terribly urgent, my advice and counsel absolutely crucial? I'd filed my next day's column, my dance card was inexplicably empty, of course I'd be over. I threw on my greatcoat, loped to the lift, hailed a dog sled, mushed up to Park Avenue, made super time—no one goes out anymore, what with the glacial—"

"DeBree?" Neuman said.

"Yes, Jake?"

"Cut—the—crap."

"I see. Well. Yes. All right. Devoid of *crap*, as you call it, I went to Frances McAlistair's apartment, we shook hands all around, a drink was offered and declined, she told me what you already know. I wish I knew how you know. I don't suppose you'll tell me. . . . No. Well.

"She told me she has leprosy."

Elsewhere:

A snowman with red plastic sunglasses, bottle tops for buttons and a green foam approximation of the Statue of Liberty's crown on its head stood outside the Staten Island ferry terminal.

Frances McAlistair straightened the crown and wondered about the buttons. You didn't see many soda bottles anymore, and the ones you saw had screw tops. Church keys: they were something else you saw less; having lived this long without knowing for sure why they were called church keys, she would probably die without ever knowing.

She took off a glove and touched the snowman's chest with her fingertips. Nothing. . . .

The parlor tricks you could do. That night, for example, for the benefit of DeBree, she'd waved her hand close to the flames in the fireplace. "I contracted it—Hansen's disease is the preferred name—in the Peace Corps in Colombia, from drinking contaminated water, probably. But it incubates for years, and it wasn't until years afterward that I discovered I'd been infected.

"Ironically, the occasion was my return to New York for my father's funeral. The night he was buried, I took a long walk in Central Park. It was January and bitterly cold—like now. Snow everywhere. I made a snowman with no gloves. That is, the snowman didn't have gloves, and neither did I." (She'd smiled and so had DeBree. Charles Ives hadn't smiled.)

"I'd been living in California for years and didn't own a pair. I stayed in the park for several hours. I woke the next morning to discover that the tips of my fingers were horribly blackened. Frostbite, it turned out, but I hadn't felt a thing."

Charles had interrupted right there with exegesis: "Hansen's causes damage to the nerves of the extremities, resulting in a loss of feeling in the hands and feet. It's not uncommon for sufferes to be unaware of burns or cuts. The famous Father Damien, the leper priest of Hawaii, sat down once to soak his feet in a pot of water he didn't realize had heated to nearly boiling; when he saw his skin blistering, he realized he'd caught the disease whose sufferers he'd devoted his life to caring for."

DeBree had ignored Charles, and leaned toward her. "Who else knows?"

"My mother. My doctor. Doctors who've treated me in the past. Patients at Carville. That's all."

"Any of your old chums from the Peace Corps know?"

She hadn't lied exactly, she'd just shaken her head no. And anyway, Michael Corry hadn't been a chum.

"No. Well. That incubation period you mentioned, I suppose. Risky, those patients at Carville. Your mum'll stay mum, of course, and the doctors, but patients, I don't know. . . ."

"Lepers are a fraternity," she'd said. "We're members for life."

"Ah, well," DeBree had said, "but every club has its misfits, doesn't it, the bad egg whose self-contempt is such that he thinks nothing of pointing a finger at another member and saying she's a *leper*. Pardon me, Counselor, but you used the L word, so I did. Who's Hansen?"

"A Norwegian scientist who—"

"Excuse me a moment," Charles had said. "But I'm afraid you misunderstand, DeBree. There hasn't been a leak. We're not asking for help in keeping a lid on. On the contrary, we—Frances—doesn't want to keep her condition a secret any longer; she wants to make it public."

DeBree sat back, fingertips together, not Buddha-like exactly—more like Sydney Greenstreet. "Public."

"Yes."

"And you hoped I'd help cope with the media blitz that would surely follow her egress from the so-to-speak closet."

"Yes."

"Why? Not why should I help, but why effect an egress?"

"So that others can benefit," Charles had said. "It wasn't very long ago that there were laws prohibiting lepers from voting, from marrying. That's changed, but most people with Hansen's must still keep it a secret or risk losing their jobs, risk ostracism by their communities."

"How many people are we talking about?"

"Five thousand," she had said. To say something. "In this country."

"A drop in the electoral bucket," DeBree had said.

That had offended her. "I'm not talking about someday getting them to vote for me. I'm talking about giving them a leader—someone with the clout to dispel the myths."

"Myths don't dispel easy," DeBree had said. "A leader to do what? Win them the right to sit in the front of the bus?"

She had ignored the sarcasm. "There *is* a problem in need of an urgent solution. Hansen's is incurable, but it *is* treatable. Do you understand the distinction? The standard drug of control, dapsone, is becoming ineffective in an alarming number of cases. There're other drugs, but they're much more expensive and have unpleasant side effects. Thalidomide is one of them. Obviously, it can't be used on people still young enough to reproduce."

Charles again: "There're twenty million cases world-wide—not a drop in any bucket—and eighty percent of them untreated. If dapsone continues ineffective, it'll be more like ninety percent. With the immigration situation the way it is, more cases are showing up all the time—one or two a week in New York alone. It might be twice that because most doctors have never seen a case and make wrong diagnoses. We're talking about a major health and social problem. Frances could make a difference."

"I can see her now," DeBree had said, "in some hole-in-the-wall office off Union Square, National Hansen's Disease parenthesis Please Don't Call It Leprosy close parenthesis Committee, Frances McAlistair, chairperson, a view of an air shaft, a rickety desk, one ancient rotary phone, shoeboxes for file drawers, and last year's calendar on the wall. That's the sad and inevitable outcome of full disclosure, which is what you're proposing.

"On the other hand, continued secrecy would have the salutary effect of permitting Frances's political ambitions to flourish. A leper governor or senator or President—even a leper U.S. Attorney for the Southern District of New York—even if no one knew that's what she was, could do a hell of a lot more for lepers than a leper civilian, even if everyone knew that's what she was. My advice to you, therefore, is no, no, a thousand times no, emphatically not, under no circumstances, quoth the raven nevermore."

Charles wouldn't look at her. "You're asking her to *lie*," he said to DeBree, his voice shriller than she'd ever heard it.

"Chas, Chas," DeBree had said. "Since when're you such a stickler for probity? I know, I know, *après* Watergate, the *déluge* of confessional morality. That binge lasted a nanosecond, Chas. As far as I can tell, no one—public or private—is any more forthcoming about *any*thing than they ever were. God knows *my* job isn't any easier. And speaking of secrets, have you told Ms. McAlistair yet about Pamela Yost?"

No answer.

"I didn't think you had. . . . Once upon a time, Counselor, Chas covered a murder. A man—an actor, not that you've heard of him; he was in a few commercials—was murdered by a burglar he'd caught red-handed absconding with his Trinitron. The actor grabbed a kitchen knife to defend his castle, and managed before the burglar shot him in the gut to inflict a fatal stab wound. The only witness to this Jacobean mayhem was the victim's wife, Pamela Yost—"

"DeBree."

"—Chas fell in love with Pamela, who was a knockout. More important to Chas, who is not your run-of-the-mill romantic, she was a knockout *despite* her bearing a stigmata, a birthmark that nearly covered one side of her face. A nevus, it's called, or more popularly a port wine stain. Gorbachev, the top Commie, has one on his forehead.

"Pamela Yost's port wine stain, Counselor, equals *your* leprosy. By falling in love with Pamela notwithstanding her abnormality, he made her more than ordinarily beholden to him. He wants to inflict the same sort of emotional blackmail on you. You know about power, Ms. McAlistair. You're in the power racket, as am I, as is Chas, although he tries to pretend he's just an amateur. An amateur he may be, but what a gifted one, for it's not everyone who understands that domination is the flip side of compassion. He found out there was a year missing from your life, he found out how you'd spent it, and instead of keeping his trap shut, which would've been the saintly thing, the perfect-gentle-knightly thing to do, he waved your deep dark secret in your face and said here, two can share it as cheaply as one.

"Chas knows that in your position, aspiring for high office and all, there's a certain amount of pressure on you to have a husband. You need to look respectable, and who's more respectable than Chas? The only problem"—DeBree had spoke to Charles now—"*your* only problem—would've been that people would've thought she was marrying you because you're respectable, reasonably good-looking and a good writer: you never use 'hopefully' when you mean 'it is hoped.' They wouldn't've known what a mensch you were, what a hero, what an extraordinary thing you'd done: loved a leper.

"So you asked me here, because I'd sure be impressed that when you got back from New Orleans last September you didn't go running through the newsroom yelling, Stop the presses, Frances McAlistair's a leper and a liar and her pants are on fire. What a noble guy. You might've won the noble prize for journalism. Or were you bucking for the *peace* prize?

"But even telling me wasn't enough, because we're not talking about the heartbreak of psoriasis here, we're talking about leprosy. So you wanted to tell the whole world, wanted *me* to tell the whole world. 'Ladies and gentlemen of the press, thanks for coming, sorry there's no booze but we want you to be clear of eye and steady of hand. Over here we have U.S. Attorney for the Southern District of New York Frances McAlistair, afflicted with, that's right, I said leprosy, with a capital *L*, and it rhymes with hell, the disease of the soul'—isn't that what they call it, Chas? you're the expert—'but please stay in your seats, never fear, it ain't what you think it is, ain't what it's cracked up to be, and besides, you'll miss the other story, the more important story, the story of how this man, mild-mannered reporter Charles Ives—'"

"DeBree," Charles had said, but without saying it she had said to DeBree, *Go on.*

"You might," DeBree had said to her now, not to Charles, "you might be able to pull off a classy press conference, get your points across absolutely clearly, no mistake about it—that leprosy's treatable, that it's not contagious, that your nose doesn't fall off. But there's a press conference and then there's hearsay; I don't mean gossip, Counselor, I mean what people *hear* about what you said. What if someone who shook your hand somewhere, sometime, is running to catch a train and catches instead a glimpse of a headline—FRANCES MCALISTAIR HAS LEPROSY? They're not going to say Hansen's disease, the newspapers, as much as you might what them to. In the body of the story, sure, but not in the headline; it's just not a headline writer's word, it's not catchy. But *leprosy*'s sure catchy. He sees the headline, this individual who's running for a train, he remembers the handshake, he thinks he can kiss his future goodbye, maybe throws himself in *front* of that train. And I'm not talking about just one guy, Frances. May I call you Frances? I'm talking about thousands. You've been in public life for a long time. How many hands've you shaken? Enough to cause a panic, that's a certainty.

"I've said what I had to say; this is between the two of you. Goodbye, Frances. Nice meeting you. Chas, I'm sorry, but I meant what I said and I said what I meant. I may beat around the bush, but I don't bullshit."

24

"You *left*?" Neuman said.

"There was nothing more to say," DeBree said. "When I later heard that Chas, as you so colorfully put it, had done a brodie off F. McA.'s terrace, well, I wished I'd tarried a while longer, though I don't know what I could've said to make him feel any better about what he'd done."

"So you think he jumped, Ives?"

"Indeed."

"You think he jumped because McAlistair bought what you said about it being better for everybody if she kept quit."

"Indeed."

"And because he was humiliated at having tried to coerce her affection."

"Indeed. Well said."

"So you made up the Coblen story to ensure her secret staying a secret?"

DeBree nodded. "That was my hope. I didn't imagine you'd come at the secret from some other direction. How *did* you find out, Jake? Please tell."

Neuman walked around until he found himself looking at himself in a mirror he hadn't noticed was there. He shook his head, meaning he didn't like it. His reflection shook *its* head, meaning it didn't like it, either. When you and your reflection agree on something, you must be right: Neuman's Law. He said, "I don't like it," and his reflection lip-synced it.

Ever so sweetly, DeBree said, "Don't like what, Jake?"

Neuman moved to stand right over him. "Ives didn't do a brodie off McAlistair's terrace, he was pushed. He was pushed because it wasn't just emotional blackmail he was

going to inflict on McAlistair, it was blackmail blackmail.
He was teamed up with a guy named Michael Corry, an
epidemiologist, a guy who tracked diseases and also had a
cocaine jones. The two of them put the bite on her. Corry's
dead now—maybe McAlistair had him whacked, maybe it
had something to do with his jones, with his dealing
soda—but I think she pushed Ives off her terrace.

"Except it's not that easy to do, push somebody off a
terrace. She's a little taller than average, McAlistair, she
looks like she's in good shape, I don't remember Ives's stats
exactly, but I think he was five ten or so, one seventy or so,
meaning it'd take a certain amount of strength and coordi-
nation to get him up over the edge even if you tricked him
into looking over the side by saying, 'Look, a reindeer,' or
'Big Foot,' or something. So she had help.

"Tom McNally's big"—big enough to dismantle mountains—"and he's good at moving around in this kind of
weather. The night after the night you just told me about,
McAlistair had dinner with McNally. At a restaurant. I
never liked that she went to a restaurant and I like it even
less now that you tell me what was going on with Ives.
McAlistair told us she had dinner with McNally so she
could tell him she didn't want to see him anymore, but that
wasn't her biggest problem, so why spend time on it? It was
all a setup—that's why spend time on it: a public spat so
there'd be witnesses who'd say she went home her way, he
went home his. McNally called her when he got home—to
ask her to reconsider, she said, but in fact so there'd be a
record of the call, so she could say he'd wanted to come
over and she'd said no. He did come over, though; he left
his building without being seen and got in McAlistair's
without being seen and went upstairs. Ives was there, and
McNally tossed him off the terrace. McAlistair pretended to
be asleep, the cops from the whitetop woke her up, asked
her to ID Ives, in the ruckus McNally slipped out and went
home.

"How did Ives get upstairs without anybody seeing
him? I think he'd been there since Monday, since the night
you just told me about. He'd been there writing a speech or
article or whatever it was—the speech or article or whatever it was McAlistair pretended she was going to make to

let the world know she was a leper. She'd already decided
she was going to get rid of him, but she needed time to
work it out and she needed to keep him there and not
suspicious, so she let him think she was going along with his
idea.

"I think you were there too. I think you didn't leave
when you said you did on Monday night. I think you stayed
around long enough that McAlistair knew you didn't like
Ives's idea, she got you aside and asked you to be her ally,
maybe you even thought up the business with McNally, I
think maybe you did something to distract McAlistair's
doorman so McNally could get in. Maybe you pretended to
be somebody else's guest needing a taxi, or somebody
looking for somebody in the building and it turned out you
had the wrong address. Nobody told us about seeing
you—no doormen or neighbors or anything—because we
didn't ask if anybody'd seen any overweight bald guys or is
it girls: I hear some people think that's what you are."

"We've got to talk, Jake."

Neuman whirled to face Milner, Slick Dave Milner,
David Milner, who was standing in a doorway that wasn't
the doorway to the front hall, a doorway that felt as though
it went to a very private part of the house. It was a measure
of the staying power of their *thing*, their deep-seated
animosity, underlain by profound mutual disrespect and
contempt for each other's morals and methods and reinforced by occasional but highly fraught confrontations over
a considerable period of time, and a measure of Neuman's
suspicion that their *thing* could have been turned into a
deep-seated admiration, underlain by profound mutual
respect and regard for each other's morals and methods, on
the strength of one half-assed wrestling match and a couple
of semi-shouting matches over a couple of days—that he
wasn't surprised to see Milner, who was supposed to have
gone to talk again to Frances McAlistair. He wasn't surprised, therefore, that Milner had his gun out, not pointing
at Neuman exactly, but in his general direction.

"We've got to talk," Milner said again.

Again, elsewhere:
"Counselor."

Frances McAlistair turned without curiosity, her head down, focused on pulling on the fingers of her glove, feeling, having been caught without it on in such bitter cold, as if she'd been surprised at some antisocial act—masturbation, or picking a pocket or her nose. The figure who bore down on her was hooded and—because backlit—shadowy, but she knew it wasn't Death, surprised to see her here in New York when she ought to have been in Samara, so she didn't begin to tally up her shortcomings.

"Thanks for coming," the figure said, hands in pockets, huddled, shivering. "I didn't mean for you to stand around outside. Let's go in."

She let the figure hold the door for her and hand her onto the escalator. At the top, she stood aside as the figure scrounged for change. She went through the turnstile the figure fed a quarter, waited, followed. The figure led her through the ferry gates and onto a ferry she didn't get the name of, for she ducked her head against the wind that whirled through the slip.

The snack bar. Two coffees—one black, one extra light with sugar. Up to the bridge deck. A bench in the sun far from any other passengers (making them as conspicuous as hell, when conspicuousness was what they were to avoid), the coffee cups between them, the black near to her hand. Only now did the figure peel away layers—hood, scarf, gloves, a thick sweater, another, thinner one, and sip at the bleached and sweetened coffee.

"Jesus." Police Commissioner Franklin Montgomery nearly dropped his cup in his haste to put it down. "Boy, is that hot. You be careful."

Frances McAlistair set her cup down too, pretending she felt its heat in her fingers, glad to have been prompted.

Montgomery fanned the air above his coffee with his hand. "Look, I'll get right to it, Frances. You have a problem, I have a problem. They seem to be connected, our problems."

She raised her eyebrows.

"I'll spare you the boring details. We got two of the armory shooters. One of them, Donald Dubro, aka Air Sax, is dead. The other—"

"Ersatz?" Frances McAlistair said.

Montgomery smiled. "Air . . . Sax. He liked to pretend he was playing a saxophone. The way kids pretend they're playing guitars."

She nodded. It wasn't a *boring* detail.

"The other, Freddy Faso, wants to cut a deal. He wanted to deal Air Sax as the shooter in another hit, but we already knew that, so he dealt this: That other hit was set up by a woman who gave Air Sax a phone number to use in emergencies. Air Sax shot off his mouth about the number to Faso, who has a cousin who works for the telco. The cousin spotted the prefix as one assigned to law enforcement agencies for fronting undercover operations. The number was one of your backups, Frances, on the armory sting."

"Club Dead—is that the problem you were referring to?" Frances McAlistair said. "You have a problem, and Club Dead's my problem?"

Montgomery smiled, but only for a second. "The other hit Air Sax did was in a movie theater on East Eighty-sixth. The papers made a thing out of the DOA's having a popcorn box on his head."

Frances McAlistair nodded.

"What you didn't read, Frances, because we've sat on it, is that in a gym bag in the victim's apartment, along with twenty grand in untraceable bills, we found a slip of paper with your unlisted home phone number. Not your name, not your initials, just the number. Did you know Michael Corry, Frances, an epidemiologist?"

She shook her head. She hadn't *known* him.

"Sure?"

"What's *your* problem, Frank?" Frances McAlistair said.

Montgomery laughed. "My problem also has to do with telephones."

She sipped her coffee, which tasted like bile.

Montgomery shook his head. "It's not easy."

She waited.

"I, uh . . . I call a phone sex service."

She raised her head fractionally.

"I'm a regular customer."

She nodded once.

"I don't do anything stupid like use a credit card. I prepay with a money order once a month. I use a pseudonym. Each call is deducted from my balance."

She made a sound in her throat, a sound of attentiveness.

"I got a tape in the mail. A cassette. Me and the girl who, you know, talks to me. I don't say much, she does most of the talking, but I'm sure a voice print . . . Anyway, she called me, told me the, uh, terms, and gave me a number where I could reach her in emergencies. It's the same number, Frances, as the number the woman gave Air Sax."

Coffee. Then: "Michael Corry was blackmailing me, Frank."

Montgomery sighed. "Can I ask why?"

"No."

"No, of course not. Air Sax, the guy who killed Corry, also killed Karen Auburn."

Frances McAlistair nodded.

"Was she onto something? Something about you?"

"Someone probably thought she was."

"*Someone*?" Montgomery said. "Not *you*?"

She shook her head. "No."

"Well, what about this, then, Frances," Montgomery said. "What about Charles Ives jumping or falling or was he pushed from your goddamn terrace?"

Frances McAlistair stood and walked toward the bow and looked out over the dazzling sunlit harbor. Every detail on the shore was given a hard edge by the cold.

Montgomery stood next but not too close to her. "I'm sorry."

"Was there a deadline, Frank, on your blackmail threat?"

"Monday noon."

"How much does she want?"

"Ten. Ten every month."

"It's too bad we can't turn this boat around."

Montgomery laughed, then shrugged. He reached down under his layers of clothes and came out with his wallet. He opened it to his badge and ID card, studied them, shrugged again, looked apologetic. "If someone showed you a piece of tin and a piece of paper saying he was police commissioner of the City of New York, would you believe him?"

She smiled. "No."

Montgomery shrugged again, then started for the stairs to the wheelhouse. "What the hell. Let's give it a shot."

25

Why did Charles need—why had he needed—all these bags?

A duffel bag, a backpack, a shoulder bag, a flight bag, a garment bag, a tennis racket bag, a—what did they call them? Kate's father had had one during the Second World War; she'd seen pictures of him, sitting on or hefting his . . . over*seas* bag. A white canvas tool bag too clean to have ever been used for hauling tools, another shoulder bag—of superlight parachute ripstop or stopwatch or ripcord or whatever it was called fabric, an*other* shoulder bag—with straps on the side for stowing an umbrella. Bags, bags, bags. How curious, after all these years, to be sitting on the floor of Charles's closet among all his bags.

How curious, never mind how many years it had been, that she was sitting on the floor of Charles's closet, bags or no bags.

But enough about her. What to make of them, the bags? The Charles she knew—had known—hadn't traveled a particular lot: a week a winter to somewhere warm, a couple of weekends in summer to somewhere by the sea, the occasional trip to someplace odd because someone had invited him there and paid his way—to a gathering of journalists who'd reported from Vietnam, she remembered, in Reading, Pennsylvania, she couldn't remember why.

Nor was he one of those overachievers who bounded from health club to power breakfast to office to power lunch to office to French class to power dinner to Broadway opening to chic soiree, needing a bag to transport his Reeboks, squash racquet, phone beeper, Filofax, Larousse, clean shirt, laptop computer.

In fact, except for the one brief vacation they'd taken together (they'd had a fight, and she'd gone home early), Kate couldn't remember in the four years she and Charles hung out together ever seeing him with a bag on his shoulder or on his back or in his hand. On that vacation—which was hardly a vacation; they'd stayed a few days at the house in Amagansett of some friends of Charles's—she remembered clearly for no reason that she could think of that he'd packed his stuff in a navy canvas duffel with red trim.

This bag, *right* here by her hand, where she can touch it. Touches it.

Was this the bag he took to New Orleans, to Carville? She took her hand away; she stopped touching it.

God, she was scared. And why not? After all, someone was tiptoeing around Charles's apartment.

Well, not tiptoeing. Walking rather confidently, in fact.

And not *some*one. Someone named Steve.

Steve Federici.

A cop.

Or so he said.

"Kate?" he was saying now. "Kate, my name's Steve Federici. I'm a cop."

So you say.

"It's okay to come out."

So you say.

"Kate?"

Not home. There's nobody home.

"Kate?"

What a persistent cuss. As persistent as a cop.

As persistent as a killer.

"Kate, you probably heard about Karen Auburn. The newspaper reporter? She was killed by mistake, by someone who was trying to kill you. You've got something somebody wants, Kate. Let me help you."

Just what she'd expect him to say.

"Kate?"

Oh, Christ, he's right outside the closet door. "Kate?" He's opening the door. "I can see your feet, Kate." Christ.

"It's okay to come out."

"So you say."

They drank tea, Earl Grey. Steve Federici made it according to Kate's instructions—steaming the inside of the teapot for a moment, then spooning in leaves and pouring hot water over them, covering the pot, sluicing the water around awhile, pouring it through a bamboo strainer into mugs—the way Charles Ives had taught Kate.

"It's good," Federici said. "I don't drink a lot of tea—especially now that I'm . . . that my wife's pregnant—but this is good." Why was he talking about his wife, his pregnant wife, when he was finally in the company of a woman who clearly loved underwear so much she didn't just wear it—he was sure she wore it, as he'd been sure Karen Auburn wore it, even though he hadn't glimpsed it—she didn't just wear it, she sold it?

"I wanted to get pregnant once," Kate said. "With Charles, in fact—"

He didn't want to hear this.

"—I wanted a girl. I read an article in the newspaper about an English cattle breeder who discovered that he could influence the gender of calves depending on which way the cows were facing when they were impregnated. If they faced the sun, the calves were likely to be males; if they faced away from the sun, they were likely to be females. It had something to do with magnetic fields or something."

A wonderful thing, the mind: In a few seconds, his provided him with a boxed compass's worth of erotic fantasies—he and Kate facing every which way.

"When I told Charles about it, he wondered how it was that the cows and bulls were so cooperative about the direction they faced—in the heat of passion and all; he grew up in cities and didn't know the insemination was done artificially. I grew up in cities too—*a* city; Philadelphia—but my grandparents had a farm in Bucks County, and I've never forgotten the couple of times I watched a vet stick his arm into a cow up to his shoulder."

Federici had grown up in cities too—*a* city; New York City—and hadn't known it was done artificially, either. But

he snorted at the thought that anyone could think otherwise. "I guess you must've been pretty shaken up when you
heard about it—about him falling to his death and all."

Kate smiled. "Surely cops don't say someone *fell* to his
death. What *do* you say?"

Federici played with the handle of his teacup. "You
don't really want to know this, do you?"

Kate nodded. "Yes, I do."

"Well, the older guys say someone, you know, did a
brodie."

"After some guy named Brodie who was the first guy to
jump off the Brooklyn Bridge, or jumped off it a lot, or
something."

"Right."

"Is that what Lieutenant Milner says—brodie?"

"He does, yeah, pretty much."

"And what do the younger guys say? What do you say?"

"I don't know. I mean, I heard one of my partners the
other day say something—not about Charles Ives, about
another case—something about Humpty Dumpty. But, you
know, it's just talk. I mean—"

"Steve?"

"Yeah?"

"Tell me again why you came here."

"I figured you might be here. I figured you'd've heard
about Karen Auburn, you'd be afraid to go home, you might
be afraid to go to friends', you might still have keys to this
place, you'd come here. I got the keys Ives had on him from
Property."

"And you didn't tell Milner you were coming here."

"No. I mean, I would've if I'd seen him, but he was out
of pocket."

"Meaning you couldn't reach him?"

"Listen, if you want him here I can understand it. I
mean, I can understand you wanting to talk to Lieutenant
Milner or Lieutenant Neuman because they're, you know,
lieutenants."

"Steve?"

"Yeah?"

"What do you do when you think another officer's done

something wrong? Is there a regular procedure to go
through, a form to fill out?"

"I'm . . . You know, I don't know. I mean, yeah, I do
know, but usually you try to work things out without, you
know, going to the brass. Did what wrong? And who?"

"I called Lieutenant Milner after I heard about
Charles's . . . brodie. I told him Charles had sent me
some tapes of interviews with Frances McAlistair—"

Federici snapped his fingers. "So it's the tapes they
want."

"—I told him someone had been calling me and
hanging up. No matter how long I let the phone ring,
they'd stay on until I picked up, then they'd hang up. It was
as though they wanted me to know they knew when I was
home. Or something."

Federici nodded. "They want those tapes."

"He didn't tell me—Milner didn't tell me—that he'd
had an appointment last month at the Museum of Modern
Art with Charles."

"Charles Ives?" Federici said.

"Charles Ives."

"Last month?"

"A month to the day before he died."

Federici closed his eyes for a moment. "He died after
midnight Tuesday, early Wednesday morning." He opened
his eyes when she made a disgusted noise. "Hey, I'm just
trying to get it straight in my mind." Feisty, wasn't she,
underwear or no underwear? Would Karen Auburn have
been as feisty? Sure. They were all that feisty—including
Jennifer, his wife Jennifer, his pregnant wife Jennifer, who
by now must've given up wondering where he was and why
he didn't call her, must've figured that he'd fallen for a
woman with breasts, legs, ankles, collarbone, wrists, everything. "Ives and Milner had a meeting at the Museum of
Modern Art a month before Ives died?"

"Correct."

"And when you talked to Milner *after* Ives died, he
didn't say anything to you about the meeting?"

"Correct. Milner hasn't said anything to you about it,
either, has he?"

"Well, you know, he doesn't tell me everything."

"Or his partner. What's his name—Neuman?"

"Right. Neuman."

"Milner hasn't said anything to Neuman about meeting with Charles, has he?"

"Not that I know of, but there're lots of things I don't know about. Look, Kate, I'm just a detective second grade. I do the dirty work, the shit work, I'm not in on a lot of high-level conferences and stuff. I'm not in on *any* high-level conferences; I just do the dirty work."

"The shit work."

"The shit work."

"Steve?"

"Yeah?"

"I'm scared."

"I can understand that. But you're safe now. I'm with you."

"No offense, Steve—I can tell you're putting yourself down, that you do more than shit work—no offense, but I'm scared because if you found me, Milner can find me."

Federici laughed. "Hey, Milner's one of the good guys. If he *doesn't* find you, I'll let him know where you are."

"That's what I'm afraid of."

"I don't get you."

"You don't get me, Steve, because you think he's one of the good guys. He's one of the bad guys."

Federici laughed again and shook his head over and over. "No."

"Yes."

"No. No, no, no."

Kate got up and got a portable tape player off the top of the refrigerator. The cord reached to the kitchen table and she set it there and pressed Eject and checked the tape inside and closed the hatch and pressed Play. "Listen."

26

"It's simple, Noomz, really. As simple as pie." Slick Dave smoothed his hair with both hands, a gesture (*vide* Neuman's Law) that was never simple, especially when he who made it made it after tucking a .38 Smith in his belt to free his hands.

"Some of it you doped out." Slick Dave walked a figure eight on the carpet of DeBree's living room, moving on nimble Fred Astaire feet around and across, around and across, around and across, for the listening *and* viewing pleasure of DeBree the fat androgyne on one side of him and Noomz his fat so-called partner on the other—and especially for the listening and viewing pleasure of the girl (*Cherchez* the girl: Neuman's Law) who leaned against a wall as if this weren't somebody's living room at all but a disco too trendy to have anyplace to sit, no fat on her, black eyes, long black hair piled up on her head, high black boots, a short black skirt, black tights, big black sweater, a big black coat in a big black heap on the floor at her feet—the audience to whom Slick Dave really played, played his heart out, played his dick off. She'd been behind the door with Slick Dave, the girl, there back in the rest of the house, and, it was clear from the way they moved round each other, been a lot of other places with him too—trendy discos, dark bars, candlelit restaurants, discreet hotels. "Like you doped out that Mike Corry found out about McAlistair's little skin problem—they were in the Peace Corps together, he stumbled on her picture in a Carville yearbook or something—and put the bite on her to finance his jones."

Around and across, around and across, taking his .38 Smith out of his belt again and using it to give a tempo to

217

the unseen unheard orchestra. "Some of it you doped out wrong. Like that Corry teamed up with Ives. The meet between Corry and Ives was a coincidence; it went down because Ives wanted to talk to an expert on leprosy, which was what Corry was. Who Corry *did* team up with was DeBree.

Neuman didn't look at DeBree but couldn't not notice that the fat androgyne waved at him from his nest of pillows. And he couldn't not notice that the girl, however much Slick Dave might be strutting for her, never took her eyes off him—him Neuman. There may be three or twenty or a hundred dangerous people in a room, the one to keep your eye on is the one who never takes his eyes off you—or her eyes: Neuman's Law.

"Before it occurred to Corry to put the bite on McAlistair, he thought he'd sell his story to a newspaper, because that's all he thought he had—a one-week stand in the nation's supermarkets. He read DeBree every morning with his Wheatena, he went to see DeBree. He was a fucking fan, Corry—a DeBree groupie. He must've once upon a time been a smart guy—med school and all—but his jones made chopped liver out of his smarts. He had a golden egg all to himself, and he scrambled it up and made an omelet."

Slick Dave didn't sound like the Slick Dave Neuman knew. The Slick Dave he knew didn't use so many food images. Either the guy doing figure eights wasn't Slick Dave (had Slick Dave worn all those jewels, all those rings? or doing figure eights with a .38 Smith in his hand, a great-looking girl watching him (or pretending to, anyway) telling his so-called partner what a stupid fuck he'd been not to have seen what was going down—maybe doing all that brought out a different side of a guy, turned him into someone who saw the world in terms of food, for who life was just a bowl of cherries, a colorful, wisecracking guy who'd be fun at parties, fun on a cruise ship, fun on a desert island if the cruise ship sank: Neuman's Law.

"DeBree knows a scoop from a long-term investment a jones when he sees one. He figured a guy with a jones could be persuaded to go partners; he called me, knowing I'm good at persuading. We go back a long way, me and

DeBree. He's helped me out now and then with background on people I wanted to know about, in exchange for advance word on maybe who spent the night in jail for beating up all over some teenaged girl they met at a party and did a few lines with. We'd both decided that maybe it was time we started making a buck out of the fact that we know things other people don't want known, if you get my drift, Noomz."

A pirouette, a coming to a stop, an adjustment of the cuffs, a touch to the knot of his necktie—Slick Dave as guest host on *The Tonight Show*. *H-e-e-e-re's David*. "It sounded to me like something McAlistair would pay ten large a month to keep under wraps, Noomz, and of course she did, she had no choice, what was she going to do, holler cop? Besides, she's got a trust fund the size of the national debt. Corry was the front man, did the negotiating, made the phone calls, hit the drops, for which he got two large. DeBree and I split the rest.

"Next month'll be ten months we've had the bite on. The setup's changed a little because of two recent developments, the first of which was the appearance on the scene of Charles Ives, the poor dumb fuck, the second of which was Mike Corry, on account of his jones was getting bigger all the time, upped without telling his partners the size of the bite. As it turned out, the two things sort of nicely dovetailed." Slick Dave smiled right into the camera, so supine America could smile with him. *We'll be r-i-i-i-ght back*.

"The story DeBree just told you, that's the story: Ives tumbled for McAlistair, he tried to get her to come clean about her little skin problem so he could be her, you know, protector, he asked DeBree for help, not knowing what you now know, Noomz, that DeBree was not inclined to be helpful. You doped it out wrong that McNally had anything to do with Ives's brodie, Noomz, though it had a nice ring to it, it was good thinking. What did happen was this: Corry, like I just said, upped the bite without telling his partners. Mary Liz here— Have I introduced you? I haven't. Jesus, I'm sorry. Mary Elizabeth Indelicato, Jacob Neuman. Mary Liz, Noomz."

They'd been looking at each other for a while, and kept on looking, though neither spoke, or even nodded.

"Mary Liz here found out Corry upped the bite from Corry's ounceman—"

Who's your ounceman too, isn't he, Mary Liz? Because you look great, Mary Liz, there's no question about it, Mary Liz, no fat on you, Mary Liz, you're hip, you're trendy, you're whatever the word is right this second, Mary Liz, you wouldn't be caught dead being what the word used to be, and you've also got a heavy, heavy jones, Mary Liz, you're your basic yuppie junkie, aren't you, Mary Liz?

"—who said Corry was flashing a roll two or three times the size of his usual roll, making two or three times the usual buys. All of a sudden we go from a nice lucrative little scam to having too many men on the field; we've got to get rid of some of them. Mary Liz, however, realizes that in the process we can also enhance the scam.

"So we had a hit man whack Corry, and set it up so it'd look like, if the cops got that far, the hit was hired by McAlistair. Then we got Ives up to McAlistair's place when she was out, pushed him off the terrace, it looked like he either jumped or if he was pushed, McAlistair pushed him.

"We're prepared to make you a full partner, Noomz, which works out to four treys a month—Corry being out of the picture. Four treys a month works out to thirty-nine nine ninety-nine a year, Noomz, call it forty large. For doing what? For doing fucking nothing. It's beautiful, Noomz. It's the best fucking con I've ever laid eyes on. It was beautiful before Ives did his brodie, now it's beyond beautiful—it's fucking perfection."

"Can I ask you a question, Milns?"

A flip of a hand. A shrug of the shoulder. *Hey, of course.* "Sure, Noomz. Would I ask you to buy a pig in a poke?"

"You got Ives up to McAlistair's while she was out how?"

Slick Dave smiled. "You doped it out much too complicated, Noomz. Mary Liz has a key to McAlistair's pad, McAlistair went to dinner with McNally, Mary Liz called Ives and said McAlistair was out on the terrace threatening to do a brodie, to get the fuck over there, she'd meet him at the service entrance so it'd stay hush-hush, she got him upstairs, he went out on the terrace, she's not there, he looks over the side, I gave him a little push."

Neuman nodded. "Plus you knew that Ives dies a suspicious death, you'll pull the job because the computer'll flag your run-in with him on the Yost thing, right?"

"The beauties of high tech, Noomz."

"And you let me find out what I'd find out to see how much I'd find out, right? You might have to head me off, you might not."

"Right again, Noomz."

"I was all over the lot with it—a few hits, a few misses—but basically I was getting ready to bear down hard on McAlistair, which didn't fit with your script."

"It didn't, Noomz. It just didn't."

"The story about McAlistair's affair with Coblen—that was a total phony?"

"Total."

"What about Lee Coblen?" Neuman said.

"What about her?"

"Doesn't she know too much?"

"She doesn't know shit, Noomz. She thinks we're *full* of shit, but she doesn't *know* shit."

"Pignatano the cop-buff doctor," Neuman said.

Slick Dave laughed. "We tell Pignatano it's supersecret police business, five people in the whole world know about it, he's one of them, he'll keep quiet about it even if someone tortures him."

"Karen Auburn. You had her whacked. What's to keep the hit man from singing?"

Slick Dave smiled. "He's dead."

"And he's the same hit man who whacked Corry?"

"One and the same. He was a lowlife scumbag, Noomz. He was one of the shooters in the Club Dead thing."

"What about whoever whacked him?"

"DeBree whacked him. You can't go contracting everything out; you know that, Noomz."

Neuman looked at DeBree, who looked away, meaning he'd broken his cherry and still wasn't sure how he felt about it. "A lot of dead people."

Slick Dave shrugged. "The world's a tough place, Noomz. I didn't make the fucking rules. I made the rules, I'd say no guns, no sharp objects, no blunt instruments, a chicken in every pot, a week in Miami every winter."

"Is Ives's old girlfriend dead yet, or haven't you found her?"

"We're working on it."

"Those tapes she has are not something you want making the top forty."

"No, indeed, Noomz."

"You figure all these dead people're worth forty large a year?"

Looking noble now, Slick Dave said, "My share's only twenty, Noomz. Mary Liz and I split a third."

"If I don't come in you can split a half."

"If you don't come in, Noomz, we got a problem."

"I can understand that."

"Good."

"Everything you just told me, I didn't come in, it wouldn't exactly cement the relationship."

Slick Dave laughed.

"Can I just ask you a question—you, Mary Liz?"

Mary Liz craned her neck a little, like a basic yuppie junkie in a tight spot.

"What do you have against Frances McAlistair?" Neuman said.

Mary Liz laughed a basic yuppie junkie laugh. "She's got too much money."

"Hey, is that really her fault?"

"Nothing's ever anybody's fault."

Nothing's ever anybody's fault: Neuman's (plagiarized) Law. "Include me out, Milns."

Slick Dave bent an ear with a fingertip. "I didn't get that, Noomz."

"You got it, motherfucker."

Slick Dave slumped. "Are we going to start this again, Noomz?"

"Fuck you."

Slick Dave sighed. "I wish you'd think it over a while longer, Jake. It puts me—"

"Don't call me Jake."

Mary Liz bent to pick up her coat. "Waste him, David, and let's get out of here."

"Now just a moment." DeBree clambered up and waddled at Slick Dave, waving his arms. "We can't have any shooting here."

Neuman reached for his .38. "Hey, that's not a bad idea, *David*."

"Jake."

He drew it. "Shoot out a few windows, air the fucking place out." He threw down on Slick Dave. "Kind of makes you wish you were in Art Theft, doesn't it, *David*?"

"Back off, Jake."

"*You* back off!" DeBree beat at Slick Dave's chest. "*You* back off this instant! I won't have this kind—"

Slick Dave shot him.

DeBree clutched his gut, looked at his hands, looked at Slick Dave, looked at Neuman, looked at Mary Liz, looked at his hands, fell on his face.

Mary Liz had her hand to her mouth.

"Dave."

Slick Dave looked like Sick Dave. "Back off, Jake."

"Dave, this is it."

"Back off."

"Do you hear me, Dave? It's over."

"Back off."

"Dave."

"Back *off*."

"Let me call an ambulance, Dave."

"Back *off*."

"Everything right you do, Dave, from now on'll make it better for you."

"Back *off*."

Neuman lowered his gun.

Sick Dave held out his hand. "Gimme."

Neuman shook his head.

"*Gimme!*"

"No."

Sick Dave fired into the carpet at Neuman's feet.

Neuman tossed his .38 on the floor.

"Pick it up," Sick Dave said to Mary Liz, who didn't

move. He grabbed her by the arm and hurled her at the gun. "Pick—it—up."

She groveled to it on hands and knees, reached it, grasped it, backed away.

Sick Dave hauled her up.

Sick Dave threw down on Neuman.

Sick Dave shook his head. "I can't."

And he opened the door to the street and hauled Mary Liz out with him.

The usual:

Mouth-to-mouth, CPR, 911.

Then the wait.

Four minutes till the first whitetop. Excellent.

Up here, in there, all that.

Say, young fellow, I know this is an unusual request, but give me your service revolver and don't tell anybody you did, just keep your coat on, no one'll notice, I'll owe you a big fat favor.

Well, sir. I, uh—

Do it. Now.

Out of his car before any brass turned up. Sick Slick Dave had slashed the tires with one of those sharp objects he'd outlaw if he were making the rules—which, at the moment, Sick Slick Dave kind of was.

Undaunted. Resourceful. Size nine and a half.

Neuman opened the trunk and got out the skis Sick Slick Dave had given him to cement their onetime relationship.

27

"So, do you, uh, have a boyfriend?" Steve Federici said.

Kate didn't look away from the window. "He's a magician." She snorted. "Did I just say magician? He's a mus*ician*."

One of those four-eyed faggots who plays the harpsichord, probably. "Oh, yeah. You mean like in a band or something?"

"A band, A rock band."

One of those skinny long-haired heavy-metal morons, probably. Motley Crude or whatever the fuck. "Oh, yeah?"

"Music," Kate said.

"What about it?"

"It's always been such a big part of my life, and what does it mean? How important is it? *Sergeant Pepper*. Was *Sergeant Pepper* more important than Beethoven, than Bach, than a Gregorian chant? Than *silence*? Pretty profound, hey, Steve?"

This was a weird chick, lingerie or no lingerie. "Sure. Yeah."

"Do you know what Lou Reed said about *Sergeant Pepper*?"

"What?"

"He said *Sergeant Pepper* was completely dispensable from beginning to end, and on top of that it was *cute*." Kate laughed.

"So?"

"Jesus, Steve, what's the matter with you?"

"What's the matter with *me*? What's the matter with *you*? You're the one who started yakking about *Sergeant Pepper*. What the fuck does *Sergeant Pepper* have to do with anything or anybody? I mean, shit, we're sitting here,

225

first you're telling me one of my superior officers, a veteran of twenty-five fucking years in the department or something, is a fucking crook, and then you're yakking about *Sergeant Pepper*. The fuck does *Sergeant Pepper* have to do with it, the fuck does *Sergeant Pepper* have to do with anything?"

Kate turned back to look out the window. "Maybe you should try Neuman again."

"He's out of pocket."

"Doesn't he have a beeper? Don't you guys have beepers? In the movies, cops always have beepers. *The Big Easy.*"

"Didn't see it."

"I didn't either. Well, I walked out, actually, when they fell into bed together without one single word about AIDS, about pregnancy, about what they were going to do when they got out of bed, and about anything at all to do with anything at all like life as we know it here on earth in practically the year two thousand."

Shit. That almost certainly meant she wouldn't buy his line that as long as they were both grownups, both killing time waiting for the phone to ring, both into lingerie, they should, you know, get *down*, both of them.

Kate drew circles in the condensation on the window. "I read a letter in the *Times* the other day saying the twenty-first century won't begin one minute after midnight nineteen ninety-nine, it'll begin one minute after midnight two thousand. So all those turn-of-the-century New Year's Eve parties people're planning? They're planning them a year too soon." She leaned her forehead against the glass and wept.

Federici got up and went to her and put his arm on her shoulder. "Take it easy, Kate. It's going to be all right."

"That's easy for you to say. You've got a gun."

"It's going to be all right."

"Just because you keep saying it won't make it come true."

"It's going to be all right."

"Stop it, for God's sake. Stop it, stop it, stop it, stop it, stop it, stop it, stop it."

"I stopped."

"Good."

The front door got kicked in.

Skiing in the street, I'm skiing in the street, what a glorious feeling, I'm skiing in the street.

Don't forget, Jake. Breathe slow and easy. Slow and easy. Slow and easy.

Ski, ski, ski your boat, gently down the stream. Merrily, merrily, merrily, merrily, life is but a scream. Dream.

Slow and easy, slow and easy, slow and easy.

I love to go a-ski-i-ing, along a mountain track. I love to go a-ski-i-ing, a monkey on my back.

Slow and easy, slow and easy, slow and easy.

Kate screamed.

Federici drew his gun.

"Back off, Feds," Milner said.

"Come on, sir. Hey."

"Back off."

"Sir, please don't make me—"

Kate hit at Federici's arm. "Drop your gun, for God's sake, you idiot."

Federici set it on the floor and kicked it toward Milner. A woman in black came out from behind Milner and bent to pick it up.

"Cute outfit," Kate said.

"The tapes," Mary Liz said.

"You were right, Steve, they want the tapes."

Mary Liz slapped Kate backhanded. "The tapes."

Kate spat bloodily at Mary Liz's face.

Mary Liz hit Kate on the temple with the butt of Federici's gun.

"Squad. Jones."

"This is Neuman."

"Man, everyone's looking for you, Loo. The fuck'd you disappear to—sir?"

"Federici there?"

"He's looking for you too, Loo. He's at Ives's pad, Loo, with the Naismith woman. Lieutenant Milner's on the way over there."

"What's the address, Jonesy?"

"Five-oh West one-oh, apartment five F-fox."

"McGovern with you?"

"Yes, sir."

"I want you two there yesterday. No other backup."

"You sure, Loo?"

"Yesterday."

"This is stupid, Feds," Milner said. "You didn't destroy the tapes because if you destroyed the tapes you *have* no tapes, you have nothing."

Federici stroked Kate's head. "Get her to a hospital, you son-of-a-bitch."

"Hey, Feds. Get with the program. *I* get the tapes, then you get what you want."

"David?" The woman in black. The bitch in black. Fucked up, seriously fucked up. This is what happens? You put in twenty-five years or whatever the fuck it is Milner's put in, you have a wife, you have a kid—hey, so what if she's adopted, she's still a kid, right?—you shitcan all of it for a fucked-up chippy bitch in black?

"You hear me, Feds?"

"David, don't you see?"

"Don't I see what? Will you shut the fuck up. Get over to the fucking window, will you, and keep an eye on things."

"Don't you see, David, *we're* the ones who don't want the tapes destroyed, because they're undeniable evidence of Frances's secret. But the rest of them—Frances, these people—they don't care. They'd just as soon destroy them, and keep her secret intact."

Milner waved a hand. "I don't know what the fuck you're talking about."

"Let's just go, David," the fucked-up chippy bitch in black said. "Let's get out of here."

"Not without those tapes."

"Check the garbage, check it out, motherfucker," Federici said.

Milner squinted. "What garbage?"

"I took it downstairs—down to the basement."

"You motherfucking liar, Feds."

"We burned the tapes in the wastebasket in the

bathroom. Check it out, asshole—you'll still find ashes in there, I bet. We dumped the ashes in a shopping bag and I took it down to the basement."

Milner flicked his head toward the bathroom and the fucked-up chippy bitch in black went to look.

She came back holding the wastebasket and held it out to Milner. He took it and sniffed it and hurled it in a corner of the kitchen. "What kind of shopping bag?"

"A plastic one."

He threw down on Federici. "The color, you fucking guinea wop asshole."

". . . Yellow."

"Yellow?"

"Yellow. It was a bag from the Wiz, or Crazy Eddie, one of those stores."

Milner flicked his head toward the service door to the hall.

The fucked-up chippy bitch in black went out the door.

"Get me a drink, will you, Feds. You know the layout here."

"Fuck you."

Milner threw down on him. "Feds."

"Shoot me." Federici opened his coat and turned his chest toward Milner.

Milner got up and opened the refrigerator and took out a can of Rolling Rock. "Nice of him to go shopping before he died, Ives."

"Before you killed him, you mean."

"Sit on it, will you, Steve."

Federici pointed to his chest. "Shoot me, *David*. You pussy."

Milner popped the top of the beer.

"Pussy*whipped*."

"Sit on it."

"Pussywhipped."

The fucked-up chippy bitch in black came back. "Nothing."

"Fuck do you mean, nothing?"

"It's empty. They emptied it. The cans're empty."

"Find the super. Find out when the pickup was."

"David, if it's gone, it's gone."

In one smooth, slow-motion, instant-replay, heartbeat-of-America move, Milner slammed the beer can down, got up out of the kitchen chair, slapped the fucked-up chippy bitch in black in the mouth and went to the window. Then he laughed. He looked at Federici and laughed. He looked at the fucked-up chippy bitch in black and laughed. He put his head back and laughed. "It's down there. The super put the garbage out, but there's no fucking pickup on account of the fucking snow. The stupid fuck." He flicked his head. "Go get it. The fucking bag's right on top of the fucking pile. A yellow bag. Go get it."

"Fuck you," the fucked-up chippy bitch in black said.

Milner threw down on her. "Go get it."

"It's full of ashes, David. What's the point."

Milner hesitated. "You believe that?"

The fucked-up chippy bitch in black rubbed her cheek. "What fucking difference does it make?"

Milner took a step toward the door. "You stay here."

The fucked-up chippy bitch in black shook her head. "I'm leaving."

"Leaving?"

"Leaving."

"Where? Where you going?"

"Away."

"You can't. We got a thing here."

"We don't have shit, David. We blew it."

"But—"

"Go look in the bag, David. Go look in the bag."

"But—"

"Go look in the bag. I'll stay here. I've got Steve's gun. You go look in the bag."

Steve. She liked him. He was working on her.

Milner put his hand on the doorknob. "Don't fuck around, Feds. She knows how to use that."

"Go look in the bag, *David*," Federici said.

Milner went out the door.

I'm skiing, I'm skiing, I'm ski-i-i-ing over you, I'm ski-i-i-ing over you. I'm something that you're gone, I'm something something something. I'm skiing.

Slow and easy, slow and easy, slow and easy.

I ski, you ski, we all ski for ice ski.

One ski, two ski, red ski, blue ski.

How much ski could a ski-ski ski if a ski-ski could ski ski?

"Known David long?" Federici said.

Mary Liz laughed. "You smoke?"

"No, but hey, go ahead. Kill yourself. Be my guest."

She sniffed. "You're such a child."

"Yeah, well, child this," Federici said, and with a smooth, slow-motion, instant-replay, heartbeat-of-America move of his own, he rose and stepped to the stove and plucked the top from the teakettle and tossed what was left—enough—of the still-steaming water in Mary Liz's face.

So let's see, from Twenty-second and Tenth over to Eighth Avenue, that's two crosstown blocks equals four uptown blocks, and then down Eighth to Thirteenth Street is nine more blocks is thirteen blocks, then down Greenwich to Tenth Street is about five short blocks, call it eighteen blocks to Tenth between Sixth and Fifth. Not even a mile, not even—how much is a kilometer? Six-tenths of a mile. Not even one point two kilometers, and Neuman usually did three kilometers, Neuman for whom racing a team of huskies five hundred miles over snow and ice and tundra and stuff was his idea of walking the dog. So how come his head's banging, his lungs're burning, his thighs're lead, his knees're rubber, his hands and feet're frozen? How come he's dying?

Speaking of walking dogs, coming toward him across the snow and ice and tundra and stuff is another asshole *walking* his dog. His yellow dog. Bright yellow.

No. No, that's not it. It's something else he's walking. Something bright yellow, but not a dog.

A bird, maybe. Because it's flying around and around over his head. Maybe he's an asshole for who racing a team of birds five hundred miles over snow and ice and tundra and stuff is his idea of walking the bird.

No. Not a bird, either.

A bag.

A yellow bag.

Walking a yellow bag.

Waving it, anyway.

Shaking it.

Jerking it around.

Pounding at it with one hand and ripping at it with the other.

Throwing it down on the snow and ice and frozen tundra and stuff and kicking at it.

Again and again.

Poor bag.

Holy shit, it's Sick Slick Dave Milner, just the guy Neuman wanted to see.

If only, having figured out how to get his skis and boots on, he could figure out how to get them off. If only he weren't dead.

Better figure out how to get them off before Milner shot him, which is what he was getting set to do, having thrown down on Neuman with his .38, which is where Neuman came in.

Maybe Neuman should shoot him first, skiis or no skis, commandeered gun or no commandeered gun, dead or not.

"Don't make me, Jake. Back off."

"You . . . back . . . off." Did Milner even hear him? He didn't act like it.

"Don't make me, Jake."

He didn't hear. "You . . . back . . . off."

"Don't make me."

"Back . . . off."

"Don't."

Neuman raised his commandeered gun and tried to aim it.

He fell on his face, his skis shot out from under him, what breath he had left got knocked out of him. And then while he was lying there helpless, dead, freezing, Milner shot him in the back.

Then he shot him again.

And again.

It didn't hurt, thank God. It just killed without hurting. Good to know, for future reference.

And again.

He was dead already. Why didn't Milner stop?

He stopped shooting.

Maybe it was safe to look.

Neuman looked.

Right in front of him was Sick Slick Dave Milner, down on one knee, holding his right shoulder, his shooting shoulder.

Down on both knees.

"Drop it, Dave." On Neuman's left, telling Dave to drop it, was Steve Federici.

"Stay back, Officer. He's bluffing."

And on Neuman's right, telling Federici to stay back, Sick Slick Dave was bluffing, was the police commissioner of the City of New York and next to him the U.S. Attorney for the Southern District of New York.

"Drop it, Milner," Federici said.

"Careful," the police commissioner of the City of New York said.

Somebody laughed.

Milner.

Laughed at Neuman.

Sick Slick Dave Milner looked at Neuman and laughed. His hair was a wet mess, his coat was thick with snow, his nose was running, he had blood coming out of his mouth. And he was laughing at Neuman.

"I didn't buy those skis, you fat fuck, Neuman. I got them from a cop in the Two-six who owes me a favor. He swapped them with a guy in a sporting-goods warehouse for half a gram of soda."

Fuck you, Neuman tried to say, but nothing came out. Of course—he was dead. Shot three times in the back.

Or maybe he wasn't. Maybe those shots were at other people, not him. Maybe having been thrown down on by the guy who strangled his wife, raped her, sold his story that he'd come home and found her dead and violated to everyone who heard it—maybe that was Neuman's close call of the year, maybe the rest of the year would be peaches and cream and strawberries and milk and honey and frankincense and myrrh and all the rest of that shit, maybe he was home free, golden, not to worry.

Neuman wondered one thing.

He wondered if anyone else there—Federici, the

police commissioner of the City of New York, the U.S. Attorney for the Southern District of New York, other cops who seemed to be arriving in whitetops and stuff, sirens blasting, all the usual shit—he wondered if any of them, not having been thrown down on by the guy who threw down on Neuman, remembered what happened after the guy who threw down on him pulled the trigger and missed.

Probably not.

They probably didn't remember that what happened was that the guy put the barrel of his gun in his mouth and pulled the trigger and sprayed the contents of his head on the wall of the foyer of his semiattached house in Douglaston.

"Dave," Neuman said.

Milner looked at Neuman, and Neuman knew he remembered, or if not remembered could at least imagine the possibility—could see it with his own two eyes like it was standing right there in front of him.

"Don't, Dave," Neuman said and Milner said, "Sorry, Jake," and transferred his .38 to his left hand and put the barrel in his mouth and pulled the trigger.

What happened to the contents of his head Neuman didn't see because he put his face down in the snow and his arms over his head.

I mean, what the fuck else could he do?

28

In sports last night, it was the Hawks snowed in in Atlanta and the Bulls snowed in in Chicago, giving the Knicks and the Nets, respectively, an unscheduled night off. The local hockey teams should've been so lucky: The Islanders lost to the Flyers, the Rangers dropped one to the Canadians, and the Devils lost to the Maple Leafs. The National Weather Service forecast: Snow. An inch or two in the city, two to four inches in the 'burbs. High today, fifteen to twenty, low tonight around ten. Tomorrow: More snow, maybe another inch, and a little colder. Right now in Central Park it's twelve degrees. With the wind from the northeast at ten miles an hour, it feels like . . . Tuktoyaktuk, Northwest Territories.

"Think it'll ever get warm, Jake?" Klinger said.

"Art Theft," Neuman said.

"Don't say it again, okay, Jake? There aren't any openings in Art Theft."

"Make one. Fire somebody, retire somebody, promote somebody. If you don't, I'll shoot somebody."

Klinger laughed.

"I mean it, Lou. I've had it with the street. The street sucks. Besides, no one's going to want to work with me. I'm bad luck."

"Some of the people you've worked with have been bad luck, Jake. There's a difference."

"I worked with Redfield, Redfield turned into a serial killer. I worked with Federici, Federici was under suspicion in that Nowhere Man shooting. I worked with Milner, even though I told you no; you said the computer said we were fucking compatible, we were both bucking for Art

235

Theft—I worked with Milner, Milner, among a whole lot of
other things probably, has the bite on the U.S. Attorney for
the Southern District of New York. So put me on fucking
Art Theft, will you, Lou. They work solo in Art Theft, don't
they? They better, because no one's going to want to work
with me."

Klinger moved some papers around. "DeBree's lawyer's going to try and make an illegal-search-and-seizure
case. You going to be able to handle that?"

"Art Theft," Neuman said.

"It's something, isn't it?" Klinger said. "DeBree being
a woman. The world is one weird fucking place."

"Art Theft."

"Art Theft pulls some world-class weirdos, Jake."

"Art Theft."

"The commish's got guts, I'll say that. He's going to go
on the record about the phone-sex thing. In fact, you
should be at that press conference. Tomorrow at two. In his
office. Clear with me whatever you think you'll say."

"I'll say I want a transfer to Art Theft."

More papers. "Inspectional Services says Milner and
Ives had a meet about a month ago, but both of them being
dead, nobody knows what went down. You got any ideas?"

"Art Theft."

"Come on, Jake. Take a guess."

Neuman shrugged. "Ives met with Corry, the guy who
tracked contagious diseases. Corry probably told Milner
that Ives was on the up-and-up, Milner probably didn't
believe him, since Corry wasn't trustworthy, he wanted to
give Ives the once-over himself."

Klinger nodded. "Sounds right."

"Art Theft."

Klinger sighed.

"I returned those skis, by the way. I took them down
to Property. Tell Inspectional Services that; I don't want to
take the rap for some hot skis."

"I don't see any reason why you shouldn't keep the
skis, Jake. You're kind of famous for showing up on them."
Klinger covered his mouth.

"What's so funny?"

"Nothing."

"Then why're you laughing?"

"I'm not laughing." Klinger coughed. "I've got something in my throat."

"Art Theft," Neuman said.

"Get the fuck out of here, will you please, Jake? Take the rest of the day off, be back here at two tomorrow for the press conference. Say hi to Maria."

"Art Theft."

Klinger pointed at the door. "Out."

"May I have a word with you, Lieutenant Neuman?" Frances McAlistair said. "Please don't get up."

Neuman sat down, but there was no place for her to sit, so he stood back up. He shrugged and smiled.

She shrugged and smiled. "Well."

"Yeah."

She offered her hand, then withdrew it. "Thank you."

He held out his hand. "You're welcome."

They shook hands.

"A grand jury's going to hear the case against DeBree. I plan to tell them everything, so if there's a trial, I guess I'll be telling everything there too."

Neuman nodded. "Well, good luck. In the end, it'll probably be a good thing to have done."

She smiled. "I know that feeling—of wanting to have *done* something but not wanting to do it."

Neuman shuffled. "Yeah."

"I'm sorry about your partner. Don't blame yourself."

"I don't. I blame the computer."

She shook her head. "I'm sorry. I don't understand."

"I don't, either."

Her eyes got narrow with concern. "Well . . . Goodbye. And thanks again."

"You're welcome again."

"Goodbye."

"Miss McAlistair?"

She turned back. "Yes?"

"I *don't* blame the computer. The computer just spewed out what somebody told it. In its mind, Milner and I looked like a good match; it couldn't know he was a creep and a bum and a chiseler and a cheater and a liar and a lousy cop. But I knew it. There's a guy on the radio in the morning. I don't know if you listen to the radio in the morning, but there's a guy on who whenever he gives the weather forecast, instead of saying the windchill factor makes it feel like ten below zero, or whatever, he says it *feels like* someplace in Canada."

"Skagway," Frances McAlistair said.

"You know who I mean then."

She shook her head. "But when I was a kid, I used to listen to Sergeant Preston of the Yukon on the radio. One of the places in it was Skagway. It always made me feel cold just to hear it. So I know *what* you mean."

"Anyway, I've been thinking it's funny that people're more concerned about what something feels *like* than with just feeling it. I never had a brother. I mean, I *don't* have a brother. Or a sister, either; I'm an only child. But what I found myself thinking once or twice when Milner and I would be talking about something and really getting along well, really understanding each other, was that it was probably *like* what it's like to have a brother. And that made me feel good—that I had a sort of surrogate brother. But if I'd really looked at the situation, instead of what the situation was *like*, then maybe I'd've seen where things were wrong, where it wasn't *like* being with a brother, it *was* being with a creep and a bum and a chiseler and a cheater and a liar and a lousy cop.

"Does this make any sense to you?"

Frances McAlistair nodded once. "Some. You're a responsible man; you need to identify and allocate the responsibility for what happened. You don't *blame* yourself; you should give yourself credit, though. That's important."

"For what? Falling on my face?"

She didn't smile. "For having made the effort that made you fall on your face. I have a . . . an ordeal ahead of me that's going to require some effort. I can use you as a model."

"Good luck," Neuman said.

"Thanks."

"Goodbye then."

"Goodbye."

*   *   *

"Neuman."

"Steve Federici, Lieutenant."

"Hello, Steve. I'm trying to get out of here. Can it wait?"

"I just wanted to tell you the baby came."

"That's great. Congratulations."

"Yeah, thanks. Seventeen hours labor."

"Wow. A girl, right? What's her name?"

"It's funny, you know, Loo. We had all that time, since the amnio, to think of a name, and we couldn't think of one. We still haven't thought of one. Jennifer's pushing Sarah, with an *h*, and I'm pushing Katherine—Kate for short."

"Can I say something, Steve?"

"Sure, Loo."

"Go with Sarah."

"You think so? I don't know. Kate Federici—I kind of like the sound of that."

"Jennifer's been reading the papers, right? She knows what's been going down the last few days, right?"

"Right."

"Go with Sarah."

"I guess I know what you mean, Loo. Thanks."

"Congratulations, Steve. Give my love to Jennifer—and to Sarah."

"I will, Loo. So long."

"So long."

"Neuman."

"This is Kate Naismith."

"Yes, Miss Naismith. I only have a minute. I'm trying to get out of here. How're you feeling?"

"I'm fine. I'm home—in Hoboken. It feels strange, knowing Karen Auburn died, well, because of me. But I think I'm okay."

"Don't blame yourself."

"It's hard not to." She laughed. "Actually, it's *easy* not to. It's easy—easiest—to blame Charles—Charles Ives. We were lovers once upon a time, he and I."

"I knew that, yeah."

"You want to leave."

"No, it's okay."

"I just read a book, a month or so ago, that reminded

me of Charles. I thought about him every day for a week or more. And then those tapes arrived."

"*Dawn's Husband?*" Neuman said.

"What did you say?"

"Was the book called—"

"I *heard* what you said. You said *Dawn's Husband.* How on earth did you know the book was *Dawn's Husband?*"

"Milner read it. He was talking about it. About how it reminded him of Ives."

"Milner read *Dawn's Husband?*"

"Yup."

"*Dave* Milner?"

Neuman laughed. "Slick Dave Milner, yes."

Kate laughed. "Slick Dave. That he was. Slick Dave Milner read *Dawn's Husband.* I don't know whether to laugh or cry."

"Laugh," Neuman said.

"When I called Milner to tell him about the tapes, he pretended he didn't know where I lived. But he did know, didn't he? He kept calling me, then hanging up, because he wanted me to ask him for help."

"Sounds like a long shot, but it sounds right," Neuman said.

"I didn't get to talk to Frances McAlistair," Kate said, "what with all the commotion, but I feel she should know that I know what was on the tapes, what she and Charles talked about. Her . . . her illness."

"There's going to be a grand jury investigation and, probably, a trial. She plans to testify."

"That's brave of her."

"It is, yeah."

"Will I be called?"

"Probably. Just to establish certain facts."

"And do I tell them about the tapes?"

"You'll be under oath."

"The tape that bothers me the most is the one Charles made without telling her. The one where he told her he knew she had . . . leprosy."

"I haven't heard the tapes, obviously, since they were destroyed."

"No one has, have they?"

"No. I guess. Just you. What're you driving at, Miss Naismith?"

"Charles was in love with her—with Frances McAlistair."

"Yeah. I think he was."

"She probably loved him too."

"That I couldn't say. It's pretty complicated."

"Well, for the sake of argument, let's say she did. She doesn't need to know that his journalistic reflex was so strong that it led him to make clandestine tape recordings of their conversations."

Neuman waited.

"Does she?"

Neuman thought. "I won't be in the grand jury room when you testify."

"What kind of answer is that?"

"Think about it."

". . . Okay. Oh. I see."

"Good."

"I guess I hoped you'd say that."

"Umm."

"Well. It was nice meeting you." She laughed. "It *wasn't* nice meeting you, it was *awful* meeting you. But you know what I mean."

"Yeah."

"Well. Goodbye."

"Goodbye."

"Well, well, Lieutenant Neuman. You've been keeping busy, according to what I read in the papers."

"Thanks for making the time to see me, Dr. Bernstein."

Bernstein laced his fingers together in his lap.

"This is the part I hate," Neuman said. "Where you sit there waiting for me to say something."

"Does it make you angry?"

"What I was thinking was that maybe *I* should do it more."

"With witnesses, you mean? Or suspects?"

"That too. But mainly just in, you know, real life. I

mean, I always have to say something. What's the thing
about nature abhors a vacuum. Well, I abhor a silence. I'm
always filling it up. If I kept quiet, if I let others do the
talking, maybe I'd find out what they're really like. Find
out sooner."

"Because sooner or later you do find out what people're really like?"

"Yeah. Sometimes."

Bernstein waited.

"You don't feel any, you know, guilt or anything?"

"For?"

"For Milner."

"Could you elaborate?"

"No. I mean, I don't want to."

"You want me to feel guilty."

"Yeah."

"Feel guilty that . . . he deceived you?"

"Yeah."

"And therefore I deceived you—and should feel guilty
about that too."

"You're supposed to know this stuff."

"Stuff. Meaning what's going on inside people's heads?
What they're thinking?"

"Yeah."

Bernstein unlaced his fingers. He slung one leg over
the arm of his chair.

"That makes me nuts when you sit like that," Neuman
said.

"You think I'm being too casual?"

"Yeah."

"What would you prefer?"

"I don't know. How come you don't have a couch?"

"I'm not a psychoanalyst."

"You could still have a couch."

"I didn't know what was going on inside Dave Milner's
head; I slouch in my chair; I don't have a couch: three areas
where I've let you down. Are there any others?"

"I want a transfer to Art Theft. I want you to tell
Klinger I'm not fit to work on the street."

"If I thought that I would certainly tell him."

"Forget about what you think; I want you to tell him."

Bernstein laced his fingers together.

"You know, you sometimes say I'm resistant to hearing things because I cross my arms over my chest. It's the same thing when you hold your hands like that."

"Another letdown."

"Fuck you."

Bernstein sat.

"Did you *know* about the drugs, about the girl, about the money? How could you know those things and let somebody go out in the street with him? Aren't there fucking limits to privilege?"

"If I had known, Jake, I certainly would've told someone. Yes, there are de*grees* of privilege."

"So you're just as dumb as the rest of us. You don't know shit, either."

"Dave Milner was a sociopath, Lieutenant. It's no breach of privilege to tell you that—and no surprise to you, I'm sure. As a sociopath, he had a rather poorly developed sense of responsibility. He felt none for most of his actions, which is what enabled him to act as he did—outside the law—even while sworn to uphold it. But what's more important here—"

"I know—is what I feel about it."

"Yes."

"I feel like shit."

"That's understandable."

"Thanks."

"What else do you feel?"

"Like transferring to Art Theft."

"What else?"

"Like going home."

"I understand it's been quite a while. I think you should go home."

"After this."

"Maybe you should go now. You've expressed your anger. It's not going to go away, and we'll deal with it the next time. Right now I think seeing your wife and putting on a comfortable pair of slippers would do you a world of good."

"I could read an art book," Neuman said.

Bernstein smiled. "You could."

"You don't smile much in here."

"You're rarely funny in here."

"You could still smile."

"And be a villain?"

"That's from Shakespeare, isn't it—'smile and smile and be a villain'?"

"*Hamlet,* I think."

"That's Slick Dave to a T, isn't it?"

Bernstein cocked his head. "Slick Dave?"

"Milner."

Bernstein nodded. "Ah."

The sun came out from behind a cloud, setting the window ablaze. Neuman looked toward it. "I've been working out, at least."

"I heard."

"Don't be a smartass, okay, Doc?"

"I heard you'd been working out at a health club."

"See, that's the thing, Doc. If I hadn't sneaked up on him, which is what I did going on foot like that—on the skis—then he might still be alive. He'd've gone back inside; there'd've been hostage negotiations; all that."

"As I understand it, it was Detective Federici who shot Lieutenant Milner while he was distracted by you."

"That's right."

"Have you spoken to Detective Federici?"

"Yeah."

"Does he feel any remorse?"

"He just had a baby. His wife did."

"Even so."

"No, he doesn't feel any remorse."

"He did his job."

"Yeah."

"But you . . . failed at yours?"

"Where I failed is I should've seen it."

"Should've seen that he was bad, evil, a villain?"

"Yeah."

"He was a brilliant deceiver, the man you aptly call Slick Dave. . . . It was he who told me you'd been working out. We had an appointment just last week."

"In the middle of all this, he came to see you?"

"It was part of his elaborate deception—that he was

taking steps to improve his mental and emotional health.
He said it admiringly—that you'd been working out. He
asked me if it would be appropriate to get you a present."

"Fuck," Neuman said.

"I understand that he said at the end that the skis were
obtained illicitly. I don't believe that to be the case. I'm a
regular customer at a sporting-goods store on Nassau Street
and I recommended it as a place to get the skis. They called
to thank me for the new customer."

Neuman shook his head. "It's too fucking confusing."

Bernstein slung his leg again.

"It's got to be less confusing in Art Theft." Neuman's
Law.

Bernstein laced his fingers.

"Doesn't it?"

About the Author

Jerry Oster was a reporter for UPI, Reuters, and the *New York Daily News*.

CLUB DEAD is the first Bantam novel by
Jerry Oster, and if you enjoyed this book, you
will enjoy his second novel for Bantam:

INTERNAL AFFAIRS

by Jerry Oster

Here is a special advance preview chapter
from INTERNAL AFFAIRS, which will be
available as Bantam hardcover in January
1990, at your local bookseller.

The Mercedes Benz shimmied, yawed, spun.

The front end came around and around and around until it faced the Saab.

Zimmerman hit the brake, confused, thinking the Benz was coming right at him.

The Benz receded and Zimmerman stared after it for a moment before stepping on the gas again. "What the fuck?"

The Benz spun again. And spun. And spun. This time, as the front end came about once more, Cullen noted that the windshield on the driver's side was shattered.

The front end hit a Federal Express van in the fast lane. The rear end swung into the van's path and the van clipped it. The Benz swung all the way around and bucked onto the median and down a small gully and smashed into a light pole.

Zimmerman whooped the siren and Cullen got the flasher on the roof, but the traffic on the left wouldn't give way, couldn't give way, so Zimmerman pulled off to the right.

Cullen was out the door before the Saab fully stopped. He slipped and darted and skipped between cars, showing his gun to drivers to startle them into stopping. Many of them risked frying their brains to let him know what they thought of him, rolling down their windows and sticking out their heads and calling him a scumfuckingbagcocksuckingmotherfucker. They—and others—leaned on their horns as though the horn buttons were his face.

Cullen caught a toe in the thick grass and tumbled into the gully, heels over head. He was sure he would break his neck, and nearly cried out, *No, God, please. Let me start all over again. Let me do it right.*

He rolled to his feet as if he'd meant to do it that way all along. James Bond, Bruce Lee, Rambo—he came from a long line of superheroes.

He yanked open the Benz's left front door and the driver fell into his arms like a clown doing a pratfall.

The driver had raspberry jelly for a face.

Cullen propped the driver up with a shoulder and turned off the ignition. He eased the driver down on the seat and backed out and grappled with the left rear door.

It was locked.

"Vera!"

He ducked down into the front seat again and pounded on the smoked glass partition. "Vera!"

He searched the dash for the switch, the lever, the button, the whatever the fuck, to open the glass. He couldn't find it. What did he know about stretch Benzes?

"Vera!"

He ran around to the right side and tried the rear door.

"Vera!"

The window opened a handsbreadth. He saw a pair of eyes bright with fright, then he saw nothing but black.

"Vera? Vera, it's Joe Cullen. Are you all right?"

"What happened?" A very tiny voice.

"The driver . . . Is he . . . ?"

Shit. The driver.

Cullen went back around to the driver's side. Zimmerman had the driver on his back on the seat. A knee on the floorboards, Zimmerman put his mouth over the driver's, puffed, turned his cheek to inhale. His eyes met Cullen's and he shook his head.

Cullen went back to the right rear door. The window was closed. He tapped on the glass.

"Vera? . . . Vera!"

Someone grasped Cullen's shoulder.

He whirled, reaching for his gun.

"Easy, now." A woman in a gray suit.

"Come on, lady. Just stay the fuck—"

"Cullen, right? The Dean thing. What the hell happened?"

Even out here? At a time like this? Then he recognized Deputy Commissioner Susan Price, her driver at her shoulder, a .44 Magnum in his hand, quite a piece for Public Affairs. "Sorry. There were shots. From an overpass, I think. That one there."

"You call it in?" Susan Price didn't wait for an answer. "Jack, call in a shots fired—"

"I called it in." It was Zimmerman, his shirtfront and his suit covered with blood, blood on his face, his forehead, his eyebrows, his lips.

Susan Price jerked a thumb at the Benz. "She all right?"

Cullen raised his shoulders and shook his head.

"Jesus, Cullen." Susan Price rapped a knuckle on the rear window. "Miss Evans? It's Susan Price . . .

"Miss Evans? . . .

"Vera?"

The window opened, as if she'd said the password. Susan Price bent down to it. "You okay?"

Cullen couldn't hear the answer. Zimmerman had a hand on his shoulder and was pulling him away.

On the overpass, just east of Steinway Street in Astoria—the shooter, confident of his aim as well as privy to schedules and routings, had sprayed in red paint:

RALEIGH 2

Mayor Sidney Lyons had only been trying to prove a point by telling Betsy Barclay of *Good Morning, New York* (why did all women television newspersons have alliterative names and why, if *Good Morning America* was called *GMA* and didn't have a comma, wasn't *Good Morning, New York* called *GMNY* and why did it have a comma?) that not everyone with his hand out had his head on straight and his heart in the right place.

"I can look you in the eye, Betsy," he had said, "and tell you that while there *are* some individuals living on our streets and in our parks, camping in our sewers amid the muck and the excrement, who are *truly* undomiciled, *truly* unemployed, *truly* undernourished, *truly* ill-clothed, there are just as many, perhaps more, not to put too fine a point on it but not to beat around the bush either, who are *truly* insane. *And*—this is the important point, Betsy, this is the reality I fear many citizens have buried their heads in the proverbial sand to avoid having to face up to—many individuals who ap*pear* to be homeless, who ap*pear* to be needy, who ap*pear* unkempt and unwashed and in rags are in *fact* dissemblers, charlatans, impostors—greedy hustlers who take advantage of our credibility and our compassion. Healthy, aggressive, clever, these . . . these *crim*inals is what they are, Betsy, are depleting the public's limited reservoir of charity and reducing the *truly* downtrodden to even worse circumstances.

"I'm thinking of a woman, Betsy, about your age, which I won't be so unchivalrous as to speculate on, attractive—pretty, almost—who haunts—I don't think that's too strong a word; she has a ghostly mien—who haunts a street corner just outside the Municipal Building across from City Hall. I see her two or three times a week sometimes, sometimes two or three times a day, whenever my schedule takes me away from the Hall and I'm driven in or out of the driveway entrance closest to the Municipal Building. What this woman does, Betsy, is weep. Stands stock still, an empty delicatessen coffee container held out in front of her, and weeps. I'm told, by my staff, by police officers, by municipal employees, that she weeps for hours at a time. I myself have never seen her when she wasn't weeping. And while she weeps, passersby fill that coffee container with money—not just dimes and quarters, Betsy, bills, dollar bills, five and ten dollar bills, sometimes *twen*ty dollar bills, anything to stanch the flow of tears, to help that poor woman cope with her miserable condition.

"And of course *noth*ing does help, because there is *noth*ing the woman needs helping *with*. She's healthy, she's well-dressed and well-groomed, as well she might be given that she's probably making, at a conservative estimate, fifty or sixty dollars an hour. That works out to something in the neighborhood of five hundred dollars a day, Betsy, two thousand five hundred dollars a week—that part of town is lightly trafficked on the weekends, and she appears to take those days off. She's certainly earned it. She probably goes shopping, for some more of her designer dresses—which is what they look like to me, though I'm not at all trained in such matters. Is this the kind of person, Betsy, you have in mind when you refer, as you just did, to the, uh, Hopeless?"

Having perfectly timed the commercial break, then having been saved from Betsy's followup or rebuttal by the need, as the show ran out, for a recap of the killing of Vera Evan's driver, Lyons had been driven downtown by his Police Department driver, down Seventh Avenue and Broadway to Canal, then over to Centre Street and down Centre to City Hall.

Past the Municipal Building.

And there she was.

Not weeping at all, just half-sitting, half-leaning against one of the columns supporting the archway that formed the Muni's entrance, sipping a cup of coffee, eating a roll or a donut or a bagel like any other municipal employee with a few minutes to kill before going to work.

Lyons was discomfited to see that she didn't look as good as he'd thought, didn't look quite as he'd just described her to the morning television audience: she was gaunter, her dress was dirtier—and might very well have been the dress she'd worn the day before and the day before that and the day before that, her hair was more disheveled, her ankles more swollen, her face and arms more weathered than, were he a betting man, he would have wagered.

Still, she didn't look *bad*, didn't look anywhere near as awful as plenty of others like her he'd seen around town. He would bet, were he a betting man, he would bet a *lot* of money that that dress *did* have a designer label, and not a fake one either, the real thing—because he *did* have some training in these matters, his wife Sylvia and the harridan virgin spinster freeloaders dropped a grand a month easy on dresses, designer dresses. And not an Orchard Street either, or in Jersey, where there were outlets, where there was no sales tax on clothes.

"Tony." Lyons leaned forward and touched the shoulder of his driver, Police Officer Anthony Casales. "Tony, pull over here a minute."

"Here?"

"Right here, Tony, right here. It's okay. I'll just be a minute."

"Sir, you want me to, uh . . . ?"

"Just stay here, Tony. I'll be fine. I just want to see something."

Casales pulled over and Lyons got out and walked over to the woman—not directly, but zig zag, so as not to frighten her. "Good morning."

The woman shivered, as if it weren't already eighty-five degrees and held her arms close together in front of her, elbows nearly touching. She had finished the roll or donut or bagel or whatever it was, but she still had the container of coffee. She was going to use it to hold all the scratch she made when she started her weeping act, wasn't she?

"How are you this morning? Hot enough for you?"

The woman's teeth began to click together. Her coffee, so milky it was almost white, began to slosh out of the container she held under her chin.

"You be careful now, dear. You're spilling coffee on that pretty dress of yours," Lyons said.

The clicking became chattering. More and more coffee leapt from the container onto her dress.

"Here, let me wipe that off." Lyons took the hand-kerchief from the breast pocket of his suit coat and stepped close to the woman. Her dress had a top that kind of overlapped, sort of, that was held together by a belt and a button or a snap on the inside of the dress, kind of. Anyway, the belt was gone and the button or snap had come undone and he could see *in* rather than *down* her dress and she wasn't wearing a bra and her breast was white and firm, not veiny and floppy, like he expected, like Sylvia's. Lyons glanced over at the Chrysler; Casales, windows up in air-conditioned comfort, reading *Newsday*, just another cop in a coop, oblivious to what was going on around him. "Let me wipe that off. I won't hurt you. It's such a pretty dress. You're a very pretty young lady. Let me wipe that off."

Lyons touched the dress over her breast with his handkerchief, then with his fingertips.

The woman threw the coffee in Lyons's face.

He slapped her.

She ran, stumbling back under the archway.

Lyons ran after her, mopping the coffee from his face with the handkerchief. He caught her by the arm and yanked her to a stop. "Let me see that *dress.*"

The woman screamed.

Lyons got a sort of half-nelson on her and grappled at the collar of her dress. "Let me *see.*"

The woman kicked back at him, hissing and grunting. Lyons changed his grip, putting one arm around the woman's waist and holding her tight against him as he found the dress's label and tried to smooth it out to read it. It was dark in here under the archway and he couldn't have made it out even if she weren't struggling. "It's a de*sign*er dress, isn't it?"

The woman clawed at his arm.

"*Isn't* it?"

The woman howled.

"*Isn't* it!?"

The woman reached behind her and grabbed him by the balls and squeezed.

Lyons shrieked and thrust the woman away, and still holding on to the dress. It came away in his hands, the dress, it came off her. She stood there naked, no underwear, no nothing. Just her shoes. Brown, low-heeled shoes. The sole of the left shoe flapped loose.

"I . . ." Lyons took a step toward her. "I'm sorry."

The woman backed away. Her stomach was distended, her thighs were blubbery, she was filthy and bruised and bitten and beaten. He didn't want to look at her. He didn't want to see her ever again in his life.

Lyons took another step. "I'm so sorry."

The woman turned and ran, the sole flapping, through another archway and back into deeper shadows.

Lyons didn't run after her.

He shook out the dress and folded it neatly and placed it on a ledge of one of the columns supporting the archway. He took out his wallet and took out a twenty, then another, then another, and folded the bills lengthwise and smoothed the dress's label and fitted the bills under it:

Jaclyn Smith for K-mart, the label said.

DON'T MISS
THESE CURRENT
Bantam Bestsellers

☐	27814	**THIS FAR FROM PARADISE** Philip Shelby	$4.95
☐	27811	**DOCTORS** Erich Segal	$5.95
☐	28179	**TREVAYNE** Robert Ludlum	$5.95
☐	27807	**PARTNERS** John Martel	$4.95
☐	28058	**EVA LUNA** Isabel Allende	$4.95
☐	27597	**THE BONFIRE OF THE VANITIES** Tom Wolfe	$5.95
☐	27456	**TIME AND TIDE** Thomas Fleming	$4.95
☐	27510	**THE BUTCHER'S THEATER** Jonathan Kellerman	$4.95
☐	27800	**THE ICARUS AGENDA** Robert Ludlum	$5.95
☐	27891	**PEOPLE LIKE US** Dominick Dunne	$4.95
☐	27953	**TO BE THE BEST** Barbara Taylor Bradford	$5.95
☐	26554	**HOLD THE DREAM** Barbara Taylor Bradford	$5.95
☐	26253	**VOICE OF THE HEART** Barbara Taylor Bradford	$5.95
☐	26888	**THE PRINCE OF TIDES** Pat Conroy	$4.95
☐	26892	**THE GREAT SANTINI** Pat Conroy	$4.95
☐	26574	**SACRED SINS** Nora Roberts	$3.95
☐	27018	**DESTINY** Sally Beauman	$4.95

Buy them at your local bookstore or use this page to order.

- -

Bantam Books, Dept. FB, 414 East Golf Road, Des Plaines, IL 60016

Please send me the items I have checked above. I am enclosing $_____
(please add $2.00 to cover postage and handling). Send check or money
order, no cash or C.O.D.s please.

Mr/Ms _____

Address _____

City/State _____ Zip _____

Please allow four to six weeks for delivery.   FB-11/89
Prices and availability subject to change without notice.